THAT THE DEAD MAY REST

KAREN A. WYLE

OBLIQUE ANGLES PRESS

Dedication

The characters in this novel include two older women who come into their own and learn about their capabilities. I dedicate it to a younger woman, my daughter Alissa Wyle, who has already done the same.

Prologue

the chronicler

The creeping peril, the quietly emerging plague, was not the sort of zombie epidemic pictured in late 20th and 21st century entertainment. Living humans did not, within seconds or minutes of being attacked, become the shambling undead. It was an older menace, one with ancient, mostly abandoned, and generally ineffectual remedies, that resurfaced. The bodies that now roamed to attack the living had been resting for days or months or years before some mysterious force drove them to emerge, like shoots of noisome growth, once more above ground. All those generations of mourners who loaded stones on the lids of coffins, laid sickles across the necks of corpses or drove iron rods through their cold chests — they knew what to fear.

As you read, do not divide your attention waiting to learn of a perpetrator or virus or other cause. I will tell you now that humanity has not yet learned why this occurred.

The terrestrial portion of what follows could be happening anywhere: Concord, or Wichita Falls, or a suburb of Boise.

Picture somewhere you know, even somewhere you love. Picture its houses grand or modest, well maintained or run down; its lush greenery or desert shrubs; its asphalt or gardens; its uninterrupted flatness, or its hills that challenge the fitness of pedestrians. Picture home.

Chapter 1

Millie

Millie stretched in her warm, roomy bed, savoring the yellow-gold light that slanted into the room and highlighted just a few dancing particles of dust. From the next room came the odor of fresh-brewed coffee, a blend with just a little chocolate in it, and the warm autumnal smell of oatmeal with nuts. How she had longed for tranquil awakenings like this, with no hovering anxieties poised to descend on her nor harsh demands hounding her from her worn and lumpy mattress. How grateful she was, day after day, that the end of her life has not meant the end of mornings and evenings, or losing the chance to savor profound and simple pleasures. Others could choose adventures that no living person could undertake, flying through erupting volcanoes or exploring ocean depths lit only by the fluorescent creatures that dwelt there. Yet others could choose to leave all corporeal senses behind, spending eternity as ethereal beings without boundaries, blending with others who did the same. Millie hoped they relished those choices as much as she relished hers.

She did, in fact, have duties awaiting her, though she'd have plenty of time for breakfast first. She was one of the many who took turns welcoming newcomers, helping them realize where, or one could say what, they now were. Bearing witness to the shock, the confusion or denial, the grief or the relief with which they absorbed the news. Reassuring them that their new life would be everything they loved in the old, or everything they longed for. Promising safety, serenity, peace.

But first, she took her time over her oatmeal, her coffee, her orange juice fresh as fresh-squeezed, though she'd seen no oranges here. If she wanted them, she would see them. For now, the juice was all she needed.

Reception, where all the new arrivals came, transformed every time to reflect the arriving spirit's conception of the most benign possible afterlife. As the welcomer helped the spirit understand what had happened to them, the surroundings would gradually shift to accommodate any details the conversation revealed about what would most deeply satisfy the spirit's needs and hopes. Sometimes the result was quite different from what she'd expected. A man who arrived dressed in velvets and silks like a king (what he'd been buried in, perhaps) might turn out to cherish the thought of a sunny cottage with a ticking grandfather clock.

This time, Millie entered a spacious circular hall with pale marble columns dividing intricate mosaics, the tiles' colors as bright and cheerful as a kindergarten crayon box. The tops and bases of the pillars had gilded trim, and the same trim framed the mosaics. The scene, though grand in its way, reminded her of the needlepoint tapestry one might expect in the living room of a very traditional American Christian family, especially since the mosaics featured winged cherubs and blue-robed Madonnas and a brown-haired bearded Jesus with his arms spread wide. She had seen such living rooms through house windows in her own town, and the pillars and mosaics might have been inspired by the most opulent of the town's churches.

The man who sat on a cushioned bench along one wall looked as if he would normally carry himself with some degree of authority. A mayor, perhaps, or a councilman. He wore a suit, not closely tailored but fitting him well, though the buttons of the jacket strained slightly over his middle. She couldn't see his features as she entered, and presumably he couldn't see hers, but he started to stand with an air of polite deference, gentleman to lady. And then he froze, and staggered backward against the bench before scuttling around it and backing against the wall, arms raised, covering his face.

The man's terror made her heart pound and her pulse race. Struggling to catch her breath, she told herself over and over: *I'm safe here. I'm safe. Even if he wants to hurt me, even if he strikes out in his fear, he can't hurt me here. No one can. I'm safe. He's just scared. He's scared. I know what that feels like. I have to find out why he's so frightened, so I can help, so I can make him feel safe, so I can feel safe again.*

Another member of the welcoming committee — Johnny, a large, quiet man whose voice had the warmth and depth of melted chocolate — had appeared and was now holding the man's hands, speaking softly to him, coaxing him to sit. Millie moved quietly toward the wall and tried to remember how to blend into the background. It was a skill she'd been so happy to leave behind . . . .

Her efforts made no difference. The man had been calming down, but when he glanced her way he sat bolt upright and pointed a shaking hand at her. "You! What are you doing here? What is this place, if *you're* here? Are you here to drive me crazy? Isn't it enough that you *killed* me? That you, you — " He turned and clutched Johnny by the arms, shook him, shouted: "She *came* at me, with her fingernails like claws, and her, her *teeth*, she clawed my face and she *tore* it with her *teeth*! And the smell, she smelled like rotting flesh and, and falling-down houses, I'd never smelled anything like it . . . ." He paused, as Millie stood with eyes wide and mouth open, staring at him, trying to find any sense in what he was saying, in any of this. "She . . . ." He took a slow step toward her. He spoke to her, this time. "You don't smell like that anymore. And your clothes were rags, dripping with something like oil, or mold. And your eyes were, were *dead* eyes, you looked dead, like a corpse pulled out of the grave . . . ."

Millie shook her head, trembling. "It couldn't be. None of this. I've been here, not there. I've been here for . . . ." Did she even know? What was time, here? But surely her life had ended months ago, or years. "I've been here. And I would never have done anything like that. It couldn't have been me." She gulped. "I'm so sorry that happened, that you died that way. No one should die that way. But it's all over now, all different. You'll be all right now. You'll be safe."

The man stared at her, his large hands opening and closing spasmodically. "How can I be safe here, if *you're* here? You killed me, and now you've followed me here! Unless . . . ." His voice dropped to muttering. "Unless I'm supposed to kill you now, to make things right. But I've never killed anyone. Is that what I'm supposed to do? Is that what I'm here for?"

Johnny gripped the man's shoulders and pulled him back toward the bench. He would find something to say, some way to make things better, but Millie wouldn't stay to hear it. She backed out of the room.

She jumped when a hand landed on her shoulder, and only then realized it was warm and gentle, almost a caress. She turned to see Sofia, whose name meant Wisdom and couldn't have been a better fit. Millie didn't remember her mother, but anyone in need of mothering would hope for someone like Sofia to appear. Millie expected her to ask what happened, and knew she'd have no answer, but Sofia put an arm around her and said softly, "I heard him."

Millie closed her eyes and felt something change around her — a breeze with the smell of salt, the rhythmic shushing of waves on sand. She opened her eyes to see one of her favorite peaceful places. Sofia had brought them to a circle of fine pale sand surrounded by wind-bent grasses, sand dunes rising and falling gently behind, the beach sloping down from below their feet to meet a shore where the waves surged and subsided but never crashed. She hadn't seen the sun rise that morning, but now she was seeing the sun glow red above the waves, reflected in a ripple stretching partway to shore. They were sitting on a soft woven blanket, its colors those of sand and water and sun, and between her now-bare feet and Sofia's was a basket with a handle, a bottle of wine slanting out to one side. Millie reached out to open the basket and found a large cheese, red-purple grapes, and a warm loaf of farmer's bread.

Millie looked from the food to the shore, the horizon, the waves, while Sofia produced sturdy wooden plates, served out the picnic, and put a plate on Millie's lap. When Millie had bestirred herself enough to pick up a wedge of cheese, Sofia put a wineglass in her other hand, wrapping Millie's fingers around the stem, and carefully filled it with a chilled white wine. Once Millie started eating, Sofia did the same, saying nothing, letting the sound of the waves fill the space around them. Not until Millie had drunk half her glass of wine (neither dry nor sweet, but something in between, refreshing without being tart) did Sofia say anything else. "We have to find out."

"What? Find out what? Whether that man was crazy? Can people be crazy here, when blind people can see and everyone gets healed?"

Sofia's fists clenched into tight little balls, but then she relaxed them, one at a time. Millie could see the red-pink crescents Sofia's nails left in her palms as Sofia said, slowly, as if counting out the words, "We have to find out whether it's true."

Chapter 2

Millie

Millie spent the next two days in bed, a cool breeze coming through the window so she could burrow under quilts, her favorite meals appearing on a convenient tray. At least, it felt like two days. Time in the afterlife did not, she'd heard, march in step with time in the world she'd left behind. Was it longer there? What might be happening in those uncountable days?

She slept twice as much as usual and spoke only to Sofia, who dropped by twice to report that no newcomers had arrived with similar gruesome tales. The third time Sofia peeked through her door, Millie sat up in bed, lifted her chin, and said, "I'll take my turn on welcome duty tomorrow."

Sofia came in, sat on the bed, and leaned in to give Millie a hug. "That's good to hear." She hesitated before saying, "There's one thing we're doing a little differently now, because of what happened to you. You know some people want to talk about how they died, and others seem eager to forget it?"

Millie nodded. She'd been one of the latter, though once she'd been here for a while, Sofia had coaxed her into revealing some of the details.

"Well, for now, if people don't bring it up, we're asking them whether they're willing to talk about it. And if they say no, we're playing it by ear. Sometimes a little gentle coaxing can make the difference."

Nothing came of the asking and coaxing for a few days. One woman mentioned taking a walk through a cemetery near her home, before she became too weak for walks, and seeing a grave that had somehow been disturbed, gaping open, the scattered earth far from neatly shoveled or piled. But, she said, it could have been a dog, a large one, let to wander by some careless owner. It had given her a shock, all the same. She had hoped her own grave would never be so disturbed.

Then, one evening, came a man who responded as if her question had been an electric shock. He went rigid, his eyes wide and his jaw clenched. Millie sat quietly, trying to project reassurance, and he slowly relaxed, but all the way into a slump. Putting his head in his hands, he mumbled something she couldn't hear. He must have realized it, because he lifted his head and said in a flat, hopeless tone, "I expected this. I assume I won't be allowed to stay. Where will you send me?" The monotone changed to a high, panicked note as he added, "Is it hell? Is there a hell? Please, can I appeal somehow?" He was crying now. "Is there some way to ask for mercy?"

Millie hurried to him and put a hand on his shoulder. "Please don't be frightened. I don't think there's anything like hell. I wasn't accusing you of anything. I — we're asking everyone this question now, for a reason that has nothing to do with you." Or so she hoped. She could only hope. "Please tell me, and then I'll find the best way to help you."

The man's sobs subsided, and he took a deep, shaky breath. It reminded her to wonder, as she often had, why they still breathed, and ate, and did so many things they had done in life, but not the more unpleasant ones. But she needed to concentrate on the shaken man in the chair, who was (perhaps unconsciously) now gripping the sides of the chair as he forced out the words, "I killed myself. Committed suicide."

That would mean counseling from someone who knew much more than she did. But now that the man had brought himself to make what he obviously saw as a confession, she should do more than simply pass him along. Using both hands now to gently massage his shoulders, she asked in as soothing a tone as she could, "Do you want to tell me what was happening to you, to bring you to that point?"

It might have been a mistake. He started sobbing again, his shoulders bowing and shaking under her hands. "It was — it was what — my wife, my wife, I saw what happened, my wife, and I couldn't stop it, I tried, but I was too late, she was already — already — all torn and bloody, blood everywhere, and she'd been screaming, and then moaning, and then nothing . . . she was like a torn, bloody *blanket* on the ground, and the thing ran off into the woods, it crashed through the trees and was gone, and my wife was, she was . . . ."

Millie wanted to do some moaning herself. She let go of the man's shoulders for fear of gripping them too hard. She could have asked what the creature looked like, whether it looked human, or like anyone in particular. But it would be kinder not to press him for details, not yet. And she couldn't bear to think what he might answer.

Slowly, as one and another arrival told similar horrific stories, the word began to spread. And since no one else had been accused of somehow being a monstrous murderer, people started whispering when Millie passed by. Some of them acted as if she weren't there, and others made a point of acting normally, except that it was more like someone on stage performing "normal" and doing it poorly.

Millie stopped welcoming new arrivals. Then she stopped going places where there were people. She found empty parks, empty trails, rivers deep in woods where few people bothered to venture; or she stayed in her room, eating chicken soup or strawberries or her favorite dark chocolate. At least she wouldn't gain weight, or break out with acne.

She made short forays to libraries and came home with books she'd already read, ones she knew she loved, books she knew had no murders or hauntings, books with no bloody deaths in them. She made herself read, and eat, instead of just sleeping the days away. She tried her hardest not to think of anything but the comfort food on her plate or the familiar words on the page. She'd had practice at that.

And then, after days dragging by as if eternity would be nothing but a burden, Sofia came to her with news. Millie knew it was terrible news, and that Sofia would forgive her for being horribly, terribly glad.

A child had arrived, dead from a terminal illness, and still in shock because her fourth grade teacher had died two months before, and then had shambled into her classroom. Only an open window, and the classroom's location on the ground floor, had let the children escape . . . while the growling corpse had been busy attacking the new teacher at the front of the class.

The next was an old woman who had been placidly tending her flowers. She had heard a dragging, uneven step coming from the bed of gardenias, and had been about to protest the careless damage the stranger must be doing when the smell hit her, so wrong amidst the flowerbeds, and then the ragged nails, and then the teeth. She was more bewildered than anything else, and worried for her flowers.

Next was a young man who had been blind, still accompanied by his guide dog, who had tried to save them both. At least the restoring of his sight provided a distraction, to his own and the dog's bewilderment and dawning joy.

Slowly, the numbers grew. The count stood at twelve when a man with silver hair and beard, and a bearing that would have been dignified if he'd been less shaken, came to Millie and told her that he, too, had met a victim of his own body come to life, his own body gone mad. So at least she was no longer alone with that — that what? That insult? That shame? That guilt?

His name was Daniel, and it suited him — a name from Shakespeare and from the Bible, a noble and almost holy name. The thought of his body dripping rot and slime, moaning and snarling as it hunted, made her almost as sick as the thought of her own body doing the same. And while Millie couldn't bear to talk about it, it somehow helped, a little, to hear him. Which was just as well, because he couldn't stop.

"Sometimes I feel the way I think I'd feel if one of my boys had done something awful. I did my best to raise them right, I loved them and took good care of them — but I'd still feel somehow responsible. That doesn't make any sense, and I know that, but . . . ."

She understood. "But feelings aren't about sense."

"That's it. That's precisely it."

Or: "I've been waiting so eagerly for my wife. Oh, I want her to live as long as her life is worth living, but I've missed her terribly, and I've thought nothing could be better than being reunited here, where there's so much we can show each other and share with each other. I still can't help being eager. But what if she's heard, and I'd see that knowledge in her eyes and know she's imagining every horrible detail? And even if she doesn't know . . . " He was dignified even when crying, the tears slipping down, glinting silver like his hair. "I'll have to tell her."

Millie couldn't say she understood, not exactly. She'd never had a loving husband who thought only the best of her. But she could expose a feeling of her own. So after he'd had time to cry a little and stop crying, she said, "What I keep thinking makes less sense, probably. The, the bodies — zombies, I guess you'd call them — they probably don't have any minds at all, so they don't know what they're doing. But sometimes I feel bad for my body, for letting something awful happen to it. Even though I didn't know it would happen, and there's nothing I could have done about it. Or if there was, I didn't know what to do, or not to do."

Daniel listened and nodded. "As if it were your child."

She supposed he was right. But right or wrong . . . "What if it somehow has feelings? What if there's even some of *me* left, helpless, carried along as it's made to do all these horrible things?"

Some people avoided the whole subject. It couldn't be true; or it was just another tragic thing that happened in the old life they had thankfully left behind; or, for those few people yielding to malicious impulses, it could only have happened to the worst people, not to people like themselves, and even mentioning the subject was vulgar and rude. Even some of the kindest had no idea what to say, or thought it would be most considerate not to mention such a painful subject. After all, they no longer had any connection to the discarded remains of their flesh, and dwelling on what had befallen them could only lead to melancholy.

Others, however, made the same unthinkable discovery and needed the company of those who would understand. A few of them found their way to Daniel and Millie, and formed the nucleus of what could be called a support group. One of them, a combat veteran, said at the first meeting he attended, "I never thought I'd be here again, seeking out people who'd been through the fire, so to speak. Who didn't have to explain the things they knew that most people didn't, the memories that haunted them." He laughed a little, bitterly. "Haunted them. Now there's the right word for it."

There were plenty of people who hadn't been accused but knew others who had been, or just wanted to talk about this new and grotesque change in the world they had left behind. Such groups mulled over such questions as: could it happen to them? Was there a time limit, some number of years after which their bodies would safely rest? Was there any connection between those whose bodies were running amuck, or those who had been attacked?

Millie and Daniel asked themselves, and each other, many of the same questions. And Millie thought of seeing whether Sofia, who seemed to know so much and had connections to so many people, had heard of any way such questions could actually be answered, or at least studied.

She had actually arranged to meet Sofia for coffee and cake at a Parisian-style café. Every restaurant had its own atmosphere, the result of not only the food and décor but the servers and hosts who tended to volunteer there, along with additional staff the volunteers or customers had imagined to fill the gaps. Millie particularly liked the way those elements had come together in this place.

But as she waited, enjoying the odors of coffee and bread and pastry, a man found her first. He stalked toward her, peering at her until he got close enough to study her face, and then he stopped in his tracks, teetering back and forth as though torn between coming closer and recoiling. She stood up and willed herself not to retreat, not to run. She let him get close enough that when he spat at her, the drops fell at her feet. She waited for him to speak, and when he didn't, she forced out the words, "Did my body kill you?"

He leaned toward her, so far she thought he might fall, and hissed, "You don't even know? You killed me, and you don't even *know*?"

Millie felt an unfamiliar surge of anger, and tried to ignore it. The man had no better target, and she might well have felt the same way. "There was no way for me to know. Until that other man arrived, I had no idea anything like this was happening. Neither did anyone else, I don't think."

Would he threaten her, like that first man? Or dissolve in grief? Should she invite him to join her, try to form some connection? As she dithered, she saw with enormous relief that Sofia was approaching, moving with a speed she almost certainly couldn't have managed in life. The man saw Millie's gaze shift, and spun around; Sofia reached him and took his arm, gently but firmly pulling him away. But before they had gone more than a few steps, the man broke loose, stalked back, and shouted, "It's your body killing people! It's your fault!"

Sofia came hurrying back, and this time she succeeded in taking the man somewhere out of sight. Millie hid her head in her arms until she heard Sofia coming back, summoning today's volunteer waiter, sitting down and pulling her chair closer to Millie's. She felt Sofia's hand, on Millie's arm this time, pressing down as if to bring Millie back to this moment of friendship and fellowship. "I'm so sorry, dear. We have to expect people to have irrational demands, to look for someone to blame. You must know how wrong he is."

The waiter appeared with a café au lait and a piece of fruitcake for Millie and Sofia's usual mille feuille and hot tea. Millie took a big bite, so big a passing stranger did a double take. When she'd finished it, she said, "I know it wasn't my fault and that I couldn't have known. But — I don't know any more than that. I don't know whether there's something anyone can do, even something I can do. And I want to know. I *have* to know."

Sofia looked at her in wide-eyed surprise. She'd proba-bly never heard Millie express any strong emotion other than self-loathing or fear. It made Millie want to laugh. *Surprise, Sofia, your baby's growing up.* Or at least, she was starting to.

Chapter 3

Millie

B old declarations notwithstanding, what *could* Millie do?

Well, she told herself over a quiet cup of tea at home, she could try to find out if anyone else knew more than she did. And one way to do that was to systematically visit the different groups that had formed in the wake of the news. But would they recognize her? Maybe not, if she disguised herself.

She tried to imagine how a bolder woman, a painter of colorful expressionist canvasses taller than she was, a lover of loud jarring music, would dress, and the makeup she would splash on her face. Donning the disguise she'd visualized helped her venture forth, odd as it felt to introduce herself under such false pretenses. She used her true name, Camille, which no one would normally associate with the meek and subdued Millie.

One of the groups she attended as Camille proved to be devoted to persuading themselves that nothing truly awful was happening. The spirits who had arrived with stories of shambling, decaying, murderous bodies arising from their graves must themselves be suffering from some very unfortunate ailment, an ailment causing hallucinations so intense that they literally frightened those afflicted to death — or perhaps the contagion proved fatal for some other reason, with the hallucinations merely a distressing side effect.

She almost stood up and shouted at them that it couldn't be true. How could a hallucination take the form of a person the sufferer had never seen? But it would be unforgivably impolite to contradict them so abruptly, and she would have to explain what she meant. It would be completely unlike her. It must have been the clothes and the makeup, the Camille persona taking over, thrusting her forward, inspiring her to rudeness.

Almost like whatever had taken over her abandoned body . . . . She jumped up and ran out of the room. She hadn't known that spirits could vomit, but she ran to the closest bush and vomited at its base until she felt almost purged.

The next day, she tried again with a different group. This time she wore a simple skirt and sweater, with her hair in a loose ponytail and a necklace made by an artist who had been kind to her. The group met in a room full of comfy chairs and cushions, the breeze coming in the open windows smelling of apple blossoms. Nonetheless, in this group she found herself one of the calmest spirits present, a rare and disorienting experience. What had drawn this group together appeared to be panic, fear that their living loved ones would be attacked. She could share the first group's figures, but that would hardly make them feel better.

A woman who looked a little like Millie's grandmother ground her fist into the palm of her other hand. "If we only had some way to *reach* our families! To warn them if they don't know, and to find out if they're all right!"

If only there were a way, indeed. The living could find out so much more about what was happening: when it started, whether it was happening more or less — and maybe, what was causing it. They must have some ideas, maybe even ways to test those ideas. If she could only know whether her own body had attacked anyone else!

But there was no way to reach back into the world, to contact the living. She muttered as much, apologetically, and expected either glum agreement or anger at saying the obvious. But another member — younger than most, only a girl, thin and with the energy of an adolescent vibrating through her, said defiantly, "How do we know that? Isn't that like someone saying the dead never come back, that zombies — that's what we're talking about, we shouldn't be afraid to say it! — are just a superstition? Or saying there's no life after death, when here we all are!"

Out of the mouth of babes? Millie turned to her and asked, "If it's possible, how would we do it? What can we try?"

A man who had said nothing so far stirred in his chair, cleared his throat, and raised his hand as if it were up to someone else to let him speak. When everyone else went silent and waited for him, he cleared his throat again and finally said, "Maybe it's like the other things that are coming true. Maybe things like Ouija boards or crystal balls or séances actually work."

Millie felt a thoroughly inappropriate giggle trying to rise out of her chest and clamped down on it. When she was sure it wouldn't escape, she said, "How would anyone, anyone still living, know to try those things?"

Before anyone could answer, a stirring in the group, its members turning toward the door, signaled Johnny's arrival.

From the reduction in the general tension, Millie deduced that many of them already knew him, and welcomed him as she did. Unnecessarily in her view, he asked quietly, "May I come in and join you? I have an idea about what you were just discussing."

When no one objected, he made his way to one of the few empty chairs, a straight-backed wooden one that looked less comfortable than the others, especially for someone his size. He sat down, clasped his hands in his lap, and said, "We could ask around to find out about friends or family or acquaintances — people still living — who would be most likely to hold séances or tarot sessions or the like. And then some of us could all try together to, to reach out to that person, over and over, in the hope of getting through."

He stopped there, and the silence quickly filled with murmurs and exclamations quiet and less quiet. The thin girl leaned forward so far she looked folded and said, tripping over her words, "Yes! We've got to try that! If we get through, what should we say?"

Suggestions came from all over the room. "Ask if they've heard about bodies rising from the grave!" "Are people being attacked by zombies?" "Are people being attacked by anything unexplained? Are they finding bodies ripped up as if by animals?" And from the man who'd suggested Ouija boards, "Has anyone encountered a revived body that *didn't* attack?" There was an idea that tempted one to hope. . . .

It was like a different group, now that people had something that passed for a plan of action. It was a plan that could fail at the very first step, let alone the later ones, but for the moment, at least, it eased the overwhelming helplessness that had been choking them. With relief, they adjourned until the next day, too anxious to delay longer.

Millie invited Daniel to go with her the next day. After initial introductions, it soon became clear that no one had made much progress so far. They should probably have left themselves more time to talk to other spirits about people they could try to reach. As Millie wondered what to say that wouldn't sound like a scold, the thin girl spoke up, her voice as urgent and clear as a trumpet call. "Let's all tell each other who we're worried about back on earth — who we're trying to save, beyond just everybody." She paused and then said more quietly, "I have a twin sister."

Murmurs of sympathy filled the room. A motherly woman sitting next to her reached over and patted her arm, letting her hand rest there for a moment, and then said, "I have two children, a girl and a boy. And my husband, for a little while longer."

The large dark-eyed man had an aging mother, tiny and frail. He clenched his fists as he said in a growl, "She's survived so much. It would be utterly wrong if *that* was how she died."

Around the room they went, naming fathers, sons, brothers, wives, girlfriends, daughters. One man, wearing dungarees and flannel, with a bristling beard, started to speak and stopped, as if overcome by embarrassment. Then he pushed through it to say, "It's my dog. He's probably grieving. It might keep him from paying as much attention to things. Or he might try to take the critter down. If any dog could do it, he could." He rubbed at his eyes with his sleeve. "But he prob'ly couldn't."

Almost everyone had named a loved one except Millie. But Millie had no one to name. Inspiration struck, and she sat straighter and said, "How about we go around again and say which other spirits we're going to talk to, in the hope of finding living people we might be able to reach?"

If anyone noticed that she had changed the subject, they were tactful enough not to mention it.

———◆◆◆———

Rosie

Madame Rebecca (or Rosie, when not in professional mode) sat at the table, the heavy velvet curtains blocking the inconvenient sunlight, and sniffed the incense her assistant Diane had lit, assessing it and finding it good. Not strong enough to irritate nasal passages, but plenty for providing atmosphere, as did the deep bass notes of the music playing at the other end of the house, just at the threshold of audibility. The black tablecloth covered the round walnut claw-foot table, and her painstakingly recruited clients held hands around it, staring at the single candle in the center. The heat was turned up high enough that her clients would welcome it after the February chill — and would be all the more susceptible to the breeze from the fan Diane would turn on at the appropriate moment.

"Welcome, friends," she intoned. "You have come together out of a shared yearning, a need to reach beyond the boundaries accepted by so many as impermeable, to welcome the spirits who themselves yearn to communicate with us." She paused to look around the room, projecting warmth without anything so ordinary as a smile. "Now let all distractions and trivial concerns fall away, and open yourselves to the ineffable, as I await the touch of my spirit guide."

Maybe it was time for a new spirit guide — a man, a warrior or shaman, instead of the Egyptian courtesan she'd been trotting out for so long. She could almost hear the man's voice, a warm baritone rumble, authoritative and masculine . . . .

Was she bored enough that her imagination had become intrusive? It almost seemed that she was hearing such a voice, that it was even demanding her attention. How ridiculous! She shoved aside the memory of her teenaged years, when her daydreams would be interrupted by the faint echo of mysterious voices, tantalizing, fading in and out. Without the naive hope that the voices would grow louder and prove real, and then the disappointment and anger when they faded away, she might never have seized on becoming a medium. It had been a sort of revenge on those thwarted hopes.

And now she was letting those old memories sabotage her. What expression had been on her face, these last minutes? She had better get down to business.

"She comes, she approaches! Welcome, Aya, gentle helper, and tell me what spirits you bring with you to speak to the living. . . ."

A wearisome time later, after "Aya" had conveyed her messages of love and reassurance, Diane collected payments from the clients and ushered them out. When they were all gone, Rosie pushed back from the table, stood up, stretched, and went to open the curtains. But the sunlight had fled.

Emma

Emma was trying to write a letter to her son. If people knew, they'd shake their heads and say sympathetically that she must be too grief-stricken, or simply too old, to know how pointless it was. But what else could she do?

When Robert was alive, she had somehow thought it a better use of her time to clean the house, or look at pictures of her ex-husband, or do exercises, or search for new clients, or do any number of things rather than to write to him. There would always be time later. She might deserve the agony that made up her days and her nights, for so idiotically assuming there would be time.

It was still hard to find things to say when she no longer had news to tell him, or new books to recommend, or any advice to give. Nor could she ask him about his day, or his job, or whether he had gotten serious about some woman, or when he would come to see her.

If she had written to him then, when he was still there to read it, would he have written back? What would he have said? Would his letters have been impatient, as he sometimes had been when she phoned him more than once a day? Or would he have been kind? If she closed her eyes, she could almost see his jagged handwriting slanting across the page, starting with *Dear Mom* . . . .

She closed her eyes, imagining it, and didn't open them until she felt a strange spasm in her hand, almost as if her pen had twitched. On the page, under her own cramped handwriting, there was a line slanting down from left to right, a line she hadn't meant to write. A line starting with an uneven shape, a sort of squashed circle, almost like a D.

Was she seeing things? Was the twitch in her hands the beginning of some sort of seizure? She should be frightened, but she was too tired to care. She left the letter on the table and shuffled to her bedroom. There was nothing, after all, more worth doing than to sleep.

Janna

It never surprised Janna to dream about her sister. In fact, it would have terrified her if she stopped dreaming about Jeri. They had, after all, been together since the moment that one small cluster of cells had decided to become two. And while they hadn't spent every minute, or even every day, at each other's sides, separation had always felt temporary, even when Jeri's anorexia had become so extreme that an ambulance screamed its way to the hospital, carrying her out of reach until Janna could get someone to drive her there.

And then she'd died, and Janna's world had fractured into unrecognizable pieces — but at least she had her dreams.

In this one they were watching TV, but not in the hospital. She wasn't even sitting on Jeri's bed, the way they had that last year. Instead, they were curled up on the living room couch, sharing the big fuzzy blanket, watching *Ghostbusters: Afterlife* and sharing a big bowl of popcorn —

Janna couldn't help it — she jerked herself awake. *Popcorn*? Jeri sitting there casually snacking? And they hadn't been little kids. They'd been about the age Janna was now. What the hell?

And there'd been something else. Jeri hadn't looked exactly healthy, the way she was in some dreams, the ones it hurt to wake up from. But she hadn't been the near-skeleton Janna had seen so often, and which Jeri had somehow never been able to see. Yes, she'd been thin, but not thin enough to make anyone wonder, let alone worry or stare. And her hair had color in it, the brown-red their mother liked to call auburn, and the bit of wave that made it different from Janna's, instead of hanging dark and colorless and breaking off like worn-out thread.

But that wasn't all. There'd been one more thing, but what was it? She squeezed her eyes shut, concentrated hard, and then she had it — and it made chills run down her spine and then settle in her stomach. Jeri's clothes. She'd been wearing the outfit their parents had bought for her, the dark orange corduroys and forest green pullover that would've fit Janna, that they bought for the day they couldn't stop hoping for, the day Jeri would come home to stay. They'd insisted in dressing Jeri in it for the funeral, even though it was so much too big. She'd been wearing it in the dream, sitting there next to Janna under the blanket, eating popcorn . . . and it had only been a little loose.

Janna fell back down on the bed and curled up small. It should be real. That should be their life, and it wasn't and never would be again. She slammed her fist into the mattress and let the tears come.

Chapter 4

the chronicler

The active group of spirits was growing. Most of those whose bodies had been desecrated had joined it, as had the most inquisitive or restless members of other groups. They eagerly questioned the people who had tried to make contact: what did they do, exactly? How did it feel? Were they sure they hadn't gotten the message across?

But the effort had taken its toll. It wasn't only exhaustion, of a kind none of them had thought they would ever feel again. They'd had little enough hope of getting through to the living, and that hope had come to nothing. Jeri had taken to snarling at any would-be new members, driving them away with sarcasm so creative it brought home to the others how promising her life could have been.

But then Johnny arrived.

His presence was a healing balm. All his experience with greeting and soothing new arrivals, finding the best way to speak to them, convincing them that the trials and strife of their lives could be faced and then put aside— it all made him the ideal person to bring the group back from splintering.

He knew just how to pay attention to their different voices and turn the complaints and accusations in more productive directions. Were there people no one had tried to reach who might be worth a try? Was there some other method no one had used yet? Could they borrow expertise from some aspect of their former lives, such as advertising, or fund-raising, or missionary work?

And finally, gently, speaking privately to each of those who had loved ones among the living, he urged them to try again.

Rosie

This time, the voice came when she was alone. She'd been playing with her crystal ball, sliding her hands over its smooth surface, admiring its heft, thinking about ways she might be able to use it in her sessions. Were her clientèle ready for it, or would they see it as hokey or fake?

Rosie. Try looking in it.

It was clearer this time, and her first reaction was disappointment. It wasn't one of the voices she'd heard, just barely heard, when she was a girl. And yet it seemed familiar. And it knew her name, the one she never used in public anymore, let alone with clients.

Then she realized why, and with the recognition came rage. After so many years without the slightest contact, was this the way for Sam to reappear in her life? He must have sunk to the level of practical jokes, a passive-aggressive commentary on how she made her living. Had she missed her phone buzzing for an incoming call? And how could she be hearing a call she hadn't answered? Or had someone snuck a loudspeaker into her house somehow?

She had long since lost track of how to reach him, but she shoved the crystal ball away and stomped to where she'd plugged in her phone to charge, bringing it back to the table and searching for traces of Sam, muttering the cutting things she would say to him. And then she stared at the entry she found, dropping the phone on her lap.

His obituary.

Movement in the corner of her eye drew her attention. She turned to see something shifting in the heart of her crystal ball. She held her breath, waiting. Could it really be Sam? And if it was, would he be young, the way she remembered him, or as old as when he'd died . . . or some shriveled corpse? But no face appeared, only shifting blobs of shadow and color. And when they came together into shapes, they formed not a face, but a body, a body walking, but not as a person should walk. A body stumbling, shambling, staggering, it arms stretched halfway in front of it.

She turned convulsively away and whispered, "Why are you doing this to me?" And the voice came again:

This, what you see in the ball, how much is it happening?

What *was* she seeing there? What sort of body, what sort of thing? She'd certainly, thank God, never seen anything of the sort.

But — hadn't she heard something, muttered conversation between two of her clients before the last session? A nervous old woman had whispered to her friend, and the friend shut her down with, "It couldn't be true. It's just people spreading stories." And then something she didn't quite catch about "those sneaky movie promotions," and about "monsters."

But it was nonsense. Ridiculous. Her former boyfriend calling to her from beyond the grave, with nothing better to say than something about bodies stalking around?

And still, she found herself saying, "I'll try to find out."

Emma

An evening and night of fitful, interrupted sleep had left Emma both exhausted and restless, a miserable combination. She tried cleaning house, but could only manage the energy for the easiest jobs — the jobs she did more often, which didn't need doing again. She reread her grocery list and added a couple of items she might never use, then one more that she almost never allowed herself — dark chocolate truffles. Maybe biting into a truffle would remind her what it felt like to enjoy something.

And then she gave up on all these useless ways of stalling, and sat down to write that letter to Robert.

She reached for the pad of stationery she'd been using, almost down to the last sheet, and saw that she hadn't torn off the spoiled sheet from last time. She should call her doctor and get examined for conditions that could cause seizures. As she picked up the pen, she held it in the air for a minute, and then two. No tremors, no shaking. She got rid of the spoiled sheet, pulled the fresh sheet toward her, and started to write.

Dear Robert,

Last fall's leaves are still on the lawn, and how I wish

The pen jerked across the page again. And then, as she gripped it so tight her fingers hurt, it spelled out, in barely legible letters,

Mom Mom it's me

She almost dropped the pen, but managed to catch it. She brought it to her lips and kissed it, then held it point down on the paper again, whispering, "Robert, oh, Robert, where are you?" But it didn't matter, because now she knew that he was *some*where. "Never mind that, oh, my darling boy, what did you want to say?"

Mom, we need your help

———◆◇◆———

Janna

In this dream, Jeri had sent Janna a postcard. But it wasn't a postcard she'd ever seen in a drugstore or tourist shop. The postcards she was used to seeing had landmarks, or ocean scenes, or mountains, or cute animals like kittens and puppies. This postcard startled her, even in the dream, because it was so far from panoramic, showing only a few details, and yet looked exactly like the twins' secret hideaway. The picture would have to have been taken from the base of the willow tree, looking up and outward through the swaying green branches with the spray of the waterfall visible between them. The warm glow of the light — "golden hour" light — brought back memories of brownie-and-cookie picnics, gobbled greedily while their mother called out to them that dinner was ready. . . .

Dream-Janna turned the postcard over, only to find another image. This one was no photograph, but a tarot card. She and Jeri had just started learning about tarot when Jeri went to the hospital the last time, the time she never came back. Janna had brought a Starlit Twins tarot deck with her to the hospital on a couple of visits, using her phone to call up one of the online guides to the different cards. This card looked like The Tower, which could mean too many things — from danger or crisis to more positive changes. What was Jeri trying to say?

Then the card changed, morphing into another: Strength. They'd laughed about this one (though Jeri's laugh had an awful rattling sound that stopped Janna's laughter) because, in the deck Janna had brought, the figure on the card looked a little like them. At least, like both of them before Jeri had started to look more like the skeleton on an antique Death card.

And then it shifted again, into a card from some other deck she couldn't identify. It might be the Judgment card. She couldn't remember what that would mean, but it must mean something other than the picture on it. Because the picture showed people standing up in their graves. What did it mean?

She woke up with that question echoing in her ears.

Millie

Millie tried to comfort herself with the thought that even if it was really happening, if bodies were really coming back as monsters, it was happening very rarely. The equivalent of weeks could go by without any of the welcomers hearing tales of them.

But gradually there were more. Not a flood, but a larger trickle.

People became more reluctant to take on welcoming duties. More and more, it was the spirits who were gathering information, and hoping to somehow act on it, who could bring themselves to greet new arrivals. Even they found it harder than before to greet them with the blend of serenity, compassion, and joy that those freshly parted from the living world needed and deserved.

And all the while, the rumors swirled. If they had thought such things as gossip and speculation and jumping to conclusions, and even blaming each other, had been left behind, they began to know better.

"Surely you've heard of self-fulfilling prophecies. Not to mention the power of the mind over the body." Arabella had been an accountant and considered herself as essentially a scientist, whose views on any particular topic must be presumed to be well-founded. "So those unfortunate individuals who fall prey to superstition and irrational thinking in their lifetimes have, as a consequence, weakened the body's defenses against whatever infection — perhaps something fungal, absorbed from the surrounding soil — has given rise to this unfortunate behavior."

Norman, to whom these remarks had been addressed, bridled at being lectured in such lofty tones. "It hardly seems likely that habits of mind during life would have any effect on the activities of a fungus! — particularly after all brain activity had ceased. Besides, I've heard this notion suggested before, and one of the people whose body is involved — a very dignified sort of fellow, poor man — emphatically denied having been at all superstitious."

Arabella sniffed. "Naturally he would. I'm not saying he was indulging in an untruth, but the same mental habits that support superstition in the first place might lead to selective memory."

Monica had cornered Millie on her way out of the welcoming hall and insisted on questioning her, apparently hoping to support her latest hypothesis. And she was almost impossible to discourage. "Of course I don't want to embarrass you," she said earnestly, "but it would be so helpful if you could tell us what unfinished business you weren't able to deal with before you died. I'm not saying you wanted to *kill* anyone, but everyone knows that ghosts linger because of the things they weren't able to get done." She nodded in satisfaction at her own good sense. "It does seem likely, doesn't it, that some similar principle is involved?"

"I assure you, I had no thwarted tasks to complete." Millie made herself smile, though she doubted the result was convincing. "And I was *not* a violent person."

Monica would have patted Millie's hand if Millie hadn't evaded her reach. "That's rather the point, dear, isn't it? You're so, ah, *mild-mannered*. You must have had a lifetime of unexpressed emotions, churning under the surface, repressed.

And by whatever mysterious mechanism, they came to the surface after you *couldn't* suppress them any longer. Don't you think?"

If Millie had allowed herself to feel this much anger during her lifetime, the idea of a posthumous rampage would seem less incredible. Unless . . .no, it couldn't be true. Millie's sense of justice had survived all efforts to convince her that she deserved mistreatment. If some part of her had sought belated vengeance, it would not have chosen random bystanders as targets. She turned and hurried away with all the energy in her perfected body.

Chapter 5

Rosie

By the next morning, Rosie felt like a fool for even considering that Sam might be reaching out to her. Was gullibility contagious? Was early senility setting in, luring her toward belief in things she'd long ago outgrown?

But she may as well find out more about whatever had been troubling those clients. It might give her ideas for attracting new business, for those slow times when she'd need some. She could ask them, if they came to another session, but that would run counter to her all-knowing persona. Instead, she went for a multi-pronged approach.

Digging deep in her closet, she finally found a pair of water-resistant boots with some faint claim to fashion. That should help her deal with the cold slush lining the streets. Donning the boots and her newest all-season coat, she set out on her quest. First she bought as many lurid scandal sheets as she could find, the kind that talked about women impregnated by aliens and giving birth to giant frogs. Then she dropped them off at her house and headed over to a family-style Italian restaurant that seated people around large tables, which meant strangers were seated together. Before she followed the waiter to her seat, she shifted her sweater so it sat less neatly and let her shoulders slump. Once she sat down, she glanced around timidly, looked down at her hands in her lap, and then looked back up again, making herself embody the shy teenager she had once been. As she'd hoped, one of the other diners was a middle-aged motherly sort who gave her a warm, reassuring smile and asked, "Have you been here before?"

Claiming to be entirely new to the place could backfire if a waiter recognized her. Donning a look of gratitude for the friendly tone, she said softly, "Once or twice, but it's been a while. Tonight, I was feeling a little down, because things just seemed too much, and I wanted to be someplace homey for a while. Someplace cozy and friendly."

A man two seats away looked at her and raised his eyebrows. "Are things really so bad? What's bugging you, especially?"

She opened her mouth, closed it again, and shuddered, hoping it looked natural. "I'm sorry. I just can't . . . I don't want to talk about it. I'm sorry."

A woman next to Rosie, whose long dark hair and no-makeup beauty she took a moment to envy, reached over and put a hand on Rosie's shoulder. "I wonder if what's frightened you is the same thing that scares me. I've heard about those strange attacks where the victims are left torn up, in places no one's seen any wild beasts for decades."

Rosie leaned just a bit into the pressure of the woman's hand and whispered, "Is it really true? Does anyone know for sure?"

The woman let go of Rosie to pull out and fiddle with her phone, calling up something and then handing the phone to

Rosie. It showed a news story, which Rosie quickly scanned. The report was notably cautious, saying that a body had been found in the early hours of the morning with bite and claw marks, and that the cause of death had apparently been exsanguination — bleeding to death.

Rosie took note of where the report came from and handed the phone back. She heaved a sigh that was not from any role she was playing, and said quietly to the woman, "Thank you for showing me." Meanwhile, the man who had questioned her held out his hand as if entitled to see for himself. But then their food came, and conversation turned to lighter matters.

Rosie stepped out of the restaurant into an evening as benign and welcoming as her table mates had been. Even the man she'd initially written off as obnoxious had turned out to be interesting on the subject of how Italian food had evolved in other countries, eager to share his knowledge without putting on airs about it. But she felt unsettled, and not only from having eaten too much pasta Bolognese. She had two — no, three facts with which to grapple:

— Something gruesome did seem to be going on.

— If she had really gotten a message from Sam, as now seemed more likely, she did indeed have the ability she'd been counterfeiting. Did that have to affect her career? In what way?

— She had just spent hours with a group of strangers drawn together by nothing more than some time to spend and a desire for Italian food — well, that and the willingness to talk to other strangers. She'd had nothing to gain from them, except, as it turned out, some disquieting information. And she'd enjoyed it. Enjoyed them.

How long had it been since she'd talked to a group of people with no personal agenda and no money to be made? Was it something she wanted to do more often? What would that say about how she'd been living her life? And whether in some intangible sense, she'd been wasting it?

She shook her head, drawing a curious glance from a couple passing by. She could use a drink, to help these thoughts subside into the background. And maybe she could learn a little more at the same time.

But first, she would stop by her house again and change into a dressier outfit. Something a little more sexy, but not over the top; something to make a bartender a little more likely to chat with her on a slow weekday night.

Rosie took a quick look around the first bar on her route and crossed it off her mental list. The bartenders were all young, by a depressing margin, and unlikely to have much interest in her. Indeed, she'd probably have trouble getting their attention long enough to order a drink. And it was too busy for her purposes.

The second, smaller bar proved more promising. The sole bartender looked to be in his mid-forties and was using a forefinger to draw pictures in a small puddle of spilled water when she came in. He looked up with a smile that combined relief and gratitude. She decided to walk the fine line between flirting and confiding . . . and found herself telling him what she did for a living. And without any sort of hint that he might become a client. The evening, or what had led to it, seemed to be shaking something loose.

She didn't go so far as to confess that her séances were pure performance, but she didn't claim otherwise either — not even as much as Sam's possibly making contact would have justified. Nonetheless, she assumed her semi-confession would make it impossible to steer the conversation toward lurid news items or rumors. And then he said, quite without prompting from her, "I guess you might be able to find out what's really happening. You know, if there are really people being killed by some lunatic playing at monsters. Would you be able to contact their, you know, their spirits? Their souls?"

The lime margarita in her stomach felt suddenly colder. But she answered, her voice gone hoarse, "I don't know. But I could try."

When she got home, she gladly took off her boots, rubbed the places they had chafed, and changed into her most comfortable clothes, a much-washed tee shirt and sweat pants that didn't rub or constrict or itch. Then she settled on the couch with the pile of magazines. It didn't take long to dispose of most of them, as their stories said far less than the headlines had promised and included no names, only the cities where these mysterious animal attacks had supposedly occurred. She made a note of those cities and moved on to finding the same online story she had read in the restaurant.

As she'd thought, it gave a name. And the city mentioned was one of those she'd already jotted down.

Now what? She still didn't know what had killed at least one person this way, or whether it had happened to as many people as the magazines claimed. If she hadn't imagined Sam and his message, she still didn't know enough to answer his question.

If she disliked the idea of making contact, that was by the way.

Emma

Her Robert had written to her! It was a miracle, the kind she'd no longer expected from a God who'd taken him away and turned a deaf ear to all her prayers. It was almost enough to make her grateful, as if He deserved it after all she'd suffered. And Robert had asked Emma to help him, to find out all she could about something — something horrible and unbelievable.

But how? If he'd been *here*, he'd have gone on his computer or that fancy phone of his and somehow come up with everything he needed to know. But she'd only gotten a computer because he'd nagged her into it, and hadn't touched it since he left her. And her newspaper stopped coming last year.

But there was one place, a place she used to love long ago, a place where she might find someone to help her.

It was seven blocks to the library. She could certainly walk that far. She should probably take her cane, just in case she needed it, but she wasn't as old and feeble as people imagined. She could walk the legs off plenty of young people who spent all their time on their hind ends staring at screens.

As she opened the door, she hesitated, first at the cold air that blew in and then at the doubts that seemed to blow in with it. What if the library had closed, or moved? People didn't read books anymore, or so she'd heard. But she didn't remember where she'd put her phone book, if she'd even gotten one lately. She would just go and see.

There were no familiar faces. The librarians who had welcomed her when she was a child must be long gone, and those who'd flitted about in the background when she came here with Robert were nowhere to be seen, if she'd even have recognized them. But there must be somewhere one was supposed to go to ask questions.

Wandering around looking for something like an information desk, she came upon a sight so familiar it startled her: newspapers, hanging, racks and racks of them. She almost ran to them, leafing through, like a child searching through a forest for a magical creature. She couldn't find the local paper — but maybe that was just as well. Papers from bigger cities might be the best place to start. She found the fattest sheaf of paper and tried to hoist it. By her second try, a young fellow barely old enough to shave appeared and took over, asking, "Where do you want it, ma'am?"

At least some young people were polite. She pointed to a nearby table and followed him there, waiting for him to lay the paper flat and extract the pole it had hung from. Then she settled herself in the wooden chair — solid, nicely shaped, if a little heavy for scooting toward the table easily — and started leafing through the paper. She'd gone through thirty-one pages, and her arms were getting tired, when she came to a page mostly taken up with photos. The headline above them, in big thick letters, read, *CONTROVERSY ABOUT PHOTO ALLEGEDLY SHOWING KILLER OF PHOTOGRAPHER.*

At approximately 3:15 p.m. yesterday afternoon, the Omaha Police Department received a 911 call about bloodcurdling screams coming from the vicinity of a local playground. Officers responding found the body of James Adams, longtime Omaha resident, who had achieved some degree of success with his collections of artfully composed and lit photographs of agricultural details and abandoned machinery. But the photograph he left behind had nothing in common with his established style.

The first two photos showed a body sprawled on grass and then, close up, ragged claw marks and what looked like bite marks and chunks of missing flesh. Emma swallowed the bile that welled up in her mouth and looked away from the photos to the text.

The body of a well-known local photographer would merit attention from law enforcement and media, due to the markings suggesting a fatal attack by a large wild animal in an area where no such animals had been found in more than a century. But when relatives of the deceased claimed his effects and examined the storage media in his camera, the story took an even more dramatic turn.

Between that paragraph and the next came the largest photo, with the caption beneath it reading, "last photograph in camera of photographer found dead from mysterious attack." It showed a manlike figure — arms, legs, head, body all the right size for a man — with its arms raised and fingers spread out, fingers with sharp jagged nails like claws. Its mouth was wide open, with something that might have been drool catching the light, and its eyes were wide open, staring, but somehow looking blind. The figure was just a little blurred, as if it had just stopped or just started moving.

Claims have been made that the camera had been planted, with the photo staged and inserted as a particularly ghoulish prank. However, the speed with which the police responded means

*that the camera would have had to be prepared beforehand —
possibly by a cold-blooded killer who took a photo of a dummy
or an accomplice, or created the photo artificially, in either case
to mislead the police and the public with an attention-getting
red herring. To this already murky situation, one must add the
finding of dozens of bodies with similar injuries, in locations
far enough apart that only an energetic traveling killer with
considerable resources could be responsible for them all. . . .*

Emma reached into her purse for the little notebook she
carried, then for a pen that, it turned out, had (probably long
since) run out of ink. She got up and looked around for something to write with and found a stub of pencil with no eraser,
oddly next to a computer of some kind. She took the pencil
back to the table and wrote down how many bodies the article
mentioned. Were they counting bodies from all over the state?
the country? beyond it? She didn't know. "Dozens" didn't
sound like enough. Maybe the authorities were trying to avoid
panic?

But she'd had enough of this nasty business. She put the
notebook back in her purse and walked away from the table,
leaving the newspaper sprawled open behind her.

My sweet Robert,
*I did what you asked. At least, I found out as much as I
could. . . .*

Janna

Damn it, she didn't want to count on dreams! She wanted to talk to Jeri here and now, awake, whenever she felt like it.

It wasn't *fair*.

Janna got hold of herself, giving herself an actual shake for good measure. She wasn't a child, to be thinking that way. Jeri was gone and wasn't coming back. Janna would have to go through the rest of her life without a sister. Without her twin.

And no, she would not cry. She bit her lip enough to hurt.

If only it were easier to remember Jeri as healthy, instead of a skeleton lying in a hospital bed. Or at least, as nearly healthy as in that last dream, the one with the tarot cards.

Where had she left that tarot deck? In the nightstand. In Jeri's nightstand. She hadn't touched it since Jeri died.

She would *not* cry.

She walked over, slowly, dragging her feet, and pulled out the drawer. There was the tarot deck, and the booklet that gave some meanings for the cards. She pulled them out and retreated to her own bed, sitting on it cross-legged. She would do a reading for herself. What came first? She took a deep breath, which couldn't hurt, and shuffled the cards. Her hands shook, and the deck got away from her. She put her hands down in front of her and leaned on them until they stopped, and then gathered the cards again. All right, cards shuffled, more or less. Next would be asking a question, but what could she ask? *Why am I dreaming about tarot?* As if the stupid cards could answer that.

"Okay, cards, tell me whatever you have to tell me. Surprise me by making sense."

She laid three cards down. Three was enough. Another deep breath, and she looked at what she had dealt.

The 5 and 6 of Cups, and the 10 of Swords. She didn't remember what any of them meant. Time to consult the booklet. It would start with actual meanings, and then hedge with "in conjunction with" and "depending on" and "context" and other subtleties she was in no mood for.

"5 of Cups. This card manifests longing, particularly as in mourning or loss, and wishing the recent past or present to be different."

She would *not cry*.

On the facing page: "6 of Cups. This card represents a longing for bygone days, for lost happiness."

It was getting hard to breathe as she flipped the pages to find the 10 of Swords.

"This card signifies intense longing, to the point that it causes pain and robs one of joy."

Janna flung herself down on the bed, away from the cards, and cried.

A few minutes later, eyes aching and nose clogged and soggy tissues scattered on the pillow, she turned back toward the cards. Scooping up the dealt cards without looking at them, she put them back in the deck and shuffled again. She'd do a reading for Jeri. It was a dumb thing to do, but they'd never done a reading for just one of them, so what the hell.

She scooted higher on the bed, which would have left room for Jeri to sit facing her at the foot of the bed with the cards between them. She closed her eyes, imagining her twin, healthy, in the outfit from the dream, facing Janna with that mocking expression of hers. *Come on, sis. Help me out here. Talk to me.*

She dealt out three cards and opened her eyes, carefully looking down at the cards, not letting her eyes drift up toward where Jeri should have been.

The Tower — and two reversed cards, the Eight of Wands and the Ace of Swords. They'd never done reversed cards. She must have been careless collecting the cards after she dropped them.

She reached for the booklet.

The Tower — "indicates sudden upheaval, even disaster."

Great.

The Seven of Wands — "The meanings of this card, when reversed, include panic . . . ."

Oh, this just kept getting better.

One more, the reversed Ace of Swords. "Reversed, this card signifies confusion, brutality, chaos."

Those weren't her feelings. Were they Jeri's? Were the cards predicting her future, or Janna's? Or describing some horrific conditions somehow affecting Jeri's spirit? How could she know what they meant?

It was ridiculous to think they meant anything. Since when had she become superstitious? Jeri would laugh at her. She'd laughed when Janna first bought a tarot deck. She'd entertained herself — and Janna — by looking at the pictures and making up silly meanings for them.

What had the tarot card been in the dream? The Judgment card, wasn't it? What was it supposed to mean? Back to the booklet. Judgment, Judgment — there it was. "Self-reflection, evaluating oneself, personal awakening; reversed, group conflict, poor organization, self-doubt." Well, that didn't have anything to do with the rest. Why would the postcard in the dream have ended up showing that card?

If Jeri had invented a meaning for it, just based on the picture, what would she have come up with?

Those other cards had been about disaster and violence and chaos and fear. Plenty of situations could lead to all that. Including if bodies started coming out of their graves.

Damn it, Jeri, just what are you trying to tell me?

She flopped back on the bed and closed her eyes. Was she actually thinking that Jeri was still around somewhere, somehow, and was sending her messages? Wasn't she just kidding herself?

A stubborn whisper insisted on answering, *What if it's true?*

Chapter 6

Millie

Johnny didn't so much call the meeting to order as go from one member to another, checking whether they were ready. When all of them were, he asked those who had been making contact to tell the group how things were going.

Robert went first, standing up and looking around with an air that combined surprise and a kind of pride. "My mom really stepped up! She not only got out of the house, but she went to the library where she used to take me and looked through newspapers. She found an article . . . ." He relayed Emma's description of the photos and the number the article had given for total attacks, with the caveat that it wasn't clear how wide a territory that number covered.

Jeri jumped up to go next, shifting from foot to foot. "Janna isn't so sure she believes I'm getting in touch, but I've been able to work with her using tarot cards. I think she's close to understanding me."

Sam waited for Jeri to sit back down and then slowly stood up, his hands in his pockets. It looked as if his fingers were fidgeting. "Rosie promised to find out what was happening and how often, but she hasn't tried to get in touch with me since then. And she's a professional medium! She's just decided not to cooperate." A couple of people groaned, and others muttered. Sam nodded agreement and added, "I'm about ready to pester her some more."

Millie considered the problem. Being a medium for money was a time-honored way to con people, but if Sam had gotten through before, Rosie must have some genuine ability to span the divide between the living and the afterlife. What if she hadn't realized it? And besides, it'd be natural enough to want to hide from the ugliness of what was happening. Millie would have been glad to do the same, if only she hadn't been dragged into the middle of it. She raised a hand for Johnny's attention and said, "What if she's just taking her time, or not sure what to do?"

"Stalling? Yeah, she might be doing that." Sam chewed his lip for a moment. "Well, I'll just need to get her moving."

Johnny looked around the group and said slowly, "You probably have the best chance of a real exchange, a back-and-forth dialogue. How about if we take advantage of it? Jeri, Robert, how would you feel about hitching a ride, so to speak, on Sam's channel of communication with his friend?"

Jeri jumped up again, waving her arm. "Oh, let me! I could even ask this Rosie to get in touch with my sister!" Her face suddenly crumpled, and she fought her way through tears to say, "I could tell her I love her."

Johnny came over and enveloped her in a bear hug, while Robert said more quietly, "I'd be glad to join in."

Millie looked at them, and then at the rest of the group. Could she? Did she want to? Yes and yes. "Why not some more of us?"

Jeri raised an eyebrow. "Did you want to get in on this? What could you tell them?"

Millie looked her square in the eye. "I can tell them what you couldn't. I could tell them that my body killed someone, and that I want it stopped. I want it to *STOP*."

Rosie

Rosie had spent quite enough time running errands for her overactive imagination. And now her assistant was offering a necessary distraction. "It's time for another séance, isn't it? You did spend a substantial, if not inadvisable, amount of money on the new sound system, and the bill has come in."

They arranged to set things in motion immediately for another séance as soon as they could collect enough people to attend it. They had to include some new clients along with the regulars, so extra staging would be prudent. She had Diane pull the high-end portable air conditioner out of the attic and place it where it would, at the appropriate moment, blow into the room, with the mood music on high enough volume to cover the sound. Then Diane showed the new clients where to put jackets and coats, as well as purses and other such articles. Some mediums would have their helpers search purses and coat pockets for useful information, but Rosie had no use for such crude methods. Mingling, eavesdropping, seemingly trivial questions, and Rosie's keen ability to read people would suffice.

The clients, old and new, gradually took their seats. Rosie let them converse a little longer — reading lips was one of her more useful skills — and then slowly lifted her hands. "Welcome, friends," she intoned, and went on with her usual spiel. As she uttered the words "spirit guide," the cool air began to flow into the room, and the more sensitive among the clients looked around uneasily or went pale.

But then, impossibly, a wave of warm air flowed in and overpowered it, air carrying the scent of . . . roses. And as the murmuring around the table increased, she heard a familiar male voice say, in somewhat sarcastic tones, *Time for a new spirit guide, Rosie. And I'm bringing some friends.*

She almost let her jaw drop before gaining control of it. And speaking of control, she had better make sure she retained it. Could she go through the usual greeting to her supposed guide, and follow it with the contacts whose suitability she'd pieced together? Not a chance, not with Sam saying, *Well, Rosie? Ready to meet them? They need to talk to you.*

She looked around the room with an awestruck expression, which was close enough to her actual feelings that she could easily don it. "My friends, something unprecedented is taking place! My spirit guide, Aya, has yielded to the entreaties of another spirit who urgently needs to speak to us. His name, she says, is – speak louder, please -- is Thaddeus." That'd show him. Take over her séance, would he?

Very funny. Now listen up.

— No, you just hold on a minute while I get 'em ready for you.

Rosie had always been good at creating voices. It was even easier to mimic a voice she'd recently heard. She ran Sam's words over in her head for a moment and then said in her own voice, "Listen, friends, to the urgent message Thaddeus has come so far to share with us, a danger he and his friends have sensed from the Great Beyond." And then, at a lower pitch and in Sam's rhythms: "I'm here to warn you all, and to ask you to warn others. There is danger coming your way, and you, all of you, the living, need to find out what to do about it." And then, to twist Sam's tail a little more, she added, "Thank you, Madame Rebecca, for giving me a way for my friends and me to deliver this warning."

The clients were so riveted they were barely breathing. Their eyes went even wider as the breeze shifted from warm and floral to cold again, but clammy this time, and bearing the odor of damp earth.

Now came a new voice, a woman's, not exactly old, but with the tentative, shaky sound that some women acquired before their time. Rosie obediently echoed it. "My name is Millie, and I know better than almost anyone else that something terrible is happening."

Even if it had come from someone who sounded like a storyteller or news anchor, Millie's story would have been chilling enough. Hearing it from this mouse of a woman, imagining her feelings . . . .

After Millie came a man named Daniel, with a voice so dignified it really *should* have been British. By then, the clients were twitching, almost writhing, in their chairs, and a couple of them were looking around as if planning how to run from the room. Rosie was guiltily relieved to hear Sam again, saying, "The rest won't be as intense, and they'll have some important facts to share." As if to reinforce this reassurance, the breeze warmed back up to neutral and the damp earth odor faded, letting the incense her assistant had lit make itself known once again.

The next speaker introduced himself as Robert. Apparently, he had been quite successful at making contact already, with his mother. She must be something of a natural medium herself — and it was just as well she didn't know it, or she'd offer some real competition. Anyway, the mother had collected some information, which Robert relayed and Rosie echoed. When he finished, she silently asked him, *Will your mother also be spreading the news?*

The man's voice went gravelly and gruff, the way men sounded when they didn't want to cry. *She's already done more than I could have expected. I won't ask more of her.*

The voice that came next sounded young, like a teenaged girl, and as energetic and emphatic as Millie had been soft and subdued. Not that she had anything very useful to tell. She gave her name as Jeri and mainly wanted Rosie to send a message to her sister, apparently her twin. Well, there was some irony in that, even some karmic justice. How many times had she given clients "messages" she'd invented? Rosie promised to relay Jeri's message: "I love you, always — and yes, I'm talking to you through the cards!"

Next should have come Sam. But Sam had nothing to report, because she hadn't told him what she'd learned. So she ignored Sam's *Well, Rosie, that's all for now* and said to her rapt audience, "Thaddeus is speaking to me once more. And here is what he wants you all to know." To Sam's *What are you playing at, you minx?*, she replied, *You were in such a hurry to crash my party, I didn't have a chance to report to you — so shut up and listen.* She stripped her account of the local details that would have been incongruous, hearing again the bartender's ingenuous question and the reproach he hadn't known it would carry. When she came to the end of it, Sam's only comment was, *You'll have to tell me how you dug that up, some day when you're not busy fleecing people.*

Hey, this worked out for you, didn't it? Stop being an ingrate.

She ignored his chuckle, looked gravely around the circle, and said solemnly, "S - Thaddeus and the others bid you farewell, and ask you to heed their warning. It is their profound hope that, as members of the community from which they have departed to a higher plane, you will find ways to protect that community, to put an end to the terrible scourge that has been visited upon it. They will be watching, and will assist you with their prayers."

Should she be throwing prayer into the mix? It might be a misstep. But she was exhausted, wrung out, and the ultra-low frequencies in the music that had been playing all this time had given her a headache. Or Sam had. She let her head drop dramatically into her arms and held the pose for a good thirty seconds, until the whispering and muttering around the table reached a suitable level, before she raised her head and let her weariness show in her face. She summoned a benign smile and stood up.

"Thank you, all of you, for joining me at what has proved a momentous encounter with the spirit world. If any of you wish to take up the challenge that Thaddeus and his comrades have posed us, please feel free to arrange a separate meeting with me. You all know how to contact my assistant. And now, farewell, and may peace be upon you." A moment too late, she thought about how jarring the clients might have found that usual closing.

She waited until they had all filed out, and the murmur of conversations between them and her assistant had subsided, before she heaved a huge sigh and fetched her crystal ball. Looking into it and striving for her driest tone, she thought, *Well, Sam? Did you get what you wanted, whatever that was? Are you going to be showing up without an invitation again any time soon?*

She hadn't heard Sam's snort for many years, but she remembered it well. *Depends on whether you need goosing. These people, and others like them, are really concerned about this. You're our best contact, at least so far, and you can do things we can't to find out more.*

True enough. She doubted the Internet extended to the afterlife just yet. *I guess I don't get to just forget about all this.*

Sam's "voice" went dark and sober. *That isn't just up to me. I imagine you'd rather not be attacked by one of these creatures. And I'd just as soon not see you up here real soon, even if I'd get some satisfaction yelling at you about assuming it would never happen to you.*

Chapter 7

the chronicler

The reports were increasing. And they came in from cities, from towns, from villages, from farms. Some of the living could still convince themselves the reports were only grotesque attempts to attract attention to one or another media source. But even they found it harder and harder to believe it.

Officer Grealy looked politely away as her partner threw up behind a nearby bush. While he wiped his mouth and pulled himself together, she called in a description of the body — or started to, before she saw her partner bent over again and heard more choking sounds. She moved farther away and resumed her report. They had already put flares around the corpse, splayed across the shoulder of the county highway. The morning sunshine made the flares less noticeable, but highlighted every gouge and tear in the flesh, every bright red splotch and puddle of blood.

Her partner came up to her, walking around the car and keeping its bulk between him and the body. "The photographer and evidence tech on their way?"

She thought about patting him on the shoulder, but refrained. "In just a few minutes. Then we can get the hell out of here."

He glanced back toward the body and whipped his head back around. "It's a serial killer. It's got to be. He's just too slick to leave fingerprints or a weapon anyone can find." He hesitated before adding, "Sure covers a lot of ground, though."

Grealy swallowed the bile that wanted to rise from her throat, and said, "I never thought I'd say this, but I hope that's what we're dealing with."

Being a homicide detective in Chicago meant you saw everything, sooner or later. Kowalski's mentor used to say they didn't let you retire until nothing had surprised you for years. He'd been wondering if maybe the time had come, if he should just hang on until the pension would kick in and then become a part-time security guard at a box store somewhere, chatting with old ladies and scaring teenage shoplifters.

That was before he'd seen the kind of old lady he would have chatted with, curled up beside a park bench like a dog taking a nap, with her head half torn off and her left hand grabbing the bench all by itself.

He'd vowed that the next time a gruesome call came in, he'd be prepared to do something about it. So he put his old friend Groves in the canine department on speed dial. It made him almost eager for the right call to come in. But now the waiting was over. Kowalski and Groves and Groves's dog Willie, a hefty German shepherd, were standing over the mutilated corpse of a middle-aged man. The victim looked prosperous, well-fed and well-dressed, with neatly trimmed hair and mustache. That made it likely the tattered remnants of rotted cloth that had fallen near the body, and the patches of slime near some of the ragged wounds, came from the killer.

Groves whistled Willie over and pointed to the cloth and the wounds. Willie sniffed, and then took a step away, whining softly. Groves frowned and shook his head slightly, so the dog's reaction must not have been routine. And when Groves said, "Track, boy!" Willie backed farther away and hid behind Groves's legs, pressing against them and whining again. Groves bent over to pet Willie and asked in a soothing tone, "What's wrong, boy? What is it? Here, let's move somewhere else." Man and dog walked to a nearby bench. Groves sat on one end, and Willie jumped up and laid his head on Groves's lap. Groves looked up at Kowalski and said, "He's *shivering*. I've never seen him do anything like this."

Kowalski blew out a long breath between his lips. "I guess we wait a while. The scent'll stay fresh enough, won't it?"

"Oh, sure," said Groves. "That won't be a problem." Though something else clearly was.

They waited fifteen minutes. Willie had stopped shivering and whining. Groves stood up and moved back toward the body. Willie slid off the bench . . . and moved under it, curling up and lying down.

Groves cussed softly, looked at Kowalski, and shrugged. "I don't know what the hell's going on, but I don't dare push him. It might ruin him for good. You'll have to try something else."

When he got back to the office, Kowalski investigated the fancy technical options, thermal imaging and even satellites. It took some digging, but he found out that both had already been tried in cases like this one. Thermal imaging had shown nothing that stood out against background plants and dirt and even concrete. As for satellites, what they showed, when they showed anything, looked like more of what Kowalski and Groves (and Willie) had found: bundles of rags and slime, somehow moving around before vanishing into forests or ruined buildings or piles of rubble.

The pastor tidied up the church and thought with satisfaction — he hoped it didn't amount to improper pride — of the funeral the day before, and his counseling session with the new widower after the graveside service. Attendance had been good, with extended family and neighbors and even coworkers from before the deceased retired to fuss over her husband and work in her garden. The husband had made sure there would be flowers growing near the grave, in season, and already several crocuses had popped up, which the pastor had made sure the grave diggers did not disturb. The weather for the burial had been benign, an unusually warm afternoon for March with a gentle breeze, and the grave site would be positively pastoral in the spring, the grass lush and green, the faint sound of water lapping at the manicured shore of the nearby lake.

The bereaved husband had seemed to take some comfort from the irrational, but oh-so-human thought of his beloved wife appreciating the spot and his care in choosing it. Encouraging any thoughts and feelings that helped the man cope, providing a sympathetic listener for his grief, while steering his mind toward the heavenly reward into which his wife had been received . . . it had been a good day's work, and he was grateful that such work was his lot in life.

He was not prepared for that very man to burst into the sanctuary, wild-haired and wild-eyed, beside himself, shouting, "*Where's my wife!*"

Had the man's grief driven him out of his mind? How had the pastor failed to see some warning sign? He hurried to the widower's side and placed a hand on his shoulder, steering him toward a pew. But the man shrugged him off, violently, and spun to face him. "I went to the grave! It's all torn up!"

The casket must have been defective, allowing odors to escape that had attracted some stray dog. It must have been a large dog, to do such damage. "I'm so sorry. That must have been very hard to see. We'll contact — "

"You don't *UNDERSTAND*! It's all torn up and *EMPTY*! She's gone! Someone *stole* her body. . . ." He broke down in sobs, groping for something to support him. He might be ready to sit down, now. The pastor reached out —

and froze as something banged into the church door, once, twice, and then burst in.

A lurching nightmare, the essence of desecration, had entered his church. And he recognized it. Recognized her from photographs, even though the husband had chosen a closed casket. And what he saw before him was a hideous mockery.

The pastor had never thought of himself as physically courageous. But he could not let this horror, this evil, go unopposed. He strode up to it and declared, "BEGONE, FOUL THING! THIS IS HOLY GROUND!"

It leaped for him, snarling, biting, clawing. And as it opened his throat, as his thoughts bled away, the last thought he carried into darkness was relief, even gratitude, that he wouldn't live to see whether the creature attacked the man who had been her husband.

As the number of attacks increased and the news of them spread, not all the victims were caught totally unprepared. Some tried to fight back — with knives, with sticks, with guns. But by the time someone got close enough to a zombie, as almost everyone called them, to hit or stab or slice them, they would have only moments to realize their attempts had failed. And guns just punched a hole through whatever decaying body part the bullet hit, barely slowing the creature down — though shotguns could rock them back for a few seconds. If the would-be victim was within a few steps of an unusually sturdy structure, they might be able to escape. At least for a while.

Not many people had access to such a structure. A very few people had leftover bomb shelters, and only needed to clear them of debris and make them habitable. Many of the rest started building them, or having them built. Stonemasons, and those architects and contractors that knew how to work with them, had never had so much business. As for those who couldn't afford a sturdy stone or underground shelter, or had nowhere to put one, they lobbied mayors and city councils for group shelters to be erected at government expense. Many of them, to their credit, started the process in motion. But there were all the obstacle courses to contend with: funding procedures, land purchases, zoning regulations, contract re-quirements, union negotiations, and on and on.

Some enterprising drone operators tried using their drones to spot lurking unnatural creatures. They were, however, hampered not only by the small odds of having the drones in the right place at the right time, but by the absence of a thermal signature and the operators' limited knowledge of the zombies' movement patterns. A few of the wealthiest operators, with experimental models capable of sensing odors, tried to approximate a target scent, even approaching homicide departments and morgues in the hope of some trace left on the victims, though none had yet been obtained. So far, government officials were more likely to threaten prosecution of the operators for excessive drone flights than to undertake their own efforts, unless some clandestine programs were underway.

In the meantime, people who could manage it spent less and less time outside.

The house had withstood hurricanes for more than a century, and since the year it was built, had always housed and protected the family. Over the last fifty years, the children and then their children had moved out of state, but as the fear spread, they one by one trickled back. Now they had only one more child to wait for, the second youngest daughter of the couple who currently owned the house. She would be driving, and her car had the family nickname of "the tank."

The elders had gone off to their bedroom, supposedly to sleep, and the ongoing effort to put the younger children to bed was in progress. The rest of the family sat around the big circular dining room table and played gin rummy with no one keeping score. And then, those with the most acute hearing heard the welcome note of the Land Cruiser's engine climbing the hill, and then a moment of silence before the slamming of the driver's door.

But then came a shout of alarm, and the quick rhythm of running feet. And with it, the uneven drag-and-thump sound that might mean something was following after.

The girl's father ran to the front door, grabbed the shotgun leaning against the wall next to it, and flung the door open. He hadn't had time to get the gun sighted in when his daughter burst through, panting, teeth gritted with the effort of running her fastest. The creature was a few steps behind, just far enough that he could slam and bolt the door in time. He dropped the shotgun by the door and seized his daughter in his arms, squeezing her tight, feeling her trembling. When he finally put her down, they both retreated to the table, where everyone else was standing and awaiting their turn.

Amid the general rejoicing, the exclamations and laughter, no one heard the first sound of breaking glass. But one by one, they heard the second, and the third; and by then, the room was so quiet that they could hear the tinkle of broken glass falling inward to the floor.

And then the tattered sleeve with its dripping greenish hand was reaching through. And the shotgun was still lying by the door.

Chapter 8

Millie

The way things were going, it was a relief for Millie to welcome someone who'd died of a heart attack — though he'd been living in a leftover bomb shelter, and his last few days had been spent by himself, fearfully eating canned food. He greeted the news that he had moved on with a mixture of resignation and relief. He had one request, which he made to Millie with a humble air as if it might be unreasonable. "Could I go somewhere with fresh air? Is that something you have here?"

She looked at him, sitting a little hunched over with his hands clasped on his knee and his eyes shy and hopeful, and made her decision. She had never taken anyone there except Sofia, let alone a stranger . . . but it was time to share. "I know just the place. At least, it's a favorite of mine, and you'll be able to smell fresh air, and the sea."

The man couldn't stop looking at the waves. Crouching just out of their reach, he watched them flow in and out, in and out as if mesmerized. When Millie knelt in the sand next to him, he said softly, "I've never seen the ocean. I always wanted to."

"It isn't exactly like this," Millie admitted. "In the real ocean, you get waves building up high and then crashing down, or some places crashing into rocks. You can see that whenever you like. But I wanted something quieter. Softer, if that makes any sense."

The man looked away from the water and gazed at her in wonder. "You *made* this place?"

Millie looked down as she said, "I guess you could say that. I had someone — my friend Sofia, you should meet her — help me, tell me how. But all you have to do is sit with yourself for a while and imagine a place you'd like to be. And you can make more than one place, to fit all the different ways you might be feeling." She glanced up, and the eagerness in his face made her say, "I could help you, if you'd like."

"That would be wonderful!" He looked back at the water. "Soon, anyway. I'd like to just sit here for a little while and listen to the sea."

She hadn't wanted to ask many questions while he was so clearly taking comfort in this escape from care, but in a few minutes he started talking without prompting, in murmured phrases. "We didn't know what to believe. Who to believe. People were dying in awful ways, but there weren't any clear photos or videos showing how it happened. And then a few videos did turn up, but they could have been fake. I've never believed in Sasquatch or vampires or any of that. But how would wild animals get loose in cities?"

That suggested another question: were the creatures showing up inside cities? Were any security cameras catching them?

But the man was asking Millie something. "Do you know, here? What's happening?"

There was no good reason to tell him just how much she did know, not the worst of it. It would only shock and frighten him, when he was just now feeling safe again. But she did say, "I'm afraid it really iss omething like what you said first. Something I never would have believed either, until I heard it from people coming here. It's, um, it's more or less zombies." Now he did look shocked. What could she say? "So you were right to be frightened, and to take shelter."

Neither of them had any more to say for a while. They listened to the waves, instead, and the faint shushing sound of the breeze bringing them the lightly salted air.

Finally the man spoke again. "I've been thinking about wha tyou said, about my making my own special places. I saw redwoods, once. A forest of them, one gigantic tree after another. I could never see the tops of them. I used to think that in heaven, I could see redwoods again, and I'd somehow be able to see the very tops of the trees." He stopped, and she was about to promise him again that he could create that vision when he went on, "But now, I think about that forest, with all the trees close around in every direction,and I don't want to be there again. I want to be able to see for a long way on every side." Another pause. "I know it's silly, here. There aren't any of those creatures." Then he went rigid and wide-eyed, and asked in a tight voice,"There aren't, are there? Zombies? There aren't any here?"

Millie closed her eyes for a moment and then made herself open them. No zombies here. Just the people who became them, whose bodies had hunted down men just like him and torn them apart. People like her. She made herself breathe evenly for a moment, to calm down enough to answer, "No, there are no zombies here."

When Millie's next shift came, she was glad to see Johnny sharing it. Just his presence made it feel possible to cope with whatever came.But nothing upsetting happened, and the two of them left together when their shift was over, talking about whatever came to mind while they walked nowhere in particular.

Johnny was so good at organizing people and getting them to work together, at smoothing over little flares of temper before they could ignite a bigger conflict, that Millie asked him what he'd done during his lifetime. His answer fit her unspoken metaphor, but was otherwise quite unlike what she would have guessed. "I was a firefighter," he told her as they hiked through a forest bright with autumn reds and yellows highlighted by the occasional patch of green. "I must have been good at it," he added with a smile, "because I lived long enough to retire. Though I waited until they made me. Threw a big party for me and shoved me out the door."

Still probing for an explanation, Millie asked, "Did you work for a big department, in a city?"

Johnny nodded as he jumped over a log lying across the path and held out a hand to help her over. She could, she supposed, jump every bit as high as he, and not even be left panting — but it didn't *feel* as if she could. She took his hand and nodded her thanks for the boost. When they were both back on the path, he said, "Over the years, I ended up spending a lot of my time behind a desk as an administrator. It wasn't my favorite work, but unfortunately I was competent at it. After a while I insisted on going out with a truck a couple of days a week. Threatened to quit if they said no."

She almost didn't say what came to mind. What if she dissuaded him from acting like an administrator now, when it helped their group so much? But she could tell he knew she had been about to speak. Timidly, she said, "I'm a little surprised, then, at your being willing to keep our group running smoothly. But I'm so glad you are! It would be awful if we fell apart over little squabbles and personality differences."

Johnny didn't answer for a while, long enough for them to reach a high point of the path. They both stopped to admire the view, a swooping dip into a valley and back up into another thickly forested slope with a red-painted log cabin atop it. There was smoke coming from the cabin's chimney. Did someone actually live there? Maybe she'd get up the nerve to visit someday and find out.

As they gazed across the valley, Johnny finally said, "I saw how it hurt you, finding out that your body had hurt someone else." Millie silently thanked him for the understatement as he went on, "And since then, I've been there when one of the victims showed up. It wasn't my body that killed him, but it was still heart-wrenching, seeing his pain and bewilderment and the fear he hadn't yet left behind." A pause, and then he exclaimed, "I spent my life trying to *prevent* that sort of fear and suffering. If there's anything I can do to stop it, I'm going to do it, even if it's just keeping the effort on track and making sure it's as effective as possible. Maybe later, I'll be able to do something more direct, more tangible. But for now, I can do this."

The path went on, but Millie was ready to go back and find a peaceful place to rest. She turned to face the way they'd come, and Johnny turned with her. They didn't say much more on their way back, but as they neared the bottom of the hill, Johnny said quietly, "I want the time to come when none of the welcomers have to hear that kind of story. Whatever we might each want our new lives to be like, they shouldn't be like that. People like you shouldn't have to hear stories like that, not anymore."

Millie was too choked up to speak.

She'd thought they were done talking when Johnny said slowly, "As a matter of fact, I've felt at loose ends, here. I was never one to relish the thought of an eternity of retirement, of just loafing around. I hate what's happening, but in a twisted sort of way, I'm glad of something better to do."

Millie reached for his hand and squeezed it. After searching for a reply, she finally said, "We need what you're doing, and so does everyone you'll end up helping. It was all right for you to feel good about being a firefighter. It didn't mean you wanted people to set fires. And it's all right if you feel better, more fulfilled, about what you're doing now."

Glancing at Johnny, she thought it might be his turn to be fighting tears.

The next day, Millie arrived at the end of Sofia's shift and sat watching her friend, thinking about Johnny's determination to protect people like Sofia and herself. As she cleared her mind, preparing to pay complete attention to the needs of new arrivals, a terrible scream shattered the peace. A young woman pushed her way past Sofia, pointing at Millie with a shaking hand. "It was *you*! You've got yourself all cleaned up, but it was *you*!"

Sofia hurried to place herself in between, facing the trembling, outraged spirit and murmuring the explanations that were becoming all too familiar. The young woman didn't seem to be listening. She made one attempt to shove past Sofia and then hunched over, hugging herself and shaking her head. Millie could just hear her say, "I was *engaged* . . ." before she collapsed in sobs and Sofia led her back to the chair in which she had been sitting.

And Millie could only think, *Johnny can't protect us, this poor woman and me. Nobody can.*

Janna

Janna tended to go through her email in a hurry. So much of it was spam, and the filter didn't catch half of it. When she saw an email from a "Madame Rebecca," she growled at her phone and was about to hit "delete" when she noticed the subject heading.

a message from your sister Jeri

It had to be a particularly evil scam. And she was in just the mood to let the creep have it with both barrels. She clicked on the message and hit "reply" — and then a word in the third line caught her eye.

cards

She couldn't help reading the entire line.

she really is talking to you "through the cards." Am I correct that those were tarot

She couldn't breathe. And she had to read it all.

Not long ago, I conducted a séance where — much to my surprise — I heard from several people for the first time, including a young woman who introduced herself as Jeri. Your twin sister, I believe? She was most insistent that I deliver a message to you, and I apologize for taking this long. (This Madame Rebecca didn't bother explaining the delay.) *She wants me to tell you that she really is talking to you "through the cards." Am I correct that those were tarot cards?*

She also wanted very much for you to know that she loves you, always.

Janna clung to the anger that would keep the tears away. Of course she knew Jeri loved her! How could Jeri think she needed to be told that? Maybe that was the clue that this was a scam after all. She should hunt this woman down and tell her just what sort of scum she was. Or maybe sue her for something.

Jeri's card choices were far from random. They were meant to convey a warning about something very serious. You may have heard about mysterious and disturbing deaths, and even seen speculation that they were caused by supernatural creatures. I'm afraid that is the incredible truth. If you'd like to be put in touch with the survivors of the other people who made themselves known to me, or if you have any questions about the subject matter of this remarkable discussion, please let me know. — Sincerely, Madame Rebecca

P.S. For what it's worth, I've done some investigating at the behest of the man who served as a guide for my other visitors, and these people's concerns seem to be valid.

And now this stupid email had her thinking about the tarot reading she'd done. Sudden upheaval, panic, brutality, chaos. Well, that fit some of the news she'd heard lately, much as she tried to avoid it or ignore it. And now there were people talking about zombies, for God's sake! ... which would fit with that Judgment card's picture.

But even if Jeri was — if there still *was* a Jeri, somehow, somewhere, and she had really been trying to tell Janna about some sort of goddamned zombie plague, what did she expect Janna to do about it?

What had those other ghostly people had to say? What did *they* want?

Janna read the email again, got up and paced around her bedroom, which should still be *their* bedroom ... and sat down again, calling the email back up.

Madame Rebecca, or whatever your real name is,
If by any chance you're for real, I guess I want to know more.

⬥

Rosie

Rosie looked at herself in the mirror and accused herself of stalling. She never waited this long between séances. (And she had said in her email to Janna that the last one had been "not long ago." Apparently lying had become second nature.) Was she really so cowed by what had happened last time? Looked at one way, it had been the most successful séance in quite a while. Three of those who'd attended had contacted her within the week, asking whether she'd be hosting another, or at least asking for more information. And if she got in touch with the others, she might rope in more of them.

Looked at another way, it was a distraction and possibly a financial dead end. Would these people pay for a repeat session, or would they consider themselves comrades with Rosie and each other on a quest? Did people ever pay to go on quests?

Was that why she'd stalled on scheduling another, or trying to find out any more about the creatures and their attacks? Or was change, a profound change in how she approached her life, too daunting? Or was she just paralyzed with fright?

A hot cup of tea with extra honey, and a chocolate roissant gobbled down to the crumbs, should have left her calmed — or at least sluggish with overindulgence. Instead, she found herself restless. After cleaning up after herself and pacing back and forth until her new shoes started to chafe, she gave in.

First, to respond to the most recent message, the one from Jeri's twin.

Dear Janna,

Thank you so much for responding to my message. I could certainly send you a summary of what the various voices from Beyond had to say, but much of that information is now avail-able on this side of the veil. The most productive course would be for all those who feel called to work together to meet, and to invite further participation from those spirits who have been moved to contact me. Then those of us still among the living could undertake tasks appropriate to our condition, such as research, in which the spirits might be able to guide us further.

Whether I can reestablish contact with these spirits is still to be determined, but I intend to make that attempt.

Yours in communion and hope,

Madame Rebecca

Which was all very well, but she hadn't actually tried to reach Sam. Who might still be annoyed with her, even if she could reach him instead of just having him turn up when he was good and ready.

She'd been leaving her crystal ball handy, and sat down at it now. Taking a deep breath and letting it out, she stared into it and thought, *Sam? Can I talk to you?*

Nothing happened. She was about to get up again when the depths of the crystal pulsed a little, but only for a few seconds, as if teasing her. Which was just the sort of thing Sam would do.

Sam? And gritting her teeth: *Sam, would you please answer, if you can?*

Sam? Don't you mean Thaddeus, sugar pie?

Oh, but wasn't he just enjoying having the shoe on the other foot. *I apologize. I was playing games, and it's no time for games, is it?*

The hints of color in the crystal went darker. *No, it isn't. Well, then. What do you want?*

That was blunt, but better than more sparring. *It looks like I'll be hosting a gathering of a few people, some of those who heard you and some of those your friends contacted. We'll try to figure out if there's anything useful we can do on this end. Would anyone on your end be interested in taking part?*

A snort. *Would we have to put up with the mood lighting and the incense and the woo-woo music?*

Was he giving her a tiny bit of leverage? *That depends. If I have them come over and everything's as everyday as a freaking board meeting, they may not take it well, to put it mildly. If you-all won't be showing up, I may as well do what's better for my business.*

I'll put it this way, darlin'. I've had it with your games. If you want us there, you'll drop all that crap. You're a bright girl, when you bother to remember it. I'm sure you'll think of something to say.

Was it really worth putting up with Sam pushing her around and maybe sabotaging her reputation? For what?

Maybe for people like that poor woman Millie. And all the people around her who might be at risk, not to mention herself. It wasn't like being psychic meant she could see zombies coming.

All right, damn it. We'll play it your way. How about 2 p.m. three days from now?

There was about half a minute of nothing but the pulsing colors before he said, in a funny sort of tone, *Well, I never thought about that. We're not exactly on Eastern orPacific Time, here. I'm going to have to ask around, find out how coordinating is going to work. Talk to you later, doll.*

And he was gone. She could feel the difference. Blast the man.

That evening, as Rosie tried to settle herself with a tall glass of gin and tonic, she felt a tug toward the crystal ball. With a sigh, she settled in front of it, still sipping her drink. *Well?*

Turns out we're not the first to try to coordinate schedules — not that even being in touch, let alone organized about it, is exactly common — and there's a procedure. It's not as precise as you'd like, so you'll have to leave it up to me to let you know a little ahead of time. I'm sure you'll be happy to rely on someone else.

Rosie hoped he could somehow see her "bite me" expression.

The rest is up to you, so I hope you can be persuasive.

It was Rosie's turn to snort. *How do you think I stay in business?*

She could feel him smile. *Point taken. I'll try to approximate your three days. When I tell you I have folks assembled on this end, you'll have two hours to handle your end. By the way, if you can manage it, we'd like to get Robert's mother Emma there. He'll alert her, but the logistics are up to you.*

⚬

Emma

Emma spent what anyone else would call too much time sitting at the table with pen and paper. But she had the ticking of the clock on the wall, a clock that had watched over Robert's childhood and what he'd had beyond that, to keep her company. And the times Robert had gotten in touch, that was how it had started. If she was going for a walk or washing dishes or tending the garden or taking a nap, and he tried to reach her, how could he do it? She must be ready.

So when the pen twitched in her hand and started moving across the paper, her first feeling was triumph, then intense curiosity — and then, reading his first words, embarrassment.

Dear Mom, thank you so much for going to the library and finding out so much. I know it must have been hard for you. But almost every time I check in on you, you're sitting at that table! You need to keep living your life. Please, just pick a couple of times to be ready for me, and leave it at that. And I'll try to make sure I can hear you if you try to reach me.

She wanted to purse her lips and pout, the way Robert had when he was two. But he'd been adorable doing it, and she would be anything but.

There's something else I'd like you to do, if you're willing and can get around enough. There's a group meeting, people like you who've heard from their loved ones here plus a few others. Those others — well, you may think this is weird, or even impossible, but they were at a séance, and I and the others here pushed through to talk to them, with some help from an old friend of the medium. We're setting up a sort of work group, and you could be part of it.

Emma shrank back in her chair, and the hand holding the pen trembled. Strangers! She hardly ever saw strangers anymore. Hadn't the people at the library been enough? And a séance! She'd gone to one, years ago, not long after Robert left her, and it had been awful. The woman running it had worn face paint as thick as a mime's, and the place stank of incense, and some assistant-type person tried to get information out of her, and it had all cost too much and for nothing. And when she slipped up and told someone about it afterward, they'd looked at her as if she were a pitiful old thing losing her marbles.

It's all right, Mom. The medium is the real thing, or we'd never have been able to talk to her. And everyone there will have lost someone, except maybe the medium — I'm not sure how close she was to the guy who helped us get through. Anyway, no one there will make fun of you or think you're crazy. They'll probably be impressed at how well we've been communicating.

Emma gulped and took over the pen. *How would I get there? How far away is it?*

Robert took control of the pen again. *Someone, maybe the medium or maybe someone else who's coming, will geti n touch with you about giving you a lift. You can check with me to make sure they're legit.*

A séance . . . how did those work, when they were real? *Would I be able to* hear *you? Oh, Robert, I want so much to hear your voice again!*

She waited, holding her breath, until he answered. *For most people, I think the medium just repeats what we say. But you're so good at this, you might hear something too.*

———◦◦◦———

Janna

Checking her morning email, Janna found one she'd been half hoping to see, and half afraid she would.

My dear Janna,

I have hopes of making contact with Thaddeus and his companions once again. If I can accomplish it, then we can work together toward finding some solution to this terrible scourge. But as our world grows more chaotic and disturbed, contact with the other side grows more difficult. Thaddeus will be working on fighting through the dark mists, and when he sees a path clearing, he will attempt to keep it clear until we can gather. Can you keep yourself available to come to my address (see my signature) on two hour's notice, probably the day after tomorrow?

In haste, MadameRebecca

She'd bought an old semi-wreck of a car when she got her license, and drove herself to school every since. And her school let them carry phones if they kept them on vibrate. And she could ditch easily enough if need be. Even if "Madame Rebecca" sounded like she was three-quarters full of it.

Dear Rebecca —

All right, I'll try to show up.

Chapter 9

Millie

Millie was still welcoming new arrivals to the afterlife, and it had been quite a while since she had any upsetting encounters. She tried to put the possibility out of her mind, so as to project the joy and serenity the new arrivals had a right to see.

Those emotions wavered when she saw, awaiting her, the small huddled form of a child.

Children did show up, naturally. Sometimes they came with their parents, but often enough the parents had survived whatever accident or illness the child had succumbed to. Sometimes the parents had passed over first. When they were found and reunited with the child, they often had mixed feelings, joy tempered with regret that the child had missed so much of life, but Millie could take comfort in the children's delight and relief.

She put aside those musings and went to kneel by the child's side. It was a boy, she saw, and she took his hand, saying softly, "Welcome, little one. Do you know where you are?"

The boy looked up, his body still tight and drawn together. His head jerked from side to side before he looked straight at her and asked, "Are they gone?"

Her heart sank, but she kept her voice soft and coaxing. "Who do you mean? And what's your name?"

The child looked around again. "I'm Joseph, but my mommy and daddy call me Joey. I don't know where Daddy went. Mommy wasn't home, and Daddy ran outside when something made noise and hit the windows, and he didn't come back in before — before — " He put his head down in his arms and whispered. She couldn't hear what, and when she laid her hand on his shoulder, he flinched. She waited for him to accept her touch and then said, "Please, Joey, speak a little louder. You asked me whether 'they' were gone. Did you mean your parents, or someone else?"

He said something a little louder, but still muffled. She waited, and as she'd hoped, he lifted his head and tried again. "Not my parents. The things. The things that came in the door after Daddy went out to the yard. They hurt me. Are there any here? Are they gone?"

Millie had not spent much of her life, nor her afterlife, being proud of herself. But she was proud of how she got through the rest of that welcoming session: coaxing him out of his crouch, soothing his fears, promising that she would find out where his daddy was, that they would join him soon, helping him find a safe place that would delight him to go in the meantime. She had accompanied him to that place, a summer camp filled with the friendly spirits of children, and with games and a lake to swim in — he'd loved summer camp, and was just old enough to start going. Only then, when the boy's father arrived and she could leave, had she let herself get the shakes, and then go looking for Johnny. He would help her cope, and he would know what to say to the rest of their group before they met with the living.

Rosie

Early on the targeted afternoon, Rosie heard something like a cop's whistle, and then, *It's the bat-signal, Rosie. Time to gather your troops.*

She sent her emails and made her calls, including everyone who'd been there the last time as well as the newcomers. She'd had time to decide how to set things up without all the usual trimmings, but she was still working on how to explain. With time running out, she would have to rely on her considerable talent for improvising. She'd had to, now and then, when an assistant slipped up and missed a cue, or passed her incorrect information.

And there was the doorbell. She'd sent Diane on an errand that should take just long enough.

Everyone filed in, exclaiming about the fresh spring day or predicting rain or looking around silently according to their dispositions. Soon they were gathered in a cluster in the anteroom, the regulars probably wondering why Diane wasn't ushering them farther in. She was glad to see the unfamiliar older woman who must be Robert's mother. There was a teenager who had to be Jeri's twin, young enough to make Rosie feel ancient, with long straight auburn hair and a dusting of freckles. Rosie swept in as if she were wearing her usual embroidered velvet caftan and turban. She had at least granted herself a long skirt, though a plain one. Breeze on her knees would have been simply too distracting.

They all fell silent, staring at her. She took a deep breath without showing it, and said to them all, "Welcome, friends. I can feel your questions at this unusual, this inappropriately pedestrian setting for our meeting today." And she still didn't know what to say, damn it! She could feel Sam's smirk as he stood by waiting for whatever rabbit she'd pull out of her missing turban.

A sudden rebellious wave swept through her, reckless and liberating. "What I must tell you now may shock you. Some of you will be angry, some disappointed, some confused. But I must beg you to hold to the purpose that brought you here today. Because that purpose is both real and vital, and the need ever more urgent." She took another deep breath and didn't try to hide it. "The dim lighting, the incense, the music, my usual clothing — none of them are truly necessary, at least for me. I am able to hear the spirits without it. I had forgotten that, during the years in which they failed to speak to me. I used the symbols people expect, and offered services I . . . mischaracterized. For the latter, I ask your pardon. It would be no more than I deserved, if you turned around and left. But the loved ones who have spoken to some of you about the recent attacks, and those spirits who broke through to alert us at a previous gathering, are all here, waiting to join with you in an effort to defeat a danger none of us has faced before."

In the stunned silence that followed, she heard Sam's voice, devoid of its recent ironic tone. *Attagirl, Rosie.*

It was one of her regulars who spoke first, her face twisted with growing fury. "So you've been a charlatan, all this time, making money off us and laughing behind our backs?"

Rosie sighed. "I'm not sure how to answer that. It turns out I'm a real medium who was more or less pretending to be a charlatan. I had a gift, and I betrayed it. I can't do that any longer, not when I've had my nose rubbed in it, and when the world needs real mediums more than ever. But let me ask you one question. Did you take any comfort from those sessions?"

The teenager, Janna, broke in, seeming even angrier than those who'd been tricked. "You'd better give these people back their money! It's the *least* you can do!"

Was that sinking feeling a reflection of her bank account? She looked Janna in the eye and said, "At this moment, I can't. I don't have the funds. What I can promise, for now, is to do my best — with the help of those who will be joining us — to reach those loved ones whom my previous clients thought they were talking to before. I may not be able to do that today, but I'll try to get it done as soon as possible."

Another silence, broken by a slamming door. Rosie looked around and counted heads. Two people had left, a first-timer and (she hid a wince) her most constant regular. She waited half a minute or so to see if anyone would take that departure as permission to leave also. When no one else did, she nodded soberly and said, "Thank you all. Please accompany me to the table in the next room."

She hadn't confessed that "Rebecca" was a pseudonym. She'd pushed her luck far enough for one day.

Once everyone had sat down, Rosie looked around the table. She had left the table bare, and winced at the splinters and scrapes visible around the edge. Maybe it would prompt some of her cheated clients to have mercy instead of demanding repayment. Attending from the previous séance were Meg, a wealthy divorcée who avidly collected spiritualist paraphernalia and seemed to have energy left over, and Paul, a young man who did something technical and incomprehensible in the gig economy. He'd been dragged along by the regular who'd just left, and looked bemused and vaguely alarmed at this abandonment. They were joined by those the visiting spirits had reached on their own.

There was one more confession Rosie thought she'd better make. "The guide whom I previously called Thaddeus is actually named Sam. It was something of a private joke. But now, Sam, will you join us, along with those you bring with you?" *And speak up*, she added silently. *I didn't put the crystal in the center. If you or the others need it, let me know.*

I will, but I doubt we'll need it. We're all pretty amped up over here.

Rosie nodded to him, drawing a couple of curious glances, and then raised her hands for silence. She ignored Sam's snicker. Not every gesture in her repertoire was inappropriate. Anyhow, it worked. In the ensuing hush, she said, "Welcome, everyone. We'll be starting with an update from Sam. As we know I can hear him, I'll be relaying what he says. But if anyone else can hear him also, feel free to correct me if I misstate something." *There. Unpretentious enough for you?*

You're getting there. Now listen up. We're going to start with a report from Millie.

Rosie relayed his last sentence. Across the circle, she saw Emma wrinkle her forehead as if confused. Or was she concentrating?

"We're going to start with a report from Millie. It's not that what she has to say is exactly surprising, but it should bring home the fact that we have a crisis on our hands."

She remembered Millie's voice well, but it had changed. It was stronger, and almost vibrating with outrage and pain. *I was welcoming newly arrived spirits, and a child appeared . . . .*

When Rosie had forced herself to repeat the story to its end, Janna waved a hand and then stood up for good measure. "Did the parents show up? Did you find them?"

Millie answered and Rosie echoed her. "Yes, I did, with help. They're together, and making favorite places to visit and to live in." Around the circle, faces and bodies lost some of their tension; as if in comment, Sam cut in to say, *But if you all think that's a happy ending, you don't value your earthly existence as much as I did. It's not just ignorance of the afterlife that makes your lives worth living. Or are you all ready to die? Will you be passing around the cyanide punch?*

Rosie thought it best to paraphrase. "Sam reminds us all that our lives here still matter, and that none of us want more and more lives ended too soon."

Close enough, I suppose.

What followed was surely the most peculiar brainstorming session ever. At first, they went decorously around her circle and then whatever Sam had set up, asking questions and tossing in ideas. But soon they were interrupting each other, which made things particularly chaotic when the attempted interruptions came to Rosie from the visiting spirits. It was a relief when, at one point of peak pandemonium, Emma shocked them all (probably including herself) by slamming her hand on the table. "Will you all just hush up and take your turns! How can we get anything done like this? Now, I believe young Jeri has the floor."

Rosie scribbled notes throughout the session. She usually had a surreptitious recorder going during séances, but that was hardly feasible under the circumstances: it would be at best incomplete. Two hours later, after she had thanked Sam and the others and made necessarily loose arrangements for the next session, after she served store-bought muffins and accompanying drinks to her corporeal guests and then ushered them out, she collapsed in the threadbare but comfortable armchair in the back room and finally had a chance to look over what she had written.

— Research folklore about how to make zombies: Paul. Rosie considered this make-work, but it was conceivable that some rare ingredient was involved, and knowing that fact could let them restrict it somehow.

— Research folklore and fiction (including comics and games) about how to destroy or stop zombies: Janna.

— Try to track down anyone who had actually encountered zombies (broadly defined) in the past and interview and/or recruit them: Robert, Jeri, Millie, Daniel

— Maintain a database, for the current crisis, of attacks, casualties, and any effective shelter or escape techniques: Rosie and Meg, with Meg doing more gathering and Rosie more organizing

— Obtain regular reports from the various participating spirits: Sam

— Follow up on any leads generated by the living members of the team: Daniel

No séance, no social interaction, not even any wrangle with the landlord had left her so wrung out. And they would be meeting again within weeks, though she could hope that meeting, at least, wouldn't start with acrimony.

Sam, naturally, didn't leave her in peace for long. *You did a pretty good job there, for a first honest encounter. Here's to more of the same. Get yourself a drink.*

It had been different, that was certain. Being socially productive, attempting to be of use to those around her, was a pleasant novelty. It would be hard to go back to the usual mumbo-jumbo and lies.

You think you can? I'm betting you've lost the knack. Not that you were enjoying it much.

Damn it, Sam, shut up and mind your own business for a change!

Sam's "voice" went grim. *If I mind my own business, and my friends here do the same, you're likely to be joining us before you're ready. So get yourself that drink and figure out what to do next.*

Like what, exactly? I have my assignment, just like the rest of the folks today. Isn't that enough?

Sam chuckled. *I'm going to play psychic for a change. I'm looking into the mists and I see . . . I see . . . the mists are clearing . . . I see a website. A website with classified ads. "For sale: one velvet tablecloth, one extensive collection of incense sticks, one boom box with built-in subwoofers . . . ."*

About to snap at him, Rosie paused as an unwelcome realization crept over her. The thought of donning her velvet and chiffon, intoning spiritual platitudes, making up messages and putting them in the mouths of those her clients desperately missed, made her want to vomit.

And on the heels of that epiphany, Rosie's assistant Diane opened the front door and almost hit Rosie in the stomach with the doorknob.

She looked at Rosie in surprise and then, obviously taking in her exhaustion, with sympathy. "Rough session?" She trotted on in and then stopped short. "Where is everything? And why don't I smell incense?"

And now, on top of everything, she would have to *explain*. Or would she? "Diane, please place an ad on whatever sites you think best, offering all our paraphernalia for sale separately or as a package." Running through the items in her mind, she winced at the thought of selling the crystal ball. "Except the ball. I might have a use for it." It did seem to help her hear Sam, and probably others, when she was tired. Though right now, she could still hear him just fine. *My sentimental Rosie. By all means hang onto it. You can pet it instead of a cat.*

Diane studied her face. "Are you going out of business?"

Rosie shrugged. "Not exactly. Although it might come to that. I'm not sure what I'm going to do. I'll tell you about this afternoon later, when I have the energy. And if I have to let you go, I'll give you a month's severance pay." If she was going to go broke, she may as well go bottom-of-the-barrel broke.

Diane started going around collecting the paraphernalia to be sold and packing it into a box. As she efficiently arranged the items for the best fit, she said casually over her shoulder, "You know, I've always known you actually have the sight. If you start using it on the regular, your business could be better than ever."

Rosie's jaw dropped, and she hustled to stand close to Diane so Diane would stop packing and look back at her. "What do you mean? How could you know anything of the sort?"

"It showed now and then. I guess you weren't trying to hide it, maybe because you didn't want to notice you were doing it. You sometimes put specifics in the 'messages from beyond' that I didn't see how you could have known — and from how the clients reacted, they were true. And you did it more times than I thought likely for dumb luck."

Sam, about whom Rosie had pretty much forgotten, commented, *Smart lady you've got there. Maybe you can get her to join our task force.*

Which Rosie had to admit was an awfully good idea. Obviously, she'd failed to apply the skills on which she prided herself, at least those required to assess people and identify their strengths and weaknesses, to the woman she saw more of than anyone else. It was a humbling thought, which she could put aside for the moment in favor of acting on it. She cleared her throat and said, "Don't leave today without us talking about this afternoon. There's something I could use your help with. Something important."

✳

Millie

Millie had never tried to start a rumor or gossip chain before. Indeed, she'd done her best to hide from them. But that was hardly the only new thing she'd had to try lately, so she would do her best. It took a while for her to think of asking Sofia for help, and when she thought of it, she at first felt an odd reluctance. She took a walk to let her thoughts settle and sort themselves, choosing a quaint street that was supposed to look like somewhere in France.

Why? Why would she hesitate to ask Sofia, always so helpful, to help her once again?

Her next feeling was almost like anger, a kind of resentment. It shocked her. She needed to sit down, her legs suddenly shaky, and she looked around for somewhere to sit. The closest was at a sidewalk café, and she tottered over to it and fell into the wrought-iron chair with the striped pink and white cushion. She was dimly aware that a waiter had appeared, hovered, and then left again.

She made herself breathe deeply and evenly until she felt able to examine herself. What could possibly be upsetting, even irritating, about asking Sofia for assistance?

She was *tired* of being the one who needed help. She was *tired* of being the needy one, the one Sofia had to support. Now she had a chance to do something, something important, something difficult. Something that might somehow eventually help others. And she wanted to do it by her*self*.

Which was absurd, she supposed, because she was already working with others. And Sofia knew more people than Millie did.

And Sofia wouldn't be helping Millie, exactly. She'd be helping the living, who shouldn't have their lives cut short in that horrible way; and the spirits who were finding out that their bodies had become monsters. Spirits like Millie, including Millie, but not Millie alone.

So she would talk to Sofia. She would ask Sofia whether she was interested in joining this group effort, by investigating rumors or any other way she liked.

Here was the waiter again, this time asking, "*Madame, is there anything I can get for you?*"

Millie turned to him and smiled. "Thank you. I'd like a glass of wine. White wine. Whatever you recommend."

He beamed at her. "*Mais ben sur!* I bring you the best."

That would be fine. She deserved it.

Sofia, of course, was eager to do her part, and suggested she take the first turn at investigating rumors. Millie, meanwhile, tracked down the groups she'd known about before and looked for new ones, finding surprisingly few of the latter. Many people still shuddered at the vulgarity of discussing the deaths' gruesome details, and avoided any discussion that might bring them up. Attitudes like the one Janna had (perhaps unwittingly) suggested at the meeting were also common: life was hard, life was pain, and whatever ended it was essentially a blessing, no matter when. Millie had only to look within at the pain she carried to know that was a way of ignoring and rationalizing away scars, the kind renewing the body didn't touch.

But she persevered. She still took her turn welcoming newcomers, and she gave herself time in her sand dune retreat and other favorite places to refresh her weary and daunted spirit. But the rest of the time she found people with whom she could mingle, and moved gradually toward the level of friendly acquaintance that would let her raise an unpleasant topic.

And gradually, word started trickling back to her.

First came a man named Pierre who swore he'd been made a zombie. He didn't know how; he just knew he'd been pulled out of his grave and forced to work as a slave on a plantation, and then had suddenly found his memory and willpower restored, though he was still somehow compelled to go back to his home village and die. As best he could calculate, it had all happened two hundred years ago. "I don't know as any of that helps you much," he said, holding her hand, eyes kind. "But if you think of something you want to know about it, just call me."

She hung onto his hand and asked, "Are you sure you don't remember anything about coming out of your grave, or about what freed you?"

He tilted his head, thinking, and finally said, "I remember something slimy. And I think I saw the bones of some sort of fish, and . . . there was something like tiny bits of glass on the ground when I made it all the way out." Then he flinched. "And there was a finger — just a finger, hacked off, and not mine — laying there too."

The next was even more unsettling. A woman, Angeline, had also been a zombie. "There were spiders all around when I climbed out of my grave," she said calmly, and handed Millie a piece of orange cake. Millie took it dumbly and held it as Angeline went on, "They were all dead, though. And there was a toe, a big one, a man's. And the back half of a toad. After that, I was sewing, sewing, sewing, all day and all night. I didn't mind, because I didn't feel or think. It was peaceful, in a way. And then, one day, poof! I had the taste of salt in my mouth, and I was full of rage. All I could think of, now that I was thinking, was to find the woman who had done this to me and kill her." She took a bite of her own piece of cake. "I did kill a woman. I tore her to pieces. I hope she was the one who made me a zombie. But how could I know for certain?"

Millie gathered her self-possession and said, "Thank you so much for telling me this. I must ask, is that woman the only person you killed? Or did you attack or kill anyone else?"

Angeline drew back as if shocked and offended. "Of course not! I would never do such a thing. It was only that one time."

When she had gone, and Millie had got rid of the piece of orange cake, she ran the two interviews over in her mind. The current reports were coming from more and more places, with an ever greater geographical reach. If some evil conspiracy or cult were performing the rites these accounts suggested, in all these places, surely one or more of them would have been discovered at it?

It was looking less likely that the past would provide any answers.

Chapter 10

Janna

J anna slammed her laptop closed and then opened it enough to check whether she'd broken it. All the games and movies she'd seen had people shooting zombies in the head. But according to Madame Rebecca, or whatever her real name was, that hadn't worked. Maybe the people who'd tried it weren't very good shots and didn't want to admit it.

As for the tarot cards, she'd been through two books and three websites looking at possible meanings, and the one thing she hadn't seen is any *specific advice* — just fuzziness. It was too much like what she imagined "Madame Rebecca" doing in one of her scam séances, tailoring the reading to what the customer seemed to want.

Maybe, when they next met — or even before, by email — she could ask whether the woman knew a tarot reader who might have a genuine gift. In the meantime, she had another game to play. At least the shooter games let her work off some of her frustration.

Some of the games had a monster called a "golem," and sometimes it even fought zombies, but golems seemed to come in all sorts of forms. What was the original? Did the category start out in one game and then spread to others? She checked it out and had some trouble at first finding the game maker who'd invented it. With more digging, she realized why. Golems hadn't initially come from video games at all. They were some centuries-old religious leftover out of Jewish tradition. And they weren't supposed to be made of ice or metal or fire or whatever, but out of something like clay. But what monsters would Jews have been needing to fight?

That was a question too easy to answer. Those monsters were human. Golems were supposed to protect Jews from people who wanted to hurt or kill them. The most famous golem, the Golem of Prague, had been created by a *rabbi* to protect the Jews in the Prague ghetto.

A creature that protected human beings would be awfully handy right now.

Janna grabbed the tarot deck and laid out three cards. Seven of Wands, Emperor, Hierophant. She looked them up and, after checking a few different definitions, saw a kind of theme: protection.

Well, that fit.

While they were trying to find ways to kill zombies and stop anyone from making more, it'd sure be nice if people could make their own golems to fight the creatures off. Was it all just myth, or was there any history behind it — or at least some spell, recipe, *some*thing they could try? She needed to know more. And if the rabbi in Prague supposedly made one, she should find a rabbi or two and see if they'd talk to her.

She started with a rabbi close by, in case they might want to meet in person — a woman, because much as she hated to admit it even to herself, a man who was supposed to be especially holy or learned would make her nervous. The woman served a congregation a few miles away, and the congregation's web page lacked a contact button but did have a phone number. Fine, great — but what would she say? *Excuse me, do you make golems, and what would you charge?* or *Do you have a golem recipe you could send me?*

She rehearsed saner-sounding openings for a minute — she'd be a student writing a paper, that usually worked — and made the call.

The rabbi did pick up, but she sounded harried, or at least hurried. "I'll have to leave for the Shabbat service in a few minutes. You want to know what? Something about golems? That's hardly a subject that comes up often these days." She chuckled. "Especially in a Reform congregation. But you could call Rab Horowitz, at the Lubavitcher syna-gogue downtown. He's an expert in Kabbalah — Jewish mys-ticism. He can be . . . prickly, especially with women. But if you manage to strike the right tone, I'd guess he knows as much about golems as anyone you could find. But don't call him now. Wait until Sunday."

Janna knew nothing about Lubavitchers, and what she learned in some quick research made her more nervous rather than less about approaching this apparently prickly and prob-ably misogynistic mystic. But she made the call, and then an appointment. The man with whom she spoke warned her sternly to wear "modest" attire, and listed all the parts of her that must be concealed, warmish weather notwithstanding. At least she didn't have to wear a veil.

When she arrived, she was ushered into a small and clut-tered office with a large desk, its surface covered by piles of paper and a blotter with scribbles on it. Behind it sat, she presumed, Rab Horowitz, a thin man with a long black and gray beard and deep lines around his mouth and eyes. The assistant or secretary or whatever he was pointed toward the only chair not piled high with worn and dusty books. The rabbi ignored her until she was seated and had (with difficulty) stopped fidgeting.

Sitting there, she found it surprisingly difficult to lie. But she folded her hands in her lap, spun her tale of a research paper, and waited. He took his time answering, and spoke with his eyes still on the book in front of him and his finger running along the text — except from right to left? She didn't dare ask why, just kept scribbling notes as he talked, which fit both her cover story and her real errand.

"Young woman, the making of a golem has been achieved by only the greatest masters of Kabbalah. It is justified only in the face of grave danger to the community, and even then, to control the golem may be beyond the powers of the most pious and skilled. Even Rabbi Eliyahu of Chelm of blessed memory, who created a golem to protect the Jewish people of Prague, failed in the end to keep the golem from doing harm. If you searched the world twice over, you might not find one capable of recreating his feat."

Well, that was discouraging. "Are there books you could recommend I read, to learn more about what he did, and what any others did, to make a golem, and what went wrong?"

He looked up from his book. "In English, I suppose?"

Janna bit her lip. "Um, yes. If possible."

Rab Horowitz sniffed and grabbed a sheet of slightly crumpled paper. "I will write some titles. You may be able to find them, or you may not. Books on this subject do not stay in print for long." He wrote for a few minutes and then pushed the paper in her direction. She had the odd thought that he preferred not to touch her. She should probably skip offering him a handshake. She thanked him, stood up, and had almost made it to the door when he said, "Your paper, for what course is it?"

Janna gulped, turned, said, "It's a . . . an independent study," and fled.

She was glumly unsurprised that the county library had none of the books Rab Horowitz had recommended. She tried the nearest college library and spent a frustrating half hour giving the names of the books several times, spelling "golem" out letter by letter, and promising to pay any fees for transferring the books from universities farther away. And if any of the books did turn up, she would have to come to the college and read them there, rather than taking them home.

Maybe the books wouldn't even be that helpful. The authors might be like so many experts who pretended to know more than they did.

Would dead experts be less likely to lie about things? Did dying make you care less about looking important, or whatever was wrong with experts like that?

Janna went into email and sent a message to Rosie. *If you have a chance to chat with Sam before we all meet, could you ask him if anyone there can track down any really old rabbis — any that might know about making golems? And could be counted on not to exaggerate as a way of showing off?*

Daniel

After a good deal of work, much of which had involved meandering chats with various people delighted to have a new audience, Daniel found Rab Levi, an eminent rabbi who had studied with the legendary Rabbi Judah Loew ben Bezalel of Prague and was almost as revered. They sat together sipping tall glasses of hot tea, which the rabbi drank through a sugar cube wedged in his teeth. Rab Levi was initially puzzled: "You are thinking that these attacks have been made by a golem?"

Daniel explained that the creatures appeared to have come out of graves, not merely out of the ground, and that unless someone was somehow creating a great many golems spread over hundreds of miles, the notion was unlikely. The rabbi nodded, his long beard — a vibrant chestnut, though it might have been white before he died — brushing his glass of tea. "I had also wondered if the attacks could have been caused by dybbuks — that is, demons possessing the living. What you say about the graves would exclude that idea as well, unless my understanding of dybbuks is incomplete. We should keep the possibility in mind."

Daniel had heard nothing, since his death, to suggest that demons were a reality, but he could hardly claim to be an expert. "What I was asked to explore with you is the possibility that the beleaguered living could create golems to protect them, as your teacher did. Did you learn from him how a golem is actually made? And do you think that if we could convey that information, the living could follow those instructions?"

The rabbi stroked his beard for a while and then shook his head. "So much detail, so many difficulties . . . . Even if someone can be found who would be up to the task, how many people could one golem protect against this plague?"

Daniel drained the last of his tea. "If one golem is successfully created, and proves able to defeat these zombies, then at least some human beings will have been spared to live out their intended spans. And then we could address the task of making more. Rabbis who know how could teach other people."

The rabbi looked at him, considered, stroked his beard some more, and nodded. "That is a good point. Did you know that 'rabbi' means teacher? Very well, then. We will undertake this challenge."

How had they gone so quickly from exploring a theoretical possibility to committing themselves? Somehow that crucial moment had occurred without Daniel realizing it. "Now to those daunting details," Rab Levi went on. "Do I attempt to reach one of the humans able to hear us, or to reach a sufficiently learned rabbi whom you have never contacted?"

Daniel almost stroked his much shorter beard, but stopped himself. "I would suggest we take those actions in sequence: apprise the living members of our team of my talk with you, and then have one of them contact a rabbi. It could then be up to that rabbi how to proceed from there."

The rabbi nodded again, this time with a hint of an approving expression. "I wish you success and will wait to hear what happens. Now, more tea, and some Kolaczki cookies ?"

Rosie

Rosie had one set of tasks to complete before the next meeting, whatever she would now call it. The meetings could rightly be called séances, given the participation of spirits from the realm beyond life, but after using that label dishonestly for years, it felt too tainted. The word might feel less corrupted once she made good her hasty promise and tried to reach the loved ones whose previous appearances she had faked. She could start with the two clients who had been present when Sam interrupted her last phony séance — Meg and Paul — and had still joined in the current effort. Though she didn't know if Paul had actually hoped to hear from someone, or just been dragged along.

Diane answered that question. She kept records of all the clients and their deceased loved ones. Paul, she said, had been wanting to make contact with his grandmother. So now Rosie knew who she should try to reach. Actually reaching them was another matter. Should she look into the crystal and call their names? Simply name them without such a prop, and try to push the call through the void?

She tried both, feeling more foolish by the minute, and finally sought out Sam. She fully expected him to gloat, and was taken aback when he said, *I'll be glad to help. And sometime soon, I'll find someone else you can contact when you need to, in case I'm busy. So, who should I try to find?*

She gave him the names of Meg's father and Paul's grandmother. Sam repeated them to make sure he had them right, then waited as if for more. Did Sam really want the job of tracking down *all* her client's lost ones? Did she even know where to find some of those past clients? And would their anger and embarrassment at having been, well, swindled leave them unwilling to accept her new assurances that this time, she could really do as she'd promised?

She sighed as quietly as she could, glumly aware that Sam could probably tell anyway, and said, "Let's start with those two, and later, if you're willing, you could help me find the others."

She could just imagine Sam's wry, mocking expression as he said, *Sure. Anything to further your reformation.*

Sam got in touch within days. *I've found my two. Now you round up yours.*

Rosie thought quickly. "Let's have those encounters at the end of our next group session, if they're willing."

They made the necessarily loose arrangements for that next session, and she went back to working with Meg recording what they — the living, at least — knew so far about the crisis.

The logistics for the session proved only slightly tangled, and soon enough they were gathered again. Once everyone had reported what, if anything, they'd learned, they took up Daniel's suggestion of recruiting a rabbi to, potentially, create an actual golem. Rosie soon summed up the group's initial reactions as, "All very well, but who bells the cat?"

"It'd be better for a man to go," Janna insisted. "I could just see him writing me off as a pushy female."

Everyone turned to look at Paul, the only man in the room. He shook his head vehemently and held up his hands. "Oh, no. I think this whole golem idea is crazy. I don't want any part of it."

Emma gave him an annoyed-schoolmarm glare. "Crazier than zombies killing people? We have somehow ended up living in crazy times, haven't we?"

Paul folded his arms and glared back. "People — and not just one small group of people — have been talking about zombies for centuries, and now we've got pictures of them, and eyewitnesses. Golems are just an old folk tale no one can really remember."

Rosie held up a finger while Daniel replied, and then relayed his response. "No one living, but we're no longer limited to living people."

"And I'm supposed to convince some rabbi that not only should he build a golem, but he should get the instructions from a ghost? I couldn't possibly pull that off!"

The ensuing silence grew more uncomfortable. Janna finally huffed and said, "All right! I'll make another appointment, if he'll even let me. He'll probably just tell me to run along and play. In the meantime, I'll keep studying up on tarot."

Rosie gave her a grateful smile. "Thank you, Janna. Meg and I can meet separately to update the database, based on all of your reports today. I'll be in touch with all of you — Sam included — after Janna makes her attempt. And now, I hope all of you except Meg and Paul will pick up any leftover refreshments you'd like to take with you as you leave. Meg and Paul can get theirs later, if you'll try to leave something for them. We have some unfinished business to take care of."

Janna

Janna called the Lubavitchers again, more than half hoping that the man on the other end would flatly refuse to make another appointment. He sounded even less welcoming than the first time, and repeated every word of his lecture about modest attire, but she was soon committed to show up in four days. That left Janna long enough to wash the clothes she'd flung into a crumpled heap after the last time — and fret for three days about whether she should wear something else, not that she had much in the way of suitable outfits to choose from.

Rab Horowitz's office was, in anything, more cluttered than before, as if to show how many more important things he had to do besides talk to her. He invited her to sit down on the only possible chair and, as soon as she did, asked, "So, this time, will you be telling me the truth?"

What was that word? "Nonplussed." It sounded like something arithmetical, but it captured exactly how she felt. And yet she'd get nowhere, this time, without fessing up. "Yes, Rabbi, and I apologize for not doing so before. But the truth will sound strange and get stranger as I go on."

"*Nu*, I've heard many strange things in my life. Some, it may surprise you to learn, I heard from young girls like you. So tell me, what brings you back to me?"

Her mouth felt as dry as the piles of paper all around her. "Sir, have you heard anything about strange attacks on people, attacks that seem to be made by some kind of, um, inhuman creature?"

The rabbi sat suddenly upright and flung up his hand, palm outward, face grim. "You asked about golems last time. Are your people now saying that they are being attacked by a golem? Will this be the latest excuse for hunting down the Jews?"

She backed away as far as the chair would let her. "No, nothing like that! I'm one of a group of people trying to collect information and figure out what's going on and how to stop it, but what we were wondering, why I asked about golems, was . . . ." Maybe Paul had been right, because what she was about to say sounded absolutely crazy to her. But she bulled ahead. "We were wondering whether it might be possible — because golems were made in order to protect communities, whether someone nowadays might be able to make a golem, or more than one, to protect people from whatever these creatures are."

His eyes, set deep in his wrinkled face, went wider than she would've thought they could. "You want to make a golem? A golem to fight, what have I heard these creatures called, the zombies?" He looked at her as if, for the first time, she might have an interesting thought in her head. "I have certainly not heard that suggestion. I can see now why you wanted to find out more. And I thank you for the compliment of coming to me for answers. But I'm afraid my knowledge falls far short of what would be necessary." He stroked his beard, nodding to himself, and added, "I can contact some other rabbis, see if they know more. But I can hardly give you grounds for much optimism."

Well, that was an improvement. But it was about to get even trickier.

"Rabbi, here's where I have something even stranger to say. Please, please don't throw me out before I finish, or — or stop listening."

For the first time, he looked at her with something like sympathy. "I will listen, and not eject you. Nor will I bite. Go on."

His words made her remember, in a sudden inconvenient flash, the pictures she'd seen of the people killed by the creatures. She forced the images from her mind and went on. "We would greatly appreciate you getting in touch with anyone with expertise. But, ah, we've also been getting in touch with some people. And, and not just, um, living people."

He sat, waiting, inscrutable, so she kept talking. "The, the spirits, souls, departed, whatever you'd call them, know what's happening. I guess people have been showing up who've been killed by the zombies." She decided not to mention, just now, people like Millie who had found out something worse. "And they also want to stop it. They want to help. And there are lots and lots of people from the past there. Including great rabbis. So if we can set it up, we were wondering whether you'd be willing, willing to talk to one of those rabbis through the person who, um, helps them reach us."

She ran down to a stop. The rabbi waited a moment and then said slowly, laying down each word like a game tile, "You and others have been talking to spirits."

She nodded.

"And you for some reason are sure this is real, and not a fraudulent trick."

Of course he'd think that. "It's not. Three of our members have heard from their dead loved ones on their own, and without anyone suggesting to them that it could happen or would happen. And the woman who runs things, she came clean about how she usually does, or did do, séances as scams. That's hardly a way for her to make money out of us or anything."

The rabbi nodded twice. "It would, at least, be an unusually subtle way of cheating people. So, then. Assuming these are real spirits, why do you believe they are the people they claim to be, and not something more malign?"

Malign must mean bad. "They're trying to help. That's not a 'malign' thing to do, is it?"

The rabbi sighed and looked suddenly older (even older) and weary. "They say they are trying to help, so they are trying to help." Now he was looking at her as if he was worried for her. "If the leader of your group is honest but is not accurately assessing the intentions of these visiting spirits, you may all be in danger. I will attend, if I understand correctly that you are inviting me to do so, and form my own judgment."

Had she accidentally set up a cage match between this rabbi and Rosie? Janna didn't know whether to be nervous or to look forward to it. But she said earnestly, "Yes, please come. I'll let you know when. I'm afraid it may be on short notice."

The rabbi gave her a look she read as *you poor fools* and said, "On the whim of the spirits, I am guessing?"

Janna was more than ready to escape from this cramped, paper-crammed office and get some air. "Someone said something about, um, logistics. Thank you so much, Rabbi. I'll let you know when." Once again she scurried away in retreat.

Chapter 11

Rosie

Rosie had never been fond of games of "Telephone," finding the garbling of messages to be frustrating, even infuriating, rather than funny. And here they were all stuck in one, when getting the messages right could hardly be more important. Apparently, those in the afterlife could understand each other's languages unless they found language differences piquant and worth playing with. So Daniel had been able to talk to Rab Levi, student of Rabbi Judah Loew ben Bezalel, without trouble. Rosie couldn't. That meant the rabbi would speak to Daniel, who would speak to Rosie, who would speak to whoever showed up at the meeting she'd be starting any minute — including, apparently, a very suspicious and skeptical rabbi who was crucial to the whole plan of making one or more golems. At least the rabbi on Daniel's end would be able to hear the rabbi on hers, if Daniel listened especially hard.

She'd done everything she could to keep down unnecessary friction, warning all the women to wear "modest" attire, asking everyone to keep any religious or other controversial talk to a minimum. She had also set the meeting for as soon as possible, before the rabbi had too much opportunity to change his mind. Now, she sat two yards away from the rabbi, a thin man with a long beard and an intimidating manner. He had come early and was making the sort of polite conversation one might make with a living exemplar of sleaze and criminality if one was determined to demonstrate both disapproval and good manners. She'd offered him tea, but he informed her that he could not consume any food or drink on the premises, since her dishes were presumably not kosher. Dishes could be kosher or not? Ah, well.

When all the earthbound members of the team had finally arrived — including Diane, already present, and Paul, of whose continued attendance she'd been uncertain — she asked everyone to sit and called the meeting to order. It probably took no longer than usual for everyone to quiet down, but her nerves had her feeling every fraction of a second as too long.

As before, the first afterlife visitor was Sam, but he quickly yielded to Daniel, who said, *I'm here with Rab Levi Kahane. Has Rab Horowitz consented to attend?* Echoing Daniel as usual, Rosie watched the rabbi for his reaction and saw skepticism so deep as to look very much like hostility. She quickly said, "Yes, Daniel, he's here. I must tell you, and the esteemed rabbi who has consented to speak to us, that Rab Horowitz is not inclined to believe that Rab Levi is with us and waiting to speak."

The very faint sound of an incomprehensible language, with a rhythm somewhat like German, followed before Daniel took his turn. Echoing him, Rosie said, "Rab Levi greets his colleague, thanks him for coming, and thoroughly understands his not immediately believing our connection is genuine. He stands ready to answer any questions Rab Horowitz may wish to pose to him."

Rab Horowitz sat up in his chair, then leaned forward with his elbows on his knees. He said stiffly to Rosie, "I now simply speak?"

She nodded, and he began speaking in what sounded like the same Germanic language. She'd heard about Yiddish, and guessed that was what he was using. Whatever the language, it sounded stiffly formal, and also more than a little like a cross-examination.

Daniel's replies, at least, were in English, though it wasn't always clear what questions Rab Levi was answering. Some of the replies seemed to concern the details of prayers and rituals, but none of them made any obvious reference to golems or the clay that supposedly would be used to make them. What she could hear, as the exchange went on, was Rab Horowitz's progress from implied accusation to partly concealed surprise to, finally, a tone of respect — even of submission.

As Rosie was absorbing this change, and mentally applauding how well Rab Levi had passed this apparent test, Rab Horowitz turned and spoke to her in English. "I owe you either an apology, or my admiration for a most intricate hoax. I must, in fairness, say that I am now inclined toward the former view."

Rosie allowed herself a deep, cleansing breath before saying, "Thank you, Rabbi. I know you did not expect this outcome, and I thank you for the flexibility you show by acknowledging it. How should we proceed?"

He looked around the circle. "Whoever is most skilled at taking detailed, accurate notes, that person should record whatever this Daniel says next."

Should she pick Janna, as perhaps the most likely of them to be taking notes in her daily life? But Janna had obviously failed to convince the rabbi that something authentic was going on. "Does anyone wish to volunteer?"

To her surprise and relief, Paul cleared his throat and said, "I'll give it a try. I can yield to someone else if I have trouble keeping up."

The rabbi nodded at him and replied, "Thank you, young man. I am sure Rab Levi and Daniel will do their best to keep to a pace that will not overwhelm you."

What followed was an exhaustive and exhausting list of steps to be taken, complicated by several caveats. She did her best to reproduce the various foreign-sounding words, not knowing whether they were Yiddish or Hebrew or some other archaic language, and could only hope Daniel was doing a good job of conveying them.

When Daniel came to a halt and said, *That's all, I think,* Paul handed his notes to Rab Horowitz, who read them over carefully and then did so again. He took out a pen and made a few changes, then asked two questions in Yiddish and made notes based on Daniel's relayed answers. Finally, he sat back in his chair and said something short that sounded like an expression of gratitude. Daniel responded with, *Rab Levi is in turn grateful for being invited to assist in this effort, and wishes you every success.* He paused and then said very quietly, *I have the impression that the good rabbi has some reservations, or thoughts about what might go wrong, but I don't think he's inclined to share them.*

Meanwhile, Rabbi Horowitz was saying something about "the materials I will need." His phrasing had some encouraging implications. "Rabbi," Rosie asked, "Will you be the one to . . . assemble the golem once we have everything?"

"I would certainly need to be involved. But I could use at least one assistant besides my own students. Ideally, that one would be someone with some skill at sculpting in clay."

Paul, who had laid his head in his arms on the table, looked up wearily. "I'm actually not bad at sculpting. I was an art major for a while. But it's been years, and I was never all that good at making a human form ultra-realistic."

The rabbi gave him an approving nod. "Thank you, young man. The skill level you describe may actually be better than the skill you say you lack. While the stories do not describe the golem in that much detail, I have the impression they were more crude than refined. Are Daniel and Rab Levi still, ah, available?"

Rosie checked and nodded. Rab Horowitz asked one more question in Yiddish. Daniel, in turn, told Rosie, *Rab Levi says that Rab Horowitz is correct on this point.*

"Thank you, Daniel, Rab Levi." She was about to dismiss the gathering when something occurred to her, something she should have thought of the last time. "Before you all go home, would any of you like to speak to loved ones who have joined us?" She hid a smile at Jeri's shouting over her final words, "Twin, you'd better stick around and talk to me!" Fortunately, Janna jumped to her feet, waving her hand in the air. Rosie had thought Janna was less volatile than her sister, but maybe the difference wasn't as great as she'd guessed.

On the other side of the circle, Emma hunched over, worrying at her lip. Rosie reached for her hand and said softly, "Should Robert remain while Janna and Jeri have their chat?"

Emma looked at her with what she'd have to call haunted eyes and whispered, "I'm afraid."

Rosie heard Jeri impatiently demanding, "Well?" Janna looked as if she shared the sentiment. Rosie had to say, "Girls, just a moment, please!" She forced down her own impatience and asked softly, "Afraid of what?"

Emma whispered even more quietly. Rosie had the sudden impression that she didn't want Robert to hear her. "All this time, I've been imagining talking to him, and imagining what he would say to me. I imagined him saying loving words, telling me how much he missed me. Now, I'd really be hearing him, at least through you. What if I got it all wrong? What if he never thinks about me?"

Rosie squeezed her hand. "I can't tell you ahead of time just what he'll say to you. But remember, he wrote to you. That can't have been easy. He didn't know, then, that you would be particularly good at hearing departed spirits. He must care about you deeply, to make that effort and to succeed." At least, she hoped so.

Emma gulped and squeezed back. "All right. I'll wait." Then, louder, "Robert — if you're willing, please stay so we can talk." She took a shaky breath. "We can talk, at last."

Paul and Rabbi Horowitz filed out, already deep in conversation. Rosie shepherded Janna and Jeri through tearful expressions of their fierce loving bond, and then squabbles about trivialities, and finally to goodbyes until the next time. Then it was time for Emma and Robert. "Emma," she asked, "would you like to speak first?" She wasn't surprised when Emma stared into her lap and shook her head.

Rosie was about to prompt Robert when he spoke up. *Are you all right, mama? You haven't written to me in a while, except about this ugly business. I want to know what's new with you, how you're spending your days, what's happening with people I knew.*

Emma's eyes widened, and she said, "I didn't know you still wanted letters, when we were having these meetings." Then she looked down again. "And I don't want to bother you while you're busy with important things, and — not living your life, of course, but doing whatever all of you do up there."

Rosie found it hard to do her job of faithful echo, without choking up or otherwise reacting, as Robert answered in a soft, caressing tone, *But mama, I love you. I'll always love you."* He chuckled. *"And that means always, here! I want to hear about your daily life, what's troubling you, what's going well. So please keep writing to me. That seems to be the easiest way for us to talk to each other.*

Emma had pulled a handkerchief — a real one, white cloth — out of her purse and had buried her face in it. When Rosie finished relaying Robert's words, she lifted her head, tears smeared on her cheeks, and said shakily, "Yes, my darling boy. I'll write every day. And I'll give you a chance to answer, but only when you want to."

Rosie bit her lip as Robert said, *Thank you, mama. Please imagine that I'm giving you the biggest hug. I love you, and I'll talk to you soon.*

Then there was no sound except Emma's sniffling and the house's various background clicks and hums. Everyone else had left except Meg, who would be driving Emma home, reading something on her phone while waiting. Rosie hesitated, then moved around to where Emma still sat and took the empty chair on her right. Should she? What could it hurt to offer? She cleared her throat and said, "Emma, I've already given you Robert's words. May I also give you the rest?"

Emma looked at her, confused and then startled. After a moment that felt long and awkward, she nodded and stood up. Rosie had imagined a side-hug, but that was hardly what Robert would have done. She stood up also as Emma closed her eyes, as if better to imagine Robert's presence. Rosie enveloped her in a hug, holding her as hard as she could without the risk of hurting her. Emma squeezed back so hard that Rosie couldn't breathe. But she held the pose until Emma let go and stepped back. "Thank you." And then, with a small smile: "You're a good woman, you know."

Rosie once more wanted to cry. But she was skilled at showing only what feelings were appropriate, and tried for something between a polite smile and sincere gratitude. It was hardly a moment to show guilt, or grief. She held the expression until Emma had collected Meg, or vice versa, and they left her to her thoughts.

⁎⁎⁎

Paul

The starting point seemed to be the soil. They would need "virgin soil," never built on or plowed or used in any way, as well as pure water, preferably from a mountain stream. Taking soil from the bed of the stream would be most efficient. The problem: there was no such soil and no such stream anywhere nearby.

Rab Horowitz, with his rabbinical contacts and his over-flowing library, began checking out possible sites when his other duties, apparently many, left him the time. Paul made a parallel search with more modern methods. Between them, they came up with a list of sites that were worth a try. Once Paul emailed Rosie with this update, list included, she gave him a call. "Most of these would require air travel. Apart from the expense, mightn't there be a problem with carrying soil by plane, what with local microorganisms and such? And what about the water? How much do you need?"

Paul started to say something, paused, and then cussed. "However much it is, it'd be too much liquid, wouldn't it. Wouldn't that be a pisser, to have TSA empty it into the trash."

That narrowed the possible destinations down to those within driving distance. They finally settled on a site that should work and had an alternate site not too far away. Paul pictured the various containers they would have to carry, in-spected his car, imagined cleaning out all the debris and trying to fit everything in . . . and arranged to rent an SUV.

Paul tried not to be intimidated by this man who had cowed Janna, hardly a shrinking violet. But the man's manner, as if constantly assessing whether one was a walking example of modern immorality or just hapless and contemptible, meant that the best he could do was try not to *look* intimidated.

He'd assumed he was at least in better shape than his companion, and wondered whether the rabbi could keep up. He should have worried about himself keeping up. The rabbi was leaping ahead like a mountain goat, despite the backpacks they both carried, and talking at the same time, while Paul was breathing hard just climbing. His comments were a mix of learned references to the terrain where rabbis had collected their ingredients centuries ago, and equally arcane descriptions of the flora and fauna around them, peppered with the occasional caustic comment on how young people these days didn't keep themselves in shape.

At least they'd found the stream, not far below the tree line — Paul could see the trees thinning a little ways ahead. As hot and sweaty as the climb had made him, he would have dearly loved to fall down next to it and lap up some water like a dog. He tried not to sound plaintive as he called to the rabbi, "How about we stop and take our samples here?"

"No, no, too soon, not enough up high! Surely you can climb as far as an old man like me."

Was that a chuckle he heard as the rabbi increased his speed?

Paul was just getting his second wind when the rabbi came to an abrupt halt, turned slowly around in a complete circle, and then, apparently satisfied, beckoned impatiently. "Come, come! Bring the containers you carry."

The rabbi knelt at the water's edge, and began muttering what must have been prayers as he dipped the first jug in the stream. Paul looked longingly at the cool water moving by; the rabbi, who apparently saw him without looking at him or just read his mind, snapped, "Do not touch the water upstream of me! Go downstream, if you must." Abashed, Paul crept around him, crouched as close to the water as he could without falling in (he hoped), and scooped up water with his hands. It was colder than he'd guessed, shocking his hands, and utterly delicious. Paul looked back at the rabbi and saw that he'd moved on to the hand rake, prying dirt delicately free of the bank and into a growing pile. He looked over his shoulder at Paul and pointed with his left hand at the shovel. Paul sighed and started filling containers.

When they had packed all the earth the containers could hold, Paul stared down at the result in dismay. "Do you really think we can haul all this down the mountain?"

The rabbi set his jaw. "I will not take less than we may need. If we could, I would take enough to build two golems. I have never done this before, and the golem must be large and sturdy enough for its task."

Paul said nothing more, but brought his backpack and started filling it, putting the water bottles in the outside pockets and the containers in the main compartment. He picked it up . . . and staggered before falling over backward, almost sliding down the slope. Turning to the rabbi, fighting back his embarrassment, he said, "I recommend we help each other put these on."

They made it home, in the end, with only one close call when Paul, fighting drowsiness, started to swerve toward the edge of both the road and a cliff. After that he turned the radio on, found a news station, and made a point of listening to the words. An hour or so later, the update included an all too familiar report. "A mother and child were attacked on the outskirts of Denver this afternoon. Neither survived, and the evidence indicates another of the mysterious creatures was responsible."

If he had needed a reminder of the urgency of their task, he had one. Unconsciously, he stepped harder on the gas, until the rabbi poked him with a sharp fingernail. "We will do no good to the world by driving off into an abyss. Drive slower."

He obeyed.

The next day was Shabbat, the Jewish sabbath, when apparently even the religiously charged work of constructing a golem was not allowed. The morning after that, the two of them set to work in what looked like a storage room in the Lubavitcher building, after Paul (of course) had moved out boxes of paper, boxes of what looked like shawls, cleaning equipment, and piles of used clothing. The rabbi then put down a wide plank, a little bigger than a stretcher and shaped somewhat like one, with slats of wood on the ends that could serve as handles. There was only one small window, high up on a wall, but that was just as well if they wanted secrecy.

In retrospect, they should have brought home more water. Dirt could dry and be used again, but if Paul added too little water and the mud fell apart, that water had been mostly wasted. After the first such mistake, he made himself work very slowly and painstakingly. Whenever they stopped work for any length of time, Paul or the rabbi would tuck a tarp around the growing mass, as carefully as if it were an oversized clay baby.

By the night following the second day, Paul found himself dreaming of sculpting, everything from a self-portrait to a sadly imperfect copy of Michelangelo's *David*. It was a relief when, on the afternoon of the fourth day, he could finally start shaping the mass into a figure something like human. The rabbi showed him an illustration of the Golem of Prague standing with the rabbi who had created it. That golem looked a good deal larger than their mountain soil would let him create, but he could at least try for similar proportions: much broader than a man, with a rounded triangular head sloping directly down to its very wide shoulders; deep pits for the eyes, and a round indent in the forehead which the rabbi did not explain. As for the size, maybe the Rabbi of Prague had been a short fellow.

As the golem started to take form, the rabbi kept a closer eye on Paul's progress . . . which made Paul nervous, which made him work more slowly. Finally, mid-morning on the third day since he'd started, the rabbi abruptly shouted, "Enough! Not another touch."

Paul got to his feet and took some deep breaths, surprised to find his hands shaking. He put them behind his back and asked, "What now?"

The rabbi left the room without answering him, returning a few minutes later with three younger men in similar clothes. They stood around the tarp, and the rabbi issued a stream of instructions in (presumably) Yiddish. Each of the men picked up a corner of the tarp and lifted it slowly while chanting in unison. Two of them folded the tarp and put it aside, and they all stared down at Paul's work. Then two of the men stood back, while the rabbi and the man with the longest beard — even longer than the rabbi's — started pacing around the golem in a clockwise circle, reciting more incomprehensible words with the rhythm of verse, or perhaps scripture.

Paul watched them just long enough for the circles to make him dizzy and went out for a walk.

When Paul eventually returned to where the rabbi and his helpers were — literally, Paul supposed — working their magic, they were just replacing the tarp over the golem. The three assistants bowed to the rabbi and left the room, while Paul stood awkwardly by, waiting for further instructions. As soon as the door closed behind the assistants, the rabbi turned to Paul and said briskly, "Have you been told where the golem is to go? The final steps must be done there."

"Just a moment." Paul fished out his phone and double-checked the location Rosie had picked, based on the database they'd compiled about where attacks were likely. "Yup — yes, I have it all lined up."

The rabbi looked skeptical, but merely said, "Very well. We will go now."

Paul looked at the tarp-covered form on the plank. The rabbi had been more than able to climb up the mountain in Oregon, but could he haul a heavy pseudo-stretcher? If the rabbi dropped his end, all this effort would be wasted. He tried frantically to find a diplomatic way to object, but the rabbi opened the door again and beckoned, and the tallest of the assistants strode back in. Paul shut his mouth again and suppressed his sigh of relief, texting Rosie with a quick update. As he sent it, the rabbi pointed to the crude handles, then to Paul and the assistant. "Waste no more time! We go!"

Chapter 12

Janna

Janna woke, stretched, and grabbed the notebook she had started keeping on her nightstand. She'd had another dream-visit from Jeri, and it had included a tarot card. Just one, which was strange: the Two of Swords.

She was bleary-eyed and foggy-headed from being up late the night before, so she made herself a cup of coffee before fetching her book of tarot card meanings and looking the card up. When she found it, she frowned. Recommendations of delay, of it not being time for some event, of being on the wrong path? There was nothing coming up soon in her life that suggested itself as fitting that advice. Had Rosie set a new meeting date that should actually be postponed?

She sent Rosie a quick email and then started planning her breakfast.

Paul

Paul, Rabbi Horowitz, and the rabbi's assistant reached their destination in late morning after a night spent in a motel, eating nonperishable foods the rabbi had brought with him. Fortunately, it wasn't raining — and what happened to a golem when it rained? It rained a lot in eastern Europe, didn't it? Presumably, whatever allowed a golem to come to life would protect it from such a common hazard, but it wasn't alive yet.

There was no parking lot, but there was a grassy area that looked firm enough to bear the weight of the SUV. He pulled in and got out, opened the hatch, and waited for the rabbi and assistant. Then, with the rabbi standing out of the way, he and the assistant hauled out the plank and carried it to a spot near the edge of a grove of trees like a small forest.

As he closed the hatch, the rabbi asked, "Are you carrying any modern devices on your person?"

Paul started to answer, "Well, only my phone," when he realized that he would sound like an idiot. Of course his phone fit that description. He fished it out of his pocket and slid it into the driver's side door pocket. "Nothing else."

"Good. Then follow me."

The rabbi and the assistant removed the tarp, with the same ceremonious care as before. Paul expected them both to be chanting some more, but the assistant moved a couple of yards away and began swaying and muttering under his breath. The rabbi did chant for a few minutes, then fell silent and squatted at the figure's head, drawing or writing something with his finger in the indented spot on its forehead.

Paul had spent too much time lately being curious and keeping his mouth shut anyway. He moved closer and asked in a hushed voice, "What are you doing?"

The rabbi, without pausing but also without snapping at him, said, "I am writing the Hebrew word for 'truth' and the holy name of God, which may be written but not spoken. When I have done this, a final prayer will bring it to life. Then I will give it the instructions prescribed in the ancient texts."

Paul barely stopped himself from staring at the man. Ancient texts? He couldn't restrain himself from asking, "Can't you, uh, update those instructions any?"

The rabbi looked at him gravely. "A golem is not a man, to absorb the new and unexpected." He hesitated, which Paul couldn't remember having seen him do before. "But I will attempt to supplement the instructions, in as simple a way as possible."

❖

Rosie

Rosie had been busy most of the morning, setting up the last of the free makeup sessions with clients and placating those who were angry. When she finally checked her email, she was intrigued to see an email from Janna with the subject line, *A dream you might understand better than I do.*

She read it quickly and then again more slowly, with a growing sinking feeling in her belly.

I had another dream of Jeri and a tarot card. This one was the Two of Swords. My book says it has something to do with delaying until a better time, or being on the wrong path. Is there something happening I don't know about that could make sense of this? — Janna

She grabbed her phone with a shaking hand and texted Paul, then took a few deep breaths while waiting for his reply.

No reply came.

Screw the text-first etiquette. She called . . . and listened to the phone ring over and over. Finally it picked up, and she waited for Paul to say something she could interrupt with her urgent demand. But what she heard, she realized seconds later, was a voicemail message.

* * *

Paul

It was a sight Paul would never forget: the broad, bulky figure, reddish-brown, its primitive shape like a remnant of some long-extinct culture, lifting its head and shoulders slowly from the ground and rising to its feet without using its arms, as if lifted by invisible hands.

Would it speak? But no, it had no mouth. Nor had it ears, but the rabbi seemed confident that it would listen as he directed a stream of Hebrew at it. When he came to a stop, he said in English for Paul's benefit, "I have told it to follow a route into the forest thirty-five steps, and then thirty steps to the left and to the right, and then back to this spot, then do the same in the opposite direction, and to repeat those steps all day and for the two days following, at which time we will return."

The golem began moving its massive legs, slowly but with metronomic regularity, toward the trees. Paul yanked his head around before the movement could hypnotize him into wanting to follow. To distract himself, he asked, "Ah, where do we go in the meantime?"

"If we can use your device to locate a hotel with a kosher kitchen, we will wait. Otherwise, you will drive us home and we will come back when the three days are up."

The assistant cleared his throat and said, this time in English, "If you permit, Rabbi, I will stay and observe the golem, following it except when I must stop to rest. I brought the necessary camping supplies."

Rab Horowitz considered, then replied, "Very well. Retrieve them. You know how to stop the golem in extremity?"

"Yes, Rabbi. I will rub away the writing on the creature's forehead."

Paul stared at them both. How either of them expected this pale, weedy fellow to accomplish that, if the golem was out of control to the point where it would be necessary, was beyond him. But he said nothing as the assistant retrieved his meager supplies and hurried off to trail behind the golem, which was already hard to see among the trees with their abundant leaves. The rabbi looked after him with what looked to Paul like a determined lack of expression. Paul shuddered and addressed himself to the search for a suitable hotel.

Paul had half expected the hotel to be staffed by replicas of the rabbi and his assistants, so he was pleasantly surprised by the motherly woman who checked them in. Was the rabbi at all uncomfortable with her? Paul hadn't seen him interact with a woman before, except Rosie, and he hadn't been exactly cordial with her. But he was pleasant, even jovial, and suggested to Paul that they accept her invitation to join the other guests at the midday meal. It proved bountiful, and while the roast beef was well-done and devoid of any natural juices, it still managed to be reasonably tender. The mashed sweet potatoes and carrots filled all Paul's empty corners, even before the thick slabs of honey cake the same woman pressed on them.

The rabbi inquired if the hotel had a study or library, and when assured it had the latter, headed off with an eager step to inspect it. Paul withdrew to his room and collapsed on his bed to digest. There was no television, to his bewilderment, so he took out his phone and checked his texts and other messages. A text with his name in all caps seized his attention. Opening it, he saw with some nervousness that it came from Rosie. Reading it didn't help matters. He also had a voicemail waiting, which only confirmed his impression that Rosie was both worried by the dream Janna had told her about and annoyed that Paul failed to be instantly available to hear about it.

He checked the time on both text and voicemail. He'd been driving when they came in. He could hardly, he assured himself, have attended to such distractions while driving. And by now, it was too late to call off the whole experiment. He could tell the rabbi and suggest stopping the golem by the method the rabbi and assistant had discussed . . . but what an anticlimax! After all this trouble, were they just supposed to call a halt?

Paul imagined going to the rabbi, disrupting his reading or writing or prayers or whatever, and telling them that a teenager's dream about a tarot card meant that they had to disable the golem. He was still running that awkward scenario in his head when the hours of driving and the huge meal conspired to send him into an unscheduled nap.

He woke up disoriented, looked around at the cozy, old-fashioned room, and sat up so abruptly his rear sank into the too-soft mattress. What had he been thinking about when he fell asleep? Hadn't he been trying to make some decision?

Oh, crap.

He looked at the round brass clock at the bedside and cussed. It was probably too late now to find the rabbi and pass on Rosie's qualms, even if he wanted to. But he could compromise and go see what was happening, maybe talk to the assistant about the dilemma. He could even stay with the assistant afterward. That would prove his diligence, and maybe mollify Rosie when she heard about it. He grabbed the spare blankets in the closet, then reconsidered and went back to the dining room. As he'd hoped, there were still some pieces of honey cake on a side table, along with what looked and smelled like freshly made chocolate chip cookies.

Good enough. He found a napkin and packed up a good supply of both treats, then went back to his room for the blankets and headed for the car.

the golem

The sun had been slanting golden between the tree branches when the golem had awakened. Then the sun moved higher, then lower and from another direction, with more red in it. All this time, the golem had marched along the route it had been commanded to march, feeling more and more lost. Where were the people it was supposed to guard? It had a purpose, and it hurt not to be fulfilling it.

There was a man following behind, who sometimes stopped and leaned against a tree or sat at the base of it. Had the golem been created simply to protect that one man? That didn't feel like the answer. It trudged on, as unhappy and puzzled as an abandoned dog. The light slanted lower.

And then something changed. Something was coming toward him through the trees. Soon it was close enough for the golem to see clearly. But seeing it only confused the golem more. The creature made moaning sounds, nothing like the language the golem's master had used. And the master's body had radiated heat. This figure did not.

Maybe it was another protector, a companion.

The other creature turned and started walking away, in a different direction than the golem had been walking. The golem had found no people to guard along its original route. If it went with this new companion, they might appear.

The newcomer was pulling ahead. The golem moved faster to follow.

<hr>

Paul

Paul pulled up where he had parked before and got out, awkwardly carrying the bundle of blankets and food. He knew where the golem had been awakened, but naturally nothing was there. What had the rabbi said about the route the golem was supposed to follow? He tried to remember the details, but not all of them came. It started with going into the forest, he knew that much.

But before he'd gone more than a few steps, he saw movement, and froze. With all this planning and excitement and fatigue, he'd almost forgotten about the zombies. Rosie had picked this spot as a place likely to have zombies show up, and here he was with blankets and desserts as a weapon? What was he supposed to do, throw cookies at it?

But the movement quickly resolved into the black-clad figure of the assistant, pacing in a small circle and mumbling and shaking his head. As soon as he saw Paul approaching, his head jerked up and he said, "We must go to the rabbi! Something terrible has happened!"

Paul glanced around for any gruesome evidence. No blood, no body parts. He could afford to take some time talking the assistant down. "Whatever it is, I'm sure we can handle it. We'll go see the rabbi in a minute. What is it that's upset you?"

His tone might have been too condescending. The assistant glared at him and stood up ramrod straight. "You stupid *shegitz*, do you think I would be so 'upset' over nothing? The golem is gone!"

"Um . . . weren't you supposed to follow it?"

"It was supposed to follow the route Rab Horowitz commanded! But when the zombie appeared — "

Paul took a step backward. "Wait just a minute! A *zombie* showed up, and you didn't think to mention that *first*?" He looked the assistant up and down. "It doesn't look like it attacked you. Did the golem protect you, the way it was supposed to?"

"The golem followed it! I hid behind the trees, and the golem left its path and followed the zombie!"

Paul stared at him. "Oh, *CRAP*."

The assistant startled Paul by smiling, though briefly. "My sentiments exactly. We must go to the rabbi at once."

They found the rabbi at dinner. Before they could assault him with information, the hostess spied them and waved them impatiently to seats. "You almost missed dinner! Sit, sit, and I'll get your plates."

Paul's stomach churned. He was, in fact, hungry, but he had a feeling food wouldn't sit well, if it even stayed down. From the assistant's expression, he had similar qualms. Meanwhile, the rabbi was looking them over. He spoke first to the assistant, asking (in English, to Paul's relief), "What has changed your intention to stay near the golem?"

It was a short explanation, if a somewhat incoherent one, but the heavily loaded plates arrived in the middle of it. Paul did his best to eat until the assistant finished talking, even though the rabbi stood up in the middle. As soon as the assistant stammered to a stop, the rabbi gestured impatiently, said, "We must go at once!", and walked quickly toward the door. The assistant looked at the plate, grabbed a roll, and followed, Paul trailing after. The hostess gave them a reproachful look as they left.

They drove to the site, and the rabbi urged him to drive fast, with no concern for speed limits or the possibility of deer (or worse) crossing the road around the next bend. The rabbi jumped out as soon as Paul screeched to a stop, followed quickly by the assistant. Paul finally gathered his wits enough to say, "Are you really planning to get close to a zombie, just because the golem is with it?"

Rab Horowitz patted his hand and said in benign reassurance, "The golem will not harm me. You and my student should stand clear."

"No, Rabbi!" exclaimed the assistant. "I will stand with you. I will not abandon you!"

The rabbi hushed him. "We can discuss this further while we track the golem." He closed his eyes, muttered for a moment, pointed, and set off at a trot, assistant at his heels and then, once the direction was apparently clear, moving ahead. Paul gulped and followed a few yards behind, hoping he'd have a phone signal and the time to call for help if they succeeded in tracking their quarry — not that he knew of anyone to call.

Their path led into an even denser area of forest. Paul soon became distracted by the need to avoid branches and weave between trees, all the while trying to keep the rabbi in sight and yet leave some distance. And suddenly, he burst onto a scene straight out of his fearful imaginings.

The assistant was standing as still as if petrified, his hands outspread, and the zombie was advancing on him.

the golem

The golem had been following its new companion, following, following, following, following . . . and then the other being, the man that had been following the golem, was standing in the way.

The companion made its moaning sound louder and went faster, lurching toward the man. Was the man the enemy, then, after all? It got ready to join them —

And then the golem's master appeared, thrusting his way in front of the other man, shouting a command in that language the golem didn't understand so much as recognize.

The golem hadn't known it could move so fast. It rushed ahead of the companion and stood in the way, thrusting the companion back, away from the master. The companion stopped and stared. Then, slowly, it turned and shuffled off another way.

The golem would have followed again, but here was its master, returned! Its master would tell it, somehow, what to do, what to fight against, what to protect besides the master himself.

The golem waited, trusting. It thought the master would speak again, but instead the master stood still for a long moment and then reached toward the golem. He had water in his eyes as he touched the golem's forehead, muttered something softly, and rubbed.

What was happening? Everything was slowing down, fading. Even the master's face, with the water glimmering in his eyes.

Paul

The three men looked down at the disintegrating lump of earth that had, so briefly, walked among them. Had it thought at all? They would never know. "Should we . . . do something with it?" he asked his companions.

The assistant was still breathing too fast to speak. The rabbi shook his head, beard swaying, and said, "There is hardly a point in burying it. But my student and I will spread it thin, so that not a clump remains."

They had brought no tools for the purpose, but a fallen branch served. The two of them chanted prayers as they worked, with as much concentration as when they had made the golem they were now destroying. They rejoined Paul when they were done, and he drove back to the hotel without any of them saying a word. Paul led the way back inside. It was too late to start the drive home. Still silent, they parted for their rooms.

First thing the next morning, Paul found the hostess, told her they'd be leaving, and thanked her for everything. "Wait!", she exclaimed, and disappeared briefly only to return with a package wrapped in brown paper. "You'll miss breakfast! At least take this for the journey."

It took fifty miles for them to start talking. The rabbi said in a musing tone, as if continuing some discussion, "I will write about this, and discuss it in depth with various colleagues. I suppose I will become known among the more learned as the first in hundreds of years to make a golem."

"Even better," Paul said glumly, "if it'd done what it was supposed to do."

"That was not the creature's fault." Paul suppressed his comment that he hadn't been inclined to assign blame in that direction. "It was made to hold the line at the edge of a crowded community. This situation was much more confusing. I hoped it would discern the overriding, underlying mission, but it could not. We explored, and now know more of, the boundaries of a golem's understanding. Those boundaries might have been more expansive than previously thought. It was worth finding out."

"That's all very well," Paul grumbled, "but what do we do now?"

The rabbi said something that sounded like, "Hashem ye-ra-hem," with a rasping sort of "r."

After a moment, the assistant spoke up for the first time since they left the forest. "It means 'God have mercy.'"

Chapter 13

Rosie

Rosie called the meeting to order and said brusquely, "All right, everyone, you can have ten minutes for telling me I should have told Paul and the rest to hold off, and what a bad idea the golem was, and anything else. Then we get back to work."

They were easier on her than she'd expected. Maybe if more of the living on the team had been men, they'd have had more to say about how *they* would have done things. Janna and Daniel questioned not why Rosie had given the go-ahead, but why they were all giving up so soon on the golem notion. Paul handled that one. "Rab Horowitz feels that if any golem could be made capable of understanding the mission we tried to give it, this one would have." Several of the others rolled their eyes or otherwise showed skepticism. Paul, however, seemed to accept the rabbi's assessment, and simply went on. "Also, he says he's diverted enough time from his studies and students and community. So that's it. Welcome to the Return of Square One."

Daniel, not quite ready to let the idea go, interjected, *I'm going to talk to Rab Loew again, just in case he has any ideas. And he'll probably want to know, anyway, how things went.*

There was a brief pause, of which Millie took advantage to introduce her friend Sofia, and Sofia to declare her earnest hope that she would find some way to contribute to their efforts. Rosie welcomed her, then turned back to business. "Janna, anything new from folklore and fiction and such?"

Janna shrugged and said, "I've seen some lists of weapons for fighting zombies. If I remember what was said at previous meetings, most of them don't work — but I haven't seen any news about using grenades. With the mess they make, a zombie might not be able to reassemble itself afterward — or at least, not before the human can get away. Oh, and I've been looking at animals that might come in handy. There's Komodo dragons —"

"Are there?" Meg broke in to ask. "I mean, is there some-place where there are plenty of them?"

"They mostly live in Indonesia, on five islands. And they're in some zoos."

Paul hesitantly weighed in. "Aren't they kind of sluggish? Zombies can move pretty fast."

Janna gave him an indulgent look and said in a conde-scending tone, "Well, Komodo dragons hunt a kind of *deer*, and wild pigs. They can't be as sluggish as all that."

"What about breeding them?" Rosie asked. "If we don't find a way to get rid of all the zombies at once, or in a relatively short period of time, we need ongoing solutions."

Janna (along with several others) winced at the thought of zombies becoming an ongoing hazard, but answered, "The females don't breed every year. And they like to eat the babies, once the babies hatch. But I'm sure whoever was breeding them could take precautions."

Emma raised her hand. "I have a notion that there aren't many of them. Are they . . . what is that word . . . ."

"Endangered," Diane suggested quietly "I believe so."

Rosie sighed. "Okay, grenades and endangered infanticidal Komodo dragons, check. Any other useful critters?"

Janna brightened. "There's vultures and ravens. And crows, I suppose. Also bears, wolves, and coyote. They all eat carrion."

Jeri weighed in with, *I don't know, twin. Carrion tends to lie there waiting for something to eat it. How do vultures and ravens feel about carrion that's still walking around?*

Rosie relayed the comment; Janna frowned, presumably at her sister, and said, "Well, bears and wolves and coyote eat live prey too!"

Including people, sometimes! Jeri answered. Sam, standing by in the background, seemed to be enjoying the family squabble.

Rosie passed along Jeri's rejoinder and then said briskly, "All right, Janna can keep looking at animal alternatives. And we can all do some thinking about how to persuade people that more bears or wolves or coyote are a good thing. There's already been plenty of opposition to reintroducing wolves in places like Yellowstone."

Paul piped up with, "And I'll find out more about grenades! And — what about flamethrowers?"

"Flamethrowers don't have much range," Janna pointed out in a tone now approaching impatience, and then said more kindly, "But it's a good idea to find out about grenades."

Rosie almost said something about Molotov cocktails, which would work much like a grenade without the hazard of getting so close. But they were probably illegal. And who knew whether zombies would even burn?

The day after the meeting, Paul reported glumly that to own a grenade, you were supposed to have a federal explosives license or permit. He seemed inclined to give up on the idea. Rosie refrained from observing that the failure of the golem experiment had perhaps unduly undermined his staying power. Instead, she began her own inquiries about just what would be involved in getting the necessary paperwork. As with any federal red tape, it was something of an obstacle course that would take get through. The trickiest aspect might be storage, around which the red tape clustered most thickly, and which involved an inspection process.

This wasn't, as things stood, going to work as a solution for the population as a whole — unless they could get the regulations changed. Rosie called up her growing Action Items list and added, "contact someone politically connected." Then she sent an email to the team. "Does anyone have a friend, college roommate, cousin, neighbor, *any*one who might have an 'in' with anyone in Congress or in the federal bureaucracy? Or who knows someone who does have such a connection?"

While she was at it, she checked for regulations about private ownership of wild or endangered animals. The latter ran into federal restrictions again. But crows and ravens weren't endangered, except for a very few crow species. And they were scarily smart. People could try to attract flocks of them. Could they be trained to attack zombies? That might depend on how well they fared in such combat.

She looked up the training of crows and found, to her surprise, that the federal government's reach extended even to them. Under the Migratory Birds Act, "possessing" corvids required a permit. But surely, with the zombie emergency, there would be a way to obtain one?

Rosie downloaded all the relevant forms she could find, as well as contact information for various federal officials, and realized her spine ached and her eyes smarted. She'd been sitting and staring at screens too long. It was high time she went for a walk — a short one, and keeping close track of her surroundings. It would be too damned ironic if a zombie got her.

Rosie made it home without incident. That was when things got sticky.

As she rounded the corner, she saw a car in her driveway. At first she assumed that some former, current, or future client had come to call, which could mean anything from fresh business to a confrontation about past deceit. She made sure her stride didn't falter as she came closer — only to come to an abrupt halt when two men got out, both dressed in colorless suits and black ties, and the closer one holding an open leather wallet with some sort of badge on it. The men approached, standing in front of her and well within what should have been her personal space, and the one with the badge displayed said sharply, "Rosalind Dodd?"

It passed through her mind to say indignantly, "Why are you addressing Madame Rebecca in such a fashion?" She clamped down on her renegade imagination and quietly said, "Yes. Can I help you gentlemen?"

The other man took a folded paper out of his jacket and displayed it. "We are authorized to search these premises. After you, madam."

What struck her first was his use of "madam," so like her fantasy. Half a second later, she took in the rest, and gasped. "*Search?* Whatever for? Why, for goodness' sake?"

"We are not required to answer that, Ms. Dodd. Kindly unlock the door."

She didn't want to admit that she hadn't bothered to lock it, not in this neighborhood. She took out her keys and quickly locked and unlocked the door, attempting to go through it first. But the men had no attention of letting her. One took her arm and moved her, not too roughly, out of the way.

Could two men fan out? They did something of the kind, going in different directions, turning their heads like some sort of scanner and then converging on the table where she had left her laptop. She'd even left it open for them, all unknowing. The taller, thinner man sat down at the table with a pleased grunt, while the other kept wandering. Finding no other computers, nor any stacks of books or papers, he held out his hand and said, "Your phone, please."

Rosie once again had a manic impulse to fall into character, saying, "As if someone of my talents needed such crude devices to contact whom I please!" She quickly extracted and handed over her phone before she could give way to it. Only after relinquishing the phone did she realize she had failed to actually read the paper they'd shown her. And should she be calling a lawyer?

She looked at the men who had invaded her space. The odds that they'd give her privacy to make a phone call were laughably small — and if she were going to explain things to a lawyer in their presence, she might as well answer whatever questions they were going to ask instead. For one thing, she could keep her answers short and as uninformative as possible, where a lawyer would need to know every detail that could conceivably be relevant.

Right on cue, the one who'd commandeered her laptop waved her to a chair, quite as if he were the host and she a not entirely welcome guest. As soon as her behind touched the chair, he barked out, "Why is an old fraud like you trying to get hold of restricted animals and restricted weapons?"

She bit back the defense that sprang to her lips. She might not be a professional fraud at present (and for that matter, who was he calling "old"?) — but she had been, for longer than she now cared to recall. And she could just guess at his reaction if she informed him that yes, she did genuinely chat with the souls of the departed, rather than merely pretending.

So, what to say? "I'm trying to figure out what could stop a zombie. I'm afraid of them." There. That sounded nicely feeble and female, and didn't mention any other members of the team. Though her laptop's contents would lead these infuriating snoops right to them, curse it.

The man snorted. "You're saying that after years of making money off the gullible, you've turned into one of them?"

For an instant, her old contempt for her clients surfaced and made her wonder if just possibly, she'd imagined Sam's getting in touch and everything that had happened since. She thrust the thought aside. If she started doubting herself to that extent, where would it stop?

She turned the question around. "Are *you* saying that you think all the accounts of people being attacked and torn up, in more and more places, places wild animals don't go, are just made up?"

Naturally, he didn't answer. Instead he gave her a knowing look, as if they were done playing games and would now talk turkey. "Ms. Dodd, we believe that you are involved in an endangered animal smuggling operation, and are planning to accumulate weapons to use in the event that either competing operations or governmental agencies attempt to intervene. What can you tell me to convince us otherwise?"

Rosie could now let him see a genuine expression, disbelief and amusement combined. "You think I. A medium in the suburbs. Am part of some nefarious network of smugglers. Domestic, or international?"

The other agent came over and weighed in with, "We haven't yet determined that. Would you care to tell us?"

She raised both eyebrows and said nothing. Undaunted, he went on, "Also, we'd appreciate an explanation of how crows fit in. Is a market in crows developing?"

She may as well tell them the truth, no matter how determined they were not to believe it. "Crows are smart enough to train, and common as well. They could be trained to attack zombies. They could at least distract the zombie long enough for its human target to take shelter." If a sufficiently sturdy shelter could be found.

The first agent shook his head in a theatrical exaggeration of more-in-sorrow-than-anger. "Cooperating now could save you a great deal of trouble."

So could talking to a lawyer, or calling their bluff, or both. "No, thank you."

The agent closed her laptop and put it under his arm. "We'll be taking this. Bill, is there anything on the phone worth our attention?"

Bill, apparently, tossed her phone on the table. "Naah — just some nonsense about tarot cards. There's one born every minute." He took out a business card and held it out to Rosie. "When you decide to cooperate, give us a call. Assuming we haven't taken you into custody by then."

Rosie took the card. Once she got a new laptop, she would research appropriate rituals for making trouble for someone once you had some personal possession of theirs. A possession with a person's name would be particularly useful, if those rituals proved as real as so much else had turned out to be.

⚬

Paul

Paul had made no promises to stay in touch with Rabbi Horowitz. In fact, he assumed the rabbi had little interest in staying in touch with this young upstart of an outsider. When the mailbox in the lobby of his apartment building turned out to contain not merely the few bills he still received on paper, but an actual letter, he assumed his mother had gotten fed up with his failure to call her more than once a week and was using this old-fashioned form of communication to rub it in. He took the stack of mail up to his apartment, dropped it on the table of his breakfast (and lunch and supper) nook, and forgot about it until that afternoon. But when he'd worked his way through the bills and got to the letter, he discovered it came from the rabbi.

His first, irrational reaction was worry about whether something had happened to his mother, as if he'd been expecting a letter from her and hadn't received it. He almost let the rabbi's letter sit unopened while he called her, but the rabbi's letter might be urgent — like the email from Rosie he had failed to read in time. He picked up the envelope and tore it open.

Dear Paul Turner,

(A neat compromise, that, between informal and formal.)

You will, no doubt, be surprised to hear from me. But I have news to impart, related to our recent efforts.

(Had the rabbi tried again, and without him? It would be absurd to feel hurt. But had he given up too soon after all?)

You must judge for yourself, based on your own beliefs and moral guidelines, whether to hold this information in confidence. If you find you may do so, I ask it of you.

(Well, *that* wasn't ominous.)

I have circulated an account among my colleagues, including how and with what materials we constructed the golem, the prayers and instructions I employed, and our failure to achieve the desired goal. I stated that I would not be making any further attempts and had some doubts that any could succeed, but that I did not claim the wisdom to be certain.

I have just heard that another rabbi, of deep learning and worthy of the high respect in which he is held, did construct a second golem. He added additional prayers and gave it modified instructions, which I will not take the time to spell out here. He also released it closer to a town, thinking that a location more like the towns golems were originally intended to protect might help the golem better understand its mission.

Unfortunately, being close to more people increased the chances that someone would come upon the golem and fail to recognize its nature and purpose. And that is what happened. The man who encountered the golem was brave or foolish enough to try to drive it away from the town. The golem, in turn, failed to understand that the being attacking it was not the threat it was created to fight.

Paul was finding it hard to breathe — hard to remember how to breathe, as if he had to know how or he would stop. That could have happened to him, to them. The people in the hotel, its guests and staff, the woman running it — who suddenly reminded him of his mother — what if the golem had turned on one of them? . . .

The rabbi and his assistants were nearby, near enough to see the attack. With great courage, they ran forward to confront the golem. They were able to halt its attack, and to put an end to it in the way you saw. They summoned help and, before it arrived, discussed — more briefly than they would have wished — which would be a greater sin, to leave without sharing the details of how the man was injured, or to expose their community to greater hostility by revealing the source of his injuries. They concluded that they could provide information later if more discussion, or consulting those few commentaries they did not know completely from memory, led them to conclude it was their duty; while information given could not be retracted. They quickly kicked the dirt into a less manlike form and left.

The authorities have quite naturally decided that the man was attacked by one of the "mysterious supernatural creatures." I would not have informed you otherwise if I had not concluded that as someone actively committed to battling such creatures, you should be warned of this incident and told that under no circumstances will I make another attempt or endorse any other rabbi's doing so.

As if the strain of confining himself to English had become too much or there was some religious requirement involved, the rabbi ended the letter with a few Hebrew symbols and his name.

Paul put down the letter and stared out the window. It was a small window, but he could see the leafy green branch of a tree, and a bird — a small, dark one, too small to be a crow or raven — sitting on it. When he felt he could stand and stay steady on his feet, he got up and opened the window, startling the bird into flapping away. After letting the breeze blow on his face for a couple of minutes, he turned away and sat down to send an update to Rosie. And then he called his mother.

Chapter 14

Rosie

I t was ridiculous, and intensely frustrating, for Rosie to be impeded in her mission of trying to stop a zombie apocalypse by the investigators' combination of wild imagination and stubborn incredulity.

She assumed that even when she bought a new laptop, the feds would find some way to hack it. She might be making that task particularly easy by downloading her backups, but the alternative would set their work back by weeks at best, and that she couldn't countenance. Would a new phone be just as vulnerable? She'd heard of "burner phones," used temporarily by criminals and other secretive sorts and then thrown away. But how could she research them without those men, or others like them, in effect looking over her shoulder?

The image of Emma, making her nervous but determined way to a library, came to her, and she decided to go forth and do likewise. And if she went to a library some ways away, it was less likely the feds would remain a step ahead.

But she was surprised — no, astonished — to walk around the library looking for an unoccupied computer and find

Emma at a nearby table, leafing through a copy of *The Atlantic*. It took a few seconds and Rosie clearing her throat twice before Emma noticed her. "I saw the magazines when I came before," said Emma in a near whisper. "And getting here wasn't as hard as I'd expected. So now I come sometimes."

Rosie had been wondering how best to reach Emma with the unwelcome news, and here was an ideal opportunity. "May I sit down for a minute and tell you about something that's happened?"

As Rosie related her experience, Emma's face went from curiosity to shock to an unexpected and welcome anger. "How dare they intrude like that! And how — how absolutely *stupid* of them! I do hope their superiors are paying more attention to what's happening. They're supposed to protect us, not keep us from finding out how to protect each other!"

A cogent political analysis, but not much help at the moment. "I'm afraid they might end up bothering some or all of the team. Even you."

Emma's indignation crumbled into fear. "Do you mean they might — come to my home? Insist on going inside, and pawing through all my things?"

Rosie tried to put aside paranoia, along with the urge to reassure, and answer with the truth. It still felt like using a neglected muscle. "I can't say for certain, but it seems unlikely to me. They as much as told me that they considered me a fraud, a professional bad actor; and of course my profession requires me to be in touch with many people. You're less plugged in, so to speak. And it may be presumptuous of me, but I'm guessing you've never been in trouble with the law, or at least not in the last several decades?"

Was that a blush? Emma nodded, without saying which of those two guesses was correct.

Emma

Emma tried to keep reading her magazine after Rosie went off to use a computer, but she was too unsettled. The nonsense with federal officials would have been enough to upset her, but she had been ridiculously startled at Rosie's idle comment about her past. It had just been that one time, when she let a so-called friend talk her into trying to buy a bottle of gin with the friend's phony identification. . . .

She went home, looked at the few dishes that needed washing and at the tea cozy she was in the middle of knitting for Rosie, and ignored both to fetch pen and paper. It was time to write to Robert.

My darling son,

I got some upsetting news today, and I wondered whether you can tell me what to do.

She told him what had happened to Rosie, and what Rosie had said about the agents probably not bothering Emma. Then she asked him, *Do you think she's right? Or should I stop going to the meetings?*

While she was wondering what else to say, the pen twitched in her hand. She set it back on the paper and watched Robert answer her.

Dear Mom, I don't know whether Emma's right or not. If you feel unsafe — more unsafe than just the zombies have been making you feel — then you could stop. It won't affect me one way or the other

The pen stopped and then started moving again.

unless my body turns into one. I'd hate that, but the odds are against it, at least for now.

The very thought seemed to stop her heart, and then set it to pounding as if it would break out of her chest. If there was any chance of that, and any chance she could help stop it from happening . . . .

There's something else to consider, though it's an unpleasant thought. I'm not sure that what you do going forward will make much of a difference as far as the feds are concerned. Unless you were to get a lot more active in the team's efforts, they'll probably decide whether to harass you based on what your involvement has already been. If you keep going, you'll at least know that you're doing something that could be important.

Now, what else is new? What have you been doing for fun? I'm glad you've gone back to the library. Bravo! Or brava, if you want to be picky.

Emma smiled, laughed, and wiped away a tear.

<hr>

Paul

Paul ran through Rosie's warning email in his mind and fumed. Those officious, interfering idiots had harassed Rosie?

Tried to intimidate her? Were essentially threatening to shut down what might be the most effective group trying to keep them all from being zombie snacks?

Well, screw them and the horse — no, probably a SWAT vehicle — they rode in on!

He'd been keeping track of Rosie's additions to his own weapons research. Ironically, it'd be easiest to make a weapon for which there was no legal process, even a cumbersome federal obstacle course. And people rebelling against tyrannical governments had been making them for hundreds of years. Time to look up the recipe for Molotov cocktails!

Which he'd better do somewhere the feds wouldn't be tracking yet. Hadn't Emma used libraries? He wasn't sure he'd ever actually been to one, but why not?

Once settled at a computer in a library chosen at random, which he'd reached while checking nervously for anyone tailing him, he looked up the potential ingredients. Glass bottle or similarly breakable container, flammable liquid, a soaked cloth wick held in place by the stopper. Thickening agents like baking soda and petroleum jelly were sometimes added. Okay, then! Alcohol could be used for both the liquid in the bottle and the liquid for soaking the wick. Alcohol was easy to come by, and it didn't even have to be the undrinkable kind. Baking soda was as innocuous an ingredient as you could ask for, with petroleum jelly almost as good. As for bottles . . . hmmm. Some sources said standard beer bottles weren't big enough. Some people had used vodka bottles, though one source carped that it'd take a higher proof alcohol than vodka. Rebels in Spain had used the homier jam jar.

Oh, and the wick shouldn't be a synthetic fabric. Natural fibers for the win!

Good thing he was good at remembering details. It wouldn't do to jot all this down, whether on his phone or on paper. Though the details of how to seal the bottle took rereading several times for them to lodge in his brain.

Paul left the library and headed off to do his shopping. He kept his grin under control until he reached the relative privacy of his car.

When he got home, he saw that Rosie had sent around a message about the next meeting. As was becoming usual, she proposed it be the following Tuesday afternoon. That was fine with him. Should he mention his little project? Maybe not on Tuesday. Maybe when he was further along.

He checked the rest of his email. There was one from Janna, the kid on the team.

Could you possibly give me a ride to the meeting? My car's in the shop, which may or may not be able to fix it this time, and my mom's too busy to drive me. Not to mention that I haven't told her about the team, and if I ask her to take me to a meeting, she'll want to know a meeting of what and I'll have to make something up, and she's good at smelling out anything phony. Also, she wouldn't want to hear about zombies because it's too depressing and she's depressed anyway. And she'd never believe Rosie is for real, let alone that she's helping me and Jeri finally talk to each other. She'd think I've lost my mind — and I REALLY don't need that! (I guess she doesn't either.)

She'd included her address. It wouldn't be too much out of his way. And she seemed like a nice enough kid. He didn't think much of this tarot thing she and her sister had going, but at least she was trying to do something.

Sure, he wrote back. *I'll pick you up at 4.*

* * *

Janna

Janna read Paul's reply and hugged herself in glee. It'd probably be just the two of them, and even though he was kind of quiet, he was probably friendly enough that they'd talk. He wasn't just cute — he was one of those guys who didn't seem to care that they were cute, instead of expecting you to follow them around drooling and worshiping. He probably thought of her as just a kid, jailbait — but once he got to know her, maybe he'd see her as more.

Oh, she'd love to tell Jeri! But unless they could somehow get a private moment, she wouldn't have that chance.

* * *

Rosie

Sam and his fellows reported in while Rosie was still waiting for people to show. They had started asking zombie victims where the attacks occurred, which would let Rosie integrate their reports into her own. Sam summarized what little news they brought, and she jotted it down to share with the others, now arriving. Rosie was mildly surprised to see Paul and Janna enter together, but she had more important business.

She called the meeting to order and said, "You all know about the unfortunate intrusion into our business by federal agents. Meg has decided she would rather not continue working with us, now that we've been targeted in this manner." She quietly relished the scornful looks with which Janna, Paul, and (to her surprise) Emma greeted this news. "As you'll recall, Meg was helping me compile the information all of you have been gathering, as well as doing research of her own. Originally, she was supposed to do more researching while I kept track of things — but she ended up doing plenty of the latter, though she sent me one final research report. I'm going to have enough trouble pulling information together without her. I need someone else to keep our records up to date. Diane has agreed to take that on." She nodded to Diane, who smiled agreeably.

Janna's hand shot into the air. "I can do more research! I'm about out of games to analyze, and really learning tarot cards will take so long we'll all be zombie chow by then." She responded to Rosie's lifted eyebrow with a defiantly lifted chin. "It's close enough to true!" Then, more seriously and quietly: "I could tell my mother it's a school project. Maybe she'll actually be willing to admit what's happening, then."

Or maybe she'd call the school in high dudgeon, and thus find out Janna was fibbing. But that was ultimately Janna's business. "Thank you," Rosie said. "I'll send you an email about where our current research has gaps in it."

Paul looked indulgently at Janna, which Rosie devoutly hoped she didn't notice, and said, "I can meet with Janna to show her some of my research tricks." He chuckled, still with that dealing-with-the-child air. "Though maybe she'll end up showing me some!"

Emma made some barely audible sound, probably the best she could do to attract attention. "What was in Meg's final report? Did she find out anything new?"

Rosie pulled the printout free of the pile in front of her. "That depends what you call new. She didn't say anything radically different — no new kind of zombies, no new ways of fighting them — but she did have some new data on where the attacks have been, and their number. I'm afraid that not only are the numbers increasing, but they're happening in more big and mid-size cities. Sam tells me that those keeping track of afterlife arrivals have seen this pattern as well. The silver lining, perhaps, is that it'll get harder for the authorities to keep pretending that nothing's happening, that it's all hysteria and trolling."

Paul muttered, a little too loud to ignore, "Don't say 'troll,' or we might start seeing them too!" Janna giggled and sent what Rosie would have to call a flirtatious smile in his direction. Oh, great. Paul had better watch out.

Sam interrupted this byplay to tell her, *Millie wants to know something. Has anything happened in your town? It turns out she comes from not that far away. Small world.*

Rosie skimmed Meg's report. *I don't think so. And now I'm knocking on wood.* Though she did so under the table, and quietly.

Chapter 15

Daniel

A young man Daniel didn't know came to fetch him, beaming happily. "Please come to the welcome area at once, sir!"

Daniel had been relaxing on the grass in a clearing ringed in young birch trees, trying to learn the trick of being comfortable in loose informal clothing. At the look in the young man's eyes, he sprang to his feet. "Is this what I think it is?"

The young man cocked his head. "Do you really want me to tell you?"

Daniel laughed. "No need! Just give me a moment." He pictured himself into a well-tailored three-piece linen suit, complete with pocket square in his wife's favorite lilac color. "Lead on!" But he quickly pulled ahead of his guide. He could have been there instantly, but he wanted a little time to anticipate, and to run.

And run he did, until he got close enough that Ruth could see him, and jump to her feet, and run in his direction. He stopped and braced herself, knowing she would jump into his arms.

After the wild embraces and the kisses and the tears, after he had teased her about arriving at the afterlife about which she'd always scoffed in disbelief, they sat side by side on a wrought iron bench in a park inspired by Paris's Parc Monceau. With both of them overflowing with questions, it was hard to know where to start. He asked her, "Do you want to tell me what happened?"

"How I died, you mean? It happened so fast I didn't really have time to realize I was probably about to die. I did have time to be alarmed, but I think I recall also noticing how novel and interesting the sensation was — flying."

He put an arm around her and held her tight as she went on, "It was the new car. But really, it was me. I never did learn to ask as many questions as you did." She smiled ruefully. "So when I bought the car, I just assumed it had front wheel drive. I thought all cars did, these days. But it turned out it had something fancier, an option to distribute power to front or back at any of three settings. I think it must have been set on more rear wheel drive.

"It was raining pretty hard, and had been for maybe half an hour, but I was low on mint chip ice cream. Can you believe it? I died for mint chip ice cream!"

Daniel pulled her close and kissed her forehead. "You always did love mint chip ice cream. In a few minutes, I'll take you to a terrific ice cream parlor."

Ruth beamed at him. "Then I'll keep this short. There was a lot of water on the road, and the grocery store was down a fairly steep hill. When I turned onto it, I went into a skid and couldn't pull out. I went sailing off the road and down the side of the hill. I had time to notice I was airborne, and to think about bracing myself, which I probably did, but it must not have done much good."

She was telling the story as if it didn't bother her, but he could feel her shiver. "I didn't have time to get very scared. At least, if I did, I don't remember that part." She took a deep breath. "And now let's go get that ice cream!"

They ambled slowly along the curved path that circled the park, and then onto a street with book stalls all along it, stopping to browse the books. As they walked, Daniel told her about all the places they could go, and how they could make others, and the friends he had; Ruth told him about the lives of friends they'd left behind. They were almost at the ice cream parlor when Ruth said, "There's been something rather horrible happening back on Earth. I don't know whether you've heard about it."

She hesitated; Daniel stopped in his tracks and turned toward her, chilled to the marrow. "Zombies. Is that what you mean?"

She nodded.

Daniel forced the question through his constricted throat. "Have you ever seen one?"

"No, only pictures of them. And of their victims." She shuddered. "Why do you ask?"

Daniel took both her hands. "Ruth, my darling Ruth, my beloved . . . I must tell you something terrible."

Had Ruth ever seen him cry? He doubted it. It was, he supposed, high time he put aside his dignity and the barriers it had built up around him. Better late — he could have laughed at the double meaning — than never.

Though it felt like cheating, to confess something so awful and then distract her by an emotional display.

Ruth gathered him into her arms, held him, crooned comfort to him, just as she would have done with the children they could never have, as she had done with many pupils over the years. He slumped into the warmth of her embrace and let himself accept it without second thoughts, without thoughts at all, until he had no more tears left. Then she held him away enough to look in his eyes. "It wasn't your fault."

It took him a couple of tries to force the words out. "I suppose not."

"Of course it wasn't! You were here, not there! What could you have done? You didn't even know it was happening, did you?"

He shook his head. "Not until later. Until someone came here who . . . who . . . ." He started to cry again.

She shushed him, caressed him, waited for him to go quiet again. Then she said softly, "You told me about how you can conjure up places and fill them with what soothes your soul. Do you think I can do it?"

"I should think so. You're an artist — it should come naturally."

Ruth stroked her chin in the way that always amused him, as if she missed having a beard to play with. "I'd like to start small. That park was so lovely — would anyone mind if I added something to it?"

He had no idea, but he assured her stoutly that no one would. They retraced their steps, and she stood along a path facing a small grove and closed her eyes. He could feel her concentration, and then the relief as she found what she wanted. There, fluttering around them both, was a cloud of pale pink butterflies — settling on his shoulders, perching in her hair, brushing his cheeks as if they were kissing him. He laughed in delight, and then followed their movement as they came together again and flew upward and toward the grove, to cover the branches of a new tree, then to become its petals and make it a cherry tree, a cherry tree in the full glory of spring.

He grabbed her and kissed her. "I was right! You did wonderfully. Just look at it!" He released her and took a step toward the tree, wanting to touch the blossoms. But then, as if stepping away from Ruth had broken a spell, his thoughts betrayed him, and he imagined something different, wrong — a creature of decay and horror hiding behind the tree trunk, a dangling arm and dragging leg slowly emerging from behind it . . . .

He jerked his head away violently, wiped the image out of his mind, and looked back at the tree. The specter was gone.

"Daniel, my dear, what is it?" As he was searching for something to say, a lie if nothing else, she added, "I thought I saw something moving near the tree. What could it have been?"

No, not a lie. An evasion. "Would you mind very much if I didn't talk about it? And if we went and got that ice cream?"

She studied him, and he saw her make up her mind not to pry — or not yet. "Yes, let's. Do you still prefer vanilla with a cherry swirl?"

"I've actually found a new favorite flavor — mint with a white chocolate swirl." Daniel strove for a lighthearted tone. But he knew Ruth saw through it.

Millie

Millie pondered her outfit for her coffee date with Sofia, musing about how little attention she'd paid to what she wore during the latter years of her life and much of her time since. When had that started to change? Maybe when she noticed how Sofia's clothes, sweaters and chunky knit scarves in soft warm or pastel colors, fit in so well with her aura of cozy warmth. Those sweaters even felt good to hug, as yielding and yet firm as Sofia herself.

So, what to wear? Something that would contrast nicely with what Sofia would be likely to choose. Blacks and grays? No, something brighter, a yellow-gold jacket with burnt-orange slacks. And a hat, a tan hat with a brim and a small red feather.

She looked in the mirror and almost stepped backward. She might never wear such an attention-getting outfit again. But today, with Sofia probably already waiting for her, she would brace herself and go out.

Sofia stood up and beamed when Millie appeared, exclaiming, "You look marvelous!" Millie made herself accept the compliment without protesting it. But after pushing her boundaries so far, she chose a comfortably familiar drink, hot coffee with milk and just a dash of cocoa. Sofia ordered something with whipped cream, raspberries, and some kind of deep pink syrup.

Making conversation had changed, even with Sofia, since they had learned about the zombies. It always seemed to turn in that direction, or else lapse into silences. During one of these, Millie sighed to hear that the talk at the two nearby tables concerned the same subject. She tried not to listen, studying the somewhat surprising merrie-olde-England decor of the coffee shop before she realized that Sofia was sitting very still and stiff, and had gone so pale that her soft aqua sweater made her skin a disquieting grayish color by contrast.

Millie reached out and put her hand on Sofia's arm. "What is it? What's happened?"

Sofia took a shaky breath. "Did you hear what that man said?"

"No. I didn't want to hear any more of . . . that just now. What did he say?"

Sofia's voice dropped, as if she were talking to herself. "I should have thought of it before, really. People of all sorts have risen up as zombies, old and young. I just never let myself think about the very young. About children."

What a horrible thought! But why had Sofia been so deeply affected? Then she understood. Sofia had a daughter, Iris, who had died at the age of nine, not long before Sofia did, and hadn't yet chosen to grow older. They must spend a great deal of time together, though Sofia had only once brought Iris to meet Millie. She might have thought that Millie wouldn't be interested in children, or more likely, that the child would be bored by the kind of talk and activities they usually shared.

"Were they talking about a child having been made into a zombie, then?"

Sofia went even paler and turned away from her raspberry concoction. "No. No, they were just wondering if — no, when it would happen."

What could she say? What point was there in trying to soothe her, to say it might not happen when clearly it might?

Recklessly she veered in the opposite direction. "What upsets you the most about the idea?"

Sofia's eyes widened, and she pulled her drink closer. She took a deep, if shaky, breath and said quietly, "You probably think the worst part is that Iris would come back as a zombie. And that's part of it. But the very worst thing would be . . . ." She clenched her fists, closed her eyes, and took a few more breaths before saying, "Telling Iris that it had happened. That her body was hurting people."

Millie didn't even try to answer that. At least, not directly. But after taking a few sips of her own drink (which, like all hot drinks here, stayed hot as long as she needed), she said diffidently, "It wouldn't be quite as hard, maybe, if she were older."

Sofia wiped away the tears trickling down her cheeks. "Not unless she were a lot older, and soon, from the way things are going. She shouldn't have to give up those years, not when she's come to a place where she can live them."

They sat there in silence for a few minutes, sipping their drinks, as Millie wondered what she could possibly do to help Sofia be less upset. Then, yielding to an unusually daring impulse, she sat up straight and said, "I know what we should do. Let's go to a bar. We'll let ourselves get just a little bit drunk."

Chapter 16

Rosie

People kept trying to find ways to keep bodies from rising. Some of them piled big stones on graves, whether or not they knew it had been tried centuries or millennia ago. Others took the effort further and erected ornate empty mausoleums with the graves underneath. The only result was more dramatically disrupted grave sites. Whatever brought bodies up out of the ground overcame such obstacles. The attacks went on. There were rumors, now, of government projects involving drones or more mysterious technology, but nothing concrete or certain, let alone available.

One of Rosie's longtime clients, who had forgiven her for her earlier deception once she put him in touch with his deceased wife, had left a message with Diane. All he'd said was that he had a question, and thought she was the only one who could answer it.

"You're sure he didn't say his wife needed to answer it?"

Diane fingered her chin. "He did say something about how you might be able to *find out* the answer."

A question for his wife, then, sure enough. Would it be some longstanding emotional issue left unresolved? Or more like "where did you put the spare safe deposit box key"?

When she called the man back, it proved to be neither.

"I keep hearing about these attacks." The man's voice was hushed and hurried, as if confiding a secret. "And if anyone knows how to stop them, how to keep a body from turning into one, it's you. It's got to be you."

Rosie's jaw dropped, which the man fortunately couldn't see. Diane, working nearby, did, and gave her a quizzical look; Rosie waved off her curiosity as she tried to come up with something to say. "I know how upsetting this phenomenon must be to you. You could speak to your wife about it, the next time I'm able to facilitate contact. But I'm afraid my gift does not give me any special insight — "

"No, you must know! You're closer to the spirit world than the rest of us. You can ask the spirits! They must know how it happens, how to keep it from happening to their own bodies. Why won't you help me?"

She could hear her tone becoming more crisp despite herself. "As a matter of fact, I'm sorry to say that even the spirits have no such power. I know this for a fact. You're quite right that they're desperate to prevent it, but they don't know how, any more than we do."

She heard a muttered exclamation, probably an expletive, and then the sharp click of the man hanging up the phone. It must have been a land line. Speculating on such factors helped her put the call behind her, for a while.

Millie

Rosie's team regularly provided their spirit collaborators with detailed updates about the attacks, including where they had occurred. Millie knew enough about statistical analysis that it had become her task to look for patterns, or possible patterns, or changes in what patterns might exist. She had found no useful way to predict, from the ever-longer list of place names, where the next attack would come. But the names made an impression on her all the same. Whether they were charming (Heart's Cove, First Star), or quaint (First Bridge, Little Drumming, Empty Fork) or familiar (Lincoln, South Bend), they shared a dreadful incongruity. None of them should have been the site of gory, unstoppable mayhem and terror.

And then Millie came to a name that carried a different message.

There had been an attack where she lived before the last time she had to move. In the park near the lake; a park on which she had partly based the first safe place she created, back before she let herself move further from the familiar. The park in whose gazebo she had taken shelter, and never been tracked down and found there.

Millie closed her eyes and took herself to the park she'd made. She looked around at the lush grass, grass that never needed mowing and yet always smelled like cut grass on a warm sunny day. She leaned against a tree near the water and listened to the light lapping of the waves, the bird song, the rustling of leaves in the gentle wind. So peaceful here; so peaceful that park had been, when she was able to calm herself enough to appreciate it. Had there been others, lost and in need, who fled there as she had? Where would they flee to now?

<hr>

Sofia

Sofia liked meeting new people, and had been particularly curious to meet Daniel's wife Ruth. What sort of woman had been able to get close to someone who strove for so seamless and dignified a surface? She found a woman of gentle manner, almost certainly kind, but with a lighthearted side — almost frivolous — that she hadn't expected. And Ruth had revealed, or invented, a delightful twist on gardening.

Sofia led Ruth down a path around a small lake, not much more than a pond. "What do you think? A flower bed, or a tree, or both?"

In answer, Ruth scrunched her forehead and waved her hand along the shore. Where she pointed, a wavy line of daffodils sprang up, interrupted by small patches of white and purple crocuses. She stepped lightly, almost dancing, along the line of flowers and beamed. "I've always loved those flowers, and they never lasted long enough! Now they will, won't they? If I want them to?"

"Yes, indeed. Do you want to add any trees?"

Ruth studied the newly embellished shoreline. "I'd like to put one over there, where there's a sort of nook, like a tiny bay. It could have a strong branch reaching out over the water, with a swing on it. People could swing and jump in, if they liked."

As she spoke, the tree appeared in outline, then filled in as if a swiftly working artist had finished drawing it. "Now, wouldn't you like to add something?"

Sofia walked a few feet away and made a bed of roses in colors of peach and pink. She leaned over and sniffed to make sure they were properly aromatic. Ruth joined her, breathed in, and rewarded her with an ecstatic smile. "Now *that's* how all roses should smell!"

They walked along the lake and its new border of flowers, saying nothing more for a while, the ebb and flow of the water a soothing backdrop. When they came to the newborn tree, Sofia stopped and leaned against it, asking, "How are you settling in? I gather you weren't expecting a place like this, or any place at all."

Ruth laughed and gestured around her. "I certainly wasn't! And to hear Daniel talk now, he did think it likely — but in fact, he was almost as skeptical as I was. He just hedged his bets a little." Her smile faded as she added, "But clearly, this isn't a place of mindless happiness for everyone. Daniel's struggling, though he tries not to show it. He didn't have that easy a life, you know, especially early on. He may look as if he was born upper-crust, but he wasn't. He . . . redefined himself, assembled that dignified look and manner, with a lot of effort. He held himself to a high standard. And now, he has to deal with the fact that his body has, well, betrayed him and undone all that."

What an appalling burden to bear — and it was only Sofia's good fortune that (as far as she knew) the same hadn't happened to her. "I'm so sorry both of you have to deal with that."

Ruth shrugged. "Thank you, dear. I just wish there was something I could do. Or rather, something *he* could do. It's feeling helpless that eats at him the most."

———◆○◆———

Daniel

It kept happening. Whether Daniel was alone or with friends, with Ruth or away from her, the creatures kept appearing, hiding behind trees or following behind him, then vanishing when he turned to confront them. And the more often it happened, the harder it was not to expect it, which probably made it more likely. It was only a matter of time before someone noticed. Was this happening to anyone else, or did he alone have the dubious honor of introducing the plague to this refuge from all the world's ills?

What would he do when Ruth saw one?

How could he stop it?

What could he do?

Chapter 17

Paul

Paul was still looking over his shoulder almost anywhere he went, and not just for ravening undead. He tried without success to talk Janna into doing the same. He wasn't sure whether Janna was defiant — not of him but of the feds — or just careless. At her age, it might be either or both. When he could be cautious for both of them, he was. But there were limits. They could go to a series of libraries to use their online search tools, but with her car apparently out of commission, there was no convenient way for her to get to most of them unless he drove her. He didn't mind — she was pretty good company — but if he was already a target, he was making her a target along with him.

The supposed training soon turned from him tutoring her to the two of them doing research side by side, and on a range of topics. As he'd guessed, she was thoroughly at home online, and the few resources she didn't know about were quickly taught. So why had she agreed to the tutoring scheme? Maybe she was lonely. After all, she'd lost a *twin*. All Paul had in the way of siblings was two brothers, both years younger.

He'd sometimes envied twins for having a playmate, confidant, buddy from babyhood onward, but he hadn't thought about how devastating it had to be to grow up with that closeness and security and then lose it.

The team had been meeting at least every other week, and lately Paul had been giving Janna a ride. But now Janna suggested a change. "I'm only two blocks from a bus stop," she told him, "and the bus could let us out a few blocks from Rosie's. We could go that way, when it's not raining or anything."

Paul thought quickly. It would be a pretty warm walk this time of year, but a little sweating wouldn't melt him. If the feds had put a tracer on his car, or a bug in it, the bus would be a way to evade them. They'd have less privacy . . . but that might be a good thing. He was starting to wonder whether Janna might have a little crush on him. Buddies of his had told him about girls that age, young enough to be trouble but determined to get in the game. And he could use the exercise of walking more.

"Sure," he replied. "That should work out fine."

Later, he thought of one problem. He'd finished making a dozen Molotov cocktails, and he'd been thinking of stashing a couple in the trunk of his car — very carefully padded and wedged so they wouldn't be dangerous (or as dangerous). Carrying one on a walk or a bus ride would be trickier. But he'd been carrying his laptop and a few snacks in a backpack when he and Janna made their library trips. He could fit two Molotov cocktails in there, with his spare hoodie between them. They wouldn't weigh any more than the booze he'd sometimes carried on his way to a party.

Janna

Janna had trouble not looking smug as they sat together on the bus. The bus was at least half full, and everyone could see her sitting next to this cute guy! They might even think she was older, his age or closer to it.

She scooted closer, but he glanced at her in a wary sort of way, and she inched away again. Damn it, he'd figured out she was into him. She needed to be patient, put him at ease while keeping up with him mentally, impressing him with her ideas and her maturity.

She managed to act at ease, chatting cheerfully while sneaking in questions now and then about his life and his hopes for the future. By the time they reached their stop, he'd relaxed. So far so good. They got off the bus, and as it pulled away, she took a deep breath of the fresh spring air and twirled around. She'd worn a skirt that twirled nicely. "Isn't it lovely out!" she said, almost singing the words.

Then she turned back to her left. What was it she'd spotted out of the corner of her eye?

Paul

The street wasn't crowded — it never was, when he'd been here — but Paul saw Janna see something, and turned to look where she had. Maybe it was someone in their group, also taking advantage of the weather and walking all or part of the way. He started to smile a greeting, and then froze.

No one in their group would be staggering, or holding their arms that way. Or . . . moaning. Or rushing toward them.

In the few seconds it took him to slip his backpack off his shoulders, before he could even start to open it, the creature had reached them. Reached Janna. Bowled her over, her mouth open in a scream she didn't have time to sound before her head hit the pavement. It was on her, biting and clawing, and he couldn't throw the bottle at her, even if he had time to light the rag, because he'd be burning her as well as the zombie that was killing her.

He didn't even have anything else to throw.

Something else — no, someone else, a middle-aged woman — came running up with a shotgun. She waved it around, and then actually came close enough to empty it, with a resounding blast, into the zombie's back. It shrieked and stood up. The woman ran for her life, and the zombie ran after her. Paul didn't even look to see whether it caught her. He was kneeling at Janna's side and fumbling for his phone, even as other people converged around them and did the same.

She was moving, feebly, as the blood collected around her. She was opening her mouth. He gripped her hand and bent closer to hear.

He could hardly believe he was seeing the trace of a smile as she whispered, "I just wanted to say . . . I really like you."

All he could do was bend even lower to kiss her, as her eyes closed and she started to slip away. And now he was sure she was smiling as he straightened up again

Was she saying something else? He couldn't hear the words, but he thought her mouth formed them.

"Talk to you later."

Stunned, it took him a moment to realize what she might have meant. She was hoping — no, planning — to find the others, Sam and Millie and Daniel, and of course her sister Jeri. She would talk to him as they did, if she had anything to say about it.

Was that any consolation with the strong young body, practically vibrating with life only minutes ago, lying broken and distorted on the ground?

Paul knelt by Janna's body, shouting every curse he knew or could imagine, until he felt someone's arms around his shoulders and then under his arms. It was Rosie, with a strength he wouldn't have guessed she had, hoisting him up. "Come on. An ambulance is coming. I've given them the information they need to know about Janna. But for now, we should get off the street."

How could he just leave her lying there? He ignored the warning until he could no longer see Janna's chest rise and fall. Then he made his way to the house as the siren swelled from a distant quaver to a loud blast of sound, and then went quiet as the EMTs prepared to take Janna away.

In a few minutes, everyone had trickled in, and everyone was crying.

Paul looked around to see what Rosie was doing and found her sitting at the table with a look of being absorbed in something, moving her lips slightly. He got up, aching all over, and joined her, asking, "Are you talking to Sam?"

Rosie took a shaky breath and nodded. "He's just told them all. They're in about the same shape as we are, even though they know in a way we don't that Janna isn't . . . extinguished. Millie and Jeri have gone to try and find her."

Paul winced and said, "I'll bet Jeri had a few choice words for me before she went."

Rosie sighed. "She did, yes. Loudly. She wanted to know why you didn't protect her sister. I told her it all happened too fast, and that if any of us could have, you could have." At his alarmed look, she let out a sound a little like a laugh and added, "I could hear the clanking when you stood up. I made an educated guess. From the look on your face, I was right."

At some point, he'd have to think about whether he could still stand to carry the Molotov cocktails around. Now he just asked, "What else did she say?"

"Oh, Paul — she's heartbroken. She said it had been a comfort to know her other half would still live out her life, meet boys —" Rosie gave a little nod, with an ironic half-smile, at Paul. "And find what she wanted to do with herself, and, and . . . ." Rosie was crying again. "And to remember Jeri the way she was before she got sick. All I could tell her was that Janna still remembered that. And that they would be together now, the way they should be."

Paul bit his lip to get control of himself. As he struggled, he realized he had failed to ask something important, something only a selfish poor excuse for a man would have forgotten. "The woman with the shotgun. Did she get away?"

Rosie patted his shoulder. "I think so. I haven't heard about a second person being killed. We should try to find her, ask her more about what happened. And do the same with the witnesses." She held up a finger. "Sam's trying to get my attention. Sorry, Sam, I was talking with Paul. Any news yet from Millie?" She paused. "Well, let me know when you hear. Is there anything else we here really need to know, or could we adjourn and meet when we're all in better shape to think and talk?"

By now, the others had joined Paul at the table. They started to sit down, but Rosie held up a hand for them to wait. "All right, Sam," she said. It only now occurred to Paul that she'd been talking to Sam silently before, and must be speaking out loud now for his and the others' benefit. "I'll let them know. And please tell Jeri, and Janna when you find her, how terribly sorry we all are."

In a minute she nodded, got up, and gestured to them all. "We're done with the actual meeting for today. I'll be in touch about when the next one will be. So you could go home — but if any of you want to stay for a while, to talk about how you're feeling or to share your memories of Janna, we can take as much time as a meeting would have, or more."

All of them chose to stay, though only Emma and Paul had much to say. Emma went first, while Paul was still trying to compose himself. "Janna was a sweet child," Emma said softly. "And I know she wouldn't like me to call her a child. She was also a young woman, and becoming more of one all the time. From what Rosie passed on to us, I can see that Jeri was the, the tempestuous one of the pair, and Janna had the job of steadying her, balancing her. But I think Janna was finding her way to a broader sense of herself. It's such a shame we won't see her reach that goal." Then, even more quietly: "I do wonder what'll happen now that they're back together. I hope Janna doesn't feel she has to be exactly what she was before. Maybe now that Jeri isn't sick, they can both grow up in their own ways, even if their bodies won't be changing." She stopped, looked at Rosie. "Or will they?"

"From what Sam has let slip from time to time," Rosie answered, "I think that may be up to each of them. In fact, they may be able to experiment with being less alike, physically."

Paul gave a sort of shudder. He didn't want to think of Janna changing, becoming less like herself. Growing up, yes, but not getting less like Janna in the process.

Emma was done. If he was going to say something, it was time to do it. He swallowed and began.

"When Janna was dying . . . ." It was getting harder by the word, by the second, but he kept going. "I wanted to tell her that I loved her. Not in a way that would've got me in trouble, which may have been the way she wanted." Too late, he wondered whether he'd betrayed a secret. "Not that she said that. But anyway, I think most of us loved her in some way, and I know I did. She was — she was brave, the bold kind of brave, going out to meet the hard things, the scary things. She hadn't let Jeri's death destroy her, and she wasn't going to just give up and hide." His voice started to shake; he took a moment to make it stop. "I'll bet she's royally pissed that a zombie got her. Janna, if you're listening, we won't let the damned things win. We'll finish the job for you, hon."

That was all he could say. He hoped it was enough.

Rosie

Rosie waited for everyone to depart and gradually realized that Paul didn't seem to be going anywhere. He remained in his seat, elbows on the table, head in his hands. She sat down next to him and waited in case he wanted to speak first. It took long enough that she decided he had nothing to say, and the muttered words surprised her. "I said it wrong."

The question was so obvious she refrained from asking, waiting for him to answer it.

"I said we'd finish the job for her. As if she couldn't do anything. Because she was one of them, dead, a spirit, whatever they are. Or because she was just a kid. But I was wrong, either way. She can still help." Glancing at him, Rosie saw a faint trace of a smile. "She'll insist on it."

"I'm sure she'll appreciate your understanding that." She waited a moment, to see whether he picked up on her phrasing. When he showed no sign of doing so, she went on, "Why don't I put you two in touch, and you can tell her?"

"I'm so incredibly sorry."/*I kind of told you, but not quite.* Paul and Janna spoke at once, as sometimes happened when she arranged this sort of chat. She relayed each message and asked Paul to wait for her signal before going on, assuming Janna would be less consistent about following such directions. She would have been less indulgent of teenage habits if Janna was still alive and learning mature behavior. Rosie winced at the distinction she was drawing, marveled at the turn her life had taken for her to have such thoughts, and then returned to her task of conversational traffic policewoman.

If you're apologizing for not saving me, don't. I don't see how you had time, and anyway, I wouldn't have wanted it to, to kill you instead. Partly because of the thing I was trying to tell you.

Paul spoke very gently. "What else did you want to tell me, dear Janna?"

A long pause, and then, a sudden bold burst of words. *I don't just like you. I love you. I did, and I still do. I can't . . . I still want you to know, even though I can't work to make you love me back.*

Janna presumably couldn't see that Paul had tears running down his face, nor could she hear the roughness in his voice. Rosie tried to convey the quality of it nonetheless. "Janna, my Janna, I wish so much that you could."

Neither of them said anything for a minute or so. Rosie was about to ask if they were finished when Janna added, with steady and determined demeanor, *At least we'll still be able to work together. I'm going to work even harder now, until we win. Until we defeat what . . . .* Her voice faltered again. *Until we defeat what parted us.*

Chapter 18

Millie

Due to her greater experience with how spirits were welcomed, Millie found Janna before Jeri could. Much as Jeri, and probably Janna, longed for their reunion, Millie was just as glad. She would have a chance to provide some orientation first — after, of course, telling her that Jeri would be with her soon.

It didn't take long before Janna took over the conversation, asking one question after another. "Is this the last stop, or am I just on the way to somewhere else?" "Do I have to pass some sort of test to stay here?" "What's the rest of this place like?" "Can we still eat, here? Do we have any choice, or is it all the sort of foods people always told me were healthy?" "Will I ever have a chance to finish growing up?" "Do people get to have boyfriends here? And what about sex?"

Millie answered as best she could, relieved that she had answered most of these questions before. After a few minutes, Janna interrupted herself to change the subject, giving Millie a look she found difficult to interpret before saying, "It wasn't you, you know."

"What? What wasn't me?"

"The zombie that killed me. It wasn't you — your body, I mean. It was a man."

How kind of Janna to think of reassuring her. "Thank you, dear. I'm very glad to know that."

But it could have been. It could just as easily have been my body clawing at her, going for her throat. She thrust the thought away.

Meanwhile, Janna looked around. "Where are we going next, exactly? Is it Jeri's special place, like you said you all have?"

Millie smiled at her. "Actually, it's one of my special places. Jeri is already there, waiting for you. She'll show you to one of hers."

Millie moved them to the spot, a small mountain lake nestled between green peaks with white frosting at their very tips. It was just before sunrise, the sky somewhere between gray and lilac. But Janna had eyes only for the girl waiting at the shore line.

The different clothing styles the two girls wore only highlighted how much alike they looked: the same auburn hair, though Janna's was longer and straighter; narrow nose, wide mouth, bright green eyes. Jeri was still a little thinner, but she was moving toward a healthy-looking weight. And that was all the comparing Millie had time for, because the two of them had flown together and collided.

For a minute or so, all Millie could hear was murmuring and sniffing and the quiet lapping of the lake on the shore. Then the girls pulled apart to arm's length, clasping hands and exclaiming things like, "I love your hair!" and "Where did you *get* that *blouse*?"

Then came a moment of silence, before the girls shouted, at the same time and almost in unison, "How could you go and *die* like that!" And then a babble of defensive explanation, anguished questions, defiance, and apologies.

Millie started to tiptoe away, but Janna glanced at her, turned back to Jeri, and said, "Let's go to *your* special place and talk. I really want to see it."

Jeri relaxed, beamed, and exclaimed, "Just wait!" . . . and the two of them vanished, leaving Millie to quiet and solitude.

Which would have been lovely, and was what she had sought when she made this pastoral sanctuary, but now it just meant she could no longer keep the thoughts at bay.

Janna had been attacked not that far from where Millie had lived. Not that far from the little cemetery where Millie had arranged to lie, where her body should be quietly returning to the soil, nourishing earthworms and dandelions. While she couldn't expect to have visitors, an occasional passerby might have paused to read her marker and wonder what she had been like, and what sort of story her life would make.

And now, that body had refused to lie obediently in its grave, and was rampaging around attacking people just as innocent as Janna, people just trying to live their own lives, people with loved ones who would mourn them!

Compulsively, unwillingly, her mind went back to the people who had reported that her body had killed them. The mayor with the too-tight suit; the man in the café; the woman who had been engaged, and had lost a lifetime's worth of dreams. There could easily be others whose spirits hadn't found her yet. Enough time had passed that there almost had to be more. How dare her body put families and wives and husbands through that grief! If only she could go back to the living world to grab her body by the shoulders and shake it, saying, "What are you doing? Stop it! STOP IT!!"

Millie looked around at what had been, once, a priceless bit of peace. She had made it unchanging, back when she associated all change with trauma and turmoil. The lake would never be more than barely ruffled by the breeze; the sky would never brighten all the way to sunrise. Now, burdened with grief and guilt and even rage, the sort of emotions she'd thought to leave behind forever, the static, unresponsive landscape made her half wild.

Clenching her fists, Millie left the lake for the welcoming center. She wasn't scheduled there just yet, but she could wait if necessary. Maybe she'd offer this place as a starting spot for a newcomer.

Emma

Emma woke from a nightmare, sitting bolt upright, a sharp twinge in her back from the sudden strain of it. She was panting in fright. What had she dreamed? She grasped after it before it faded away, not knowing why she did so.

It had started with a memory. She had been sitting in the chair near the window, a few days after Robert died. She had been staring out the window without seeing anything, or anything that was really there. Instead she was seeing Robert's pale, waxy face in the coffin. She should have told them to keep the coffin closed. Then her last memory of him would be his carefree smile as he waved goodbye that morning, before the accident.

But in the dream, as she was staring out the window, something appeared. A horrible creature, smeared with earth and dripping slime, holding a human hand that looked as if it had been torn off. And on one finger of the hand, Robert's class ring.

She was shaking, sitting there in her bed. She wrapped her arms around herself, trying to hold still. But sitting like this was hurting her back, so she got up. She should put on a shawl. And some hot tea might help. Or even hot water with milk in it, her grandmother's favorite alternative to tea or coffee.

Sipping her hot water, adding a touch more milk to get the temperature right, she calmed down enough to ask herself: why had she had that horrible dream?

It could be just the work she was doing with Rosie and the others. . . . The others. Paul, Meg, Diane . . . but not Janna anymore. At least, not in the flesh. Because a zombie had killed her. She was as dead as Robert.

And Janna had a mother. A mother who was going through what Emma had gone through, except worse. If anything could be worse. If it mattered why her child was dead. . . . But she had lost two children. That was worse.

Tying her shawl so that it wouldn't slip off as she moved, Emma made her way to her computer and began an email to Rosie. Should she add Paul? Not yet, not unless she had to.

Dear Rosie,

Do you know how I could reach Janna's and Jeri's mother?

Rosie, or rather Diane, had Mrs. Dallin's street address, email, and phone number.

It would be impossible, absurd, to explain herself in an email. And so much could go wrong in a phone call.

Emma picked up the phone anyway. But when she dialed, it rang, and rang, and no one answered.

But of course. Would she have answered the phone in those first days, when all she could think about was that Robert was gone?

If someone had come to the house, though, and knocked softly, not like a salesman, she might have answered. At least if they knocked again after she didn't. It would have felt rude to ignore someone standing there. And she didn't, at that point, care how she looked. Knowing someone was right outside the door might have made her feel very much alone, enough to take a chance on opening the door.

Emma took a cab. It was too far to walk, and anyway she needed to save her strength for what lay ahead. As she paid the driver and turned toward the house, it occurred to her for the first time that someone other than the mother might answer the door — a relative, or even the girls' father, though Janna had never mentioned one. But as she knocked, waited, and knocked again, the door opened and she knew at once that this was a mother like herself. Oh, she was younger than Emma had been, let alone compared to Emma's age now. But she knew, well enough that her stomach roiled and her throat ached, that flat stunned look, and the fury that waited behind it for when the numbness finished wearing off.

The woman stared at Emma, or through her. Emma cleared her throat and said, in a voice she wished shook less,

"Mrs. Dallin, my name is Emma Wells. I knew Janna. And I'm so terribly sorry. And I — I know a little of what you're going through, because I lost a child too. My only child." She had to stop and swallow hard before she could go on. "My son, years ago."

Mrs. Dallin looked at her again, this time as if seeing her through a fog, but seeing her. And hearing her, maybe, as if from a distance.

"I don't want to disturb you," Emma said. "But we could talk."

Mrs. Dallin took a small step backward, as if startled at the idea. But then a look of wanting, almost craving, pushed aside the blankness on her face, and she nodded. She started to speak, but it was more of a croak. On the second try she was able to say, "Please come in."

They were sitting in a living room, with several vases full of flowers starting to wilt, the loose petals lying un-attended on floor and furniture. After exerting herself to invite Emma in, Mrs. Dallin seemed to have run out of the energy to speak again. So Emma, hesitantly, began to talk. She told her hostess about Robert. How good it felt, in spite of everything, to be able to talk about him, as she hardly ever had a chance to do. She talked about what a good son he was, and how good at baseball, and how wild he could be at times — but still a good boy, she hurried to add. And then, the lump in her throat once again, "I'm sure he would have liked Janna. He'd have seen how pretty she was, and how smart. He'd have been a little shy around her, but he would have liked her. She was a wonderful girl. You must have been so proud of her."

That broke the dam. Emma sat quietly and handed Mrs. Dallin a handkerchief as she sobbed, and then another. She had come prepared. She remembered needing more than one.

It took another few minutes before Mrs. Dallin asked her the question Emma had been dreading. "How do — how did you know my daughter?"

Where to start? "We shared a concern about something that's been happening. Did Janna ever mention the various sightings of, of what people are calling zombies?"

Mrs. Dallin was back to staring at nothing. "She did, once or twice. I told her it was nonsense. It surprised me that Janna would listen to it. She was always the more level-headed one. Of the twins. You know she was a twin?"

"Yes," Emma said gently. "I know about Jeri."

"It went on so long, and things got worse and worse, and we still couldn't help hoping Jeri would get better, that she'd finally turn a corner. But hoping never helped. I thought nothing could be worse." Mrs. Dallin actually laughed, a horrible coughing sound. "I should have known better than to think that."

Emma had expected Mrs. Dallin to ask more about what Emma and Janna had been doing. She had even thought the woman might know, and admit, how Janna had died — might even want to help defeat what had killed her. But Emma should have known better. Mrs. Dallin's world had shattered, and she was in no condition to accept a truth that was shattering in its own way.

Maybe someday. But not today.

She got to her feet. "Thank you for seeing me." And when Mrs. Dallin stirred restlessly in her chair, as if wanting to get up but lacking the strength: "I'll see myself out. I'll leave my phone number here, on this card." She laid it on the bureau, next to the fallen flower petals. "If I can ever do anything — sit with you, bring you dinner, take you somewhere, or you could tell me more about your daughters — please, please call me."

The expression that flitted across the woman's face could almost have been the faint impression of a smile. By the time Emma turned to leave, it was gone.

Chapter 19

Millie

The man Millie was supposed to welcome was in no mood for such courtesies. Tall and burly, he towered over Millie even when she abandoned the chair she'd started out in. She suspected the zombie had been the first opponent in his adult lifetime whom he could neither defeat nor intimidate. He wasn't taking it well. "How could this happen!" he shouted. "This is something out of ridiculous superstitions and folk tales! Aren't there, I don't know, authorities here who can keep people's bodies from running around attacking people?"

Millie remembered an expression that she'd heard once or twice during her lifetime. But she doubted the man would take kindly to her saying his question was "above her pay grade."

The man wasn't giving her time to reply anyway. "I'm going to find someone to speak to about this!" He stomped out without asking for the directions she wouldn't have known how to supply. She could only wish him some encounter on his way that would calm him enough to receive actual assistance.

She sighed, sat back down, and waited for the next spirit to appear.

It seemed unfair, though an unfairness dwarfed by what had happened to the newly arrived spirit, that Millie should once again encounter someone whose life her body had destroyed.

This spirit was thin and frail. Millie's body would have been able to overpower her even if it didn't have whatever frenzied strength came with its condition. And instead of raging, the woman talked in a monotone, as if all capacity for feeling had been driven out of her. But it didn't take her long to look closely enough at Millie to recognize her. She recoiled, pointing a shaking finger, and whispered, "It was you."

In an idle moment when she was feeling especially use-less, Millie had developed a script of sorts to use if another of her body's victims appeared. She struggled to remember it. "I'm so terribly sorry. I didn't have anything to do with it — not me, my spirit. None of us know what's happening, but we don't have any control over it."

The woman slumped in her own chair and pulled a crumpled tissue out of a pocket. "I wasn't done. I wasn't ready. I didn't have an exciting life, but I had plans. I was going —" She started to sob, the tissue quickly becoming a saturated, dissolving clump. "I was finally going to go abroad. To Ireland. I was going to visit my grandparents' village. I was going to take pictures to show my children." She stopped short, mouth dropping open, face going pale. "Is the same thing happening over there? Are bodies coming out of graves and hunting peo-ple there?" She covered her face with her hands and muttered, barely loud enough for Millie to hear, "Maybe it's just as well I didn't go. I couldn't bear to see my grandma like that." She lifted her face again and peered at Millie. "Did you have grand-children?"

Millie mutely shook her head.

"You don't have to worry, then, about your grandchildren seeing . . . what I saw."

Millie bit her tongue so she wouldn't rail at the woman. Grandchildren or no, it was bad, terrible, *abominable* that anyone would see her like that, let alone have that sight as their last, terrified memory.

The woman looked at Millie with a sort of sympathy. "It must be awful for you. If only you could stop it from happen-ing. Go back into your body and put it to rest again somehow."

The echo of her own earlier thought startled her enough that she twitched in her chair. The woman, now looking around the chamber, didn't notice. In a soft voice with the first traces of wonder in it, she said, "This is lovely, if rather grand. What is the rest of this place like?"

With that opening, Millie could drop back into her usual routine. "It's anything and everything you want it to be. . . ."

Finally done with her welcoming session, Millie needed a comforting retreat. Rather than any of her existing spots, or even a new one — though she promised herself to create one soon — she decided to go exploring. There were lists of popular attractions, and these very much included places to eat. She was soon ensconced at the corner table of a bustling ice cream parlor, its decor suggesting the 1890s, awaiting her order of a chocolate and strawberry ice cream sundae, complete with whipped cream, chocolate sprinkles, and hot fudge. If she'd been less troubled, she might have rubbed her hands together in childish glee.

If only the sundae would come soon! The place was crowded to bustling, affording plenty of opportunity to people-watch, but that pastime wasn't quite enough to keep thoughts from coming into her head. She did her best to drive them out, looking at that matronly woman with a younger woman who might be her daughter, and a proud papa carrying a baby and spoon-feeding melted vanilla ice cream into its mouth; and that young couple, almost grown, sharing a banana split and gazing into each other's eyes. . . .

Janna had been about their age, or a very little younger. Was there a boy somewhere, fiercely disbelieving what had happened, left without the girl who might have been his first love?

No, she would *not* think of that! She would imagine Janna and Jeri reunited, coming here and enjoying ice cream together after their painful separation. Maybe she would bring them here. Would they order identical dishes, or share some splendidly   excessive dessert, or prove their individuality by making their orders as different as possible?

There would probably be another meeting soon, given the abrupt end to the last one. Maybe someone had thought of something useful to do, besides just keeping track of the growing number of victims.

Sitting there, she could remember as if hearing it again the woman, her body's victim, saying, "If only you could stop it from happening. Go back into your body . . . ."

Millie almost didn't notice her sundae appearing in front of her. Only the clink of the spoon on the table recalled her attention. She picked up the spoon and dug into the ice cream. Even as she relished the cold ice cream softened by the smooth whipped cream, the hot fudge against the cold, the tart-sweetness of strawberry against the welcoming lushness of chocolate, she ran those words over and over in her mind.

"Stop it from happening . . . . Go back . . . ."

So many people died untimely, or at least felt they had. Surely, over all the eons of human existence, someone — maybe several someones — must have tried to go back. It can't have worked, surely? Though there had been stories, stories that were always explained as premature burials or mistaken identification of bodies.

But assuming no one had ever found a way to go back, by pleading their case or by overwhelming willpower, those people had been trying to return to bodies lying meekly in their graves. Even if there had been zombies before, it was much less likely that their spirits had tried to return to them.

Millie couldn't imagine how to do it. But the first step toward doing something no one considered possible was to decide, firmly decide, to attempt it.

* * *

Emma

After Janna's death, Rosie had floated the idea of meeting more often. Emma knew she should be in favor, but it was taking her some time to recover from the horrible shock of Janna's death. She was grateful, if also ashamed, that Rosie instead left a little extra time before scheduling their next gathering.

Diane had been giving Emma a ride to the meetings, which saved her a trip on the often-crowded bus and the walk from the bus stop through the August heat. When they arrived, Diane vanished into the less public part of the house to do something or other. Meg helped Rosie carry a platter of brownies and a teapot to the table. Emma looked startled to see her; Meg, noting her expression, paused with platter in hand, shifting from one foot to the other. "I changed my mind." Then, tearing up: "There are so few of us, and now Janna's gone . . . I couldn't let my nerves keep me away."

When all the living members of the team had gathered, and brownie crumbs decorated all the plates and bits of the table, Rosie called the meeting to order. "Welcome, everyone. Those present on our end have already seen that Meg has rejoined the team, and we welcome her return. For a change, I have some other news besides the usual dismal increase in the casualty count." She paused, as if Sam had interrupted her, before going on to say, "And after I mention that news, Millie has an announcement for us."

Emma sat straight enough for her back to protest and had to remind herself not to hold her breath, as suspense sometimes led her to do. Rosie looked around to make sure everyone was suitably attentive and then said, with an odd little smile, "Two days ago, I received a letter from the U.S. Fish and Wildlife Service Migratory Birds Program."

Rosie waited out the various small sounds of dismay, and winced at what might have been louder exclamations from the team of spirits, before continuing. "This wordily named agency is the agency — or rather, the 'lead agency,' among goodness knows how many — in charge of making sure that the world does not run out of migratory birds. Apparently, these include corvids, like crows and ravens, though I must confess I had the impression I had seen crows in all seasons.

Perhaps they merely made an impression that failed to fade during winter."

But something was pulling at Emma's attention, like a faint voice calling to her. With an unspoken apology to Rosie, she focused on it — and almost jumped in her chair. It was Robert, trying to be loud enough for her to hear him. What must the other spirits think? But that didn't matter now. *Mama!* he was saying, or shouting. *Mama, do you remember the crows? The crows, at the park!*

Yes, Robert! I'll tell them.

Her distraction must have been obvious, at least to Rosie, whose former profession required her to have a keen eye for such things. She blushed. "I'm so sorry. I believe I missed a few words of what you were saying."

Rosie smiled at her. "Actually, I know why. I could hardly help hearing. Everyone, the connection between Emma and Robert is strong enough that they don't always need my help to communicate. It appears Emma and Robert have some past experience with crows. Emma?"

Now everyone was looking at her. Emma's back was really aching now, but she put it out of her mind. "I hadn't thought of it in years, until Robert reminded me just now. When he was a little boy — well, not so little, I suppose, old enough to play on a softball team — I used to take him to softball practice at a little park near where we lived. I drove, back then. Anyway, there was one year when every time we arrived, a big flock of crows would arrive just after us and settle in the trees around the parking lot. And then, when Robert ran off to join the other boys, about half of them would fly after him, perching in trees near the field or pecking around in the grass, and the other half would stay with me. Sometimes I would bring a library book and read in the car until he was done, and most of the crows stayed the whole time. Robert and I used to tease each other about it, saying I was the queen of crows and he was the prince."

There she went talking too much. She could have made the story shorter. But no one seemed bored or impatient, and Rosie even looked a little excited. "That's a piece of luck! As I was starting to say, the federal folks at this agency weren't writing to warn me about how they were planning to come down on us for daring to meddle. Instead, for a change, they told me about a program under development that might interest us. As I already knew, crows are very smart birds. This program is studying whether it might be possible to train crows to avoid certain hazards as they follow their migration routes. In a near miracle, someone with authority in the organization is actually paying attention to the growing zombie problem, and when they were copied on a memo about our little upstart organization, this person was senior enough to ignore the plan to intimidate us. Instead, we're going to be in the loop, getting copied on reports of various kinds."

Emma looked around and saw that Paul and Meg looked deflated. She felt much the same, and let herself slump, much to the relief of her spine. Copied on reports? So what? Rosie gave that wry little smile again and said, "I know that doesn't sound like much, but the reports aren't the important part. What this means is that we're less likely to be hassled if we pursue our own research and experiments. And it appears we have someone ideally suited to pursue the option."

Emma blushed again. "I'll certainly try. Robert and I will write to each other about it. And maybe someone here can help me — give me rides to places where crows gather, and so on."

Paul waved a hand. "I'd be glad to do that."

Emma should have guessed as much. Poor boy, he'd been right there when Janna was attacked, and before that, he'd had to see the golem destroyed. He must be feeling something like useless. She gave him a grateful smile and said, "Thank you so much."

Rosie cleared her throat and said, "Good, that's settled. As for the harassment we've experienced from that other agency, they seem to have moved on to other wild goose chases, and I for one don't intend to worry about them unless they reappear. Now, let's hear what Millie wants to tell us." She went on a few words at a time, relaying Millie's words. "Millie is very upset about the fact that her body is hurting people . . . and that no one knows what to do about it. . . . She feels that she should be able to do something . . . since after all, it's her body . . . and she wants to try something that no one has been talking about. . . ." Rosie's eyebrows shot up. "She wants to try to find a way to get back inside her body."

"How?" The question fairly exploded out of Meg, and from the looks on everyone's faces, she spoke for them all.

Rosie listened and said ruefully, "For lack of any information about past attempts, let alone past successes, she'll try what sheer willpower can do." Then she held up her hand for silence, and may have done something similar to keep any of the spirits from speaking. From her furrowed forehead, she was thinking of something, or trying to re-member something. She finally said in a musing tone, "I wonder if it could be anything like lucid dreaming."

She paused, then said, "Jeri wants to know what lucid dreaming is. For her benefit and for anyone else unsure of the meaning, it's the ability to control one's dreams while dreaming them. Some people have this talent naturally, and I'm among them." Another pause. "Like most people, Millie doesn't, or at least isn't aware of having it. But there are things people can do, drills and adopted habits, that may help. And . . . ." Yet another pause. "And it seems that the spirits have the ability to do something similar. They can — as we might say — dream up environments, places, where they want to spend time. It's actually one of the first things they do upon arrival, to make themselves a place where they feel safe and relaxed as they get used to the great change they've just experienced."

Emma looked at Rosie, at how her expression had brightened and her body language had become more energetic. The long slog with no results must have been weighing on her, as it had on Emma, and here was a way they might be able to make progress. Emma checked to make sure no one else around the table was about to speak and diffidently suggested, "Why don't you and Millie collaborate? With Sam's help, if that will make things go more smoothly."

"An excellent idea," Rosie said briskly. "Sam, Millie, I'll be in touch later about how we'll handle that collaboration — no need to keep everyone else sitting around now. Emma, Paul, I'll forward that email to you — Emma, you have email working now, don't you?" Emma nodded. "Does anyone have any other reports or business we should address today?"

No one did, and they adjourned, Rosie saying as she got up and stretched, "I don't know what they'll do on the other end, but I'm offering seconds on snacks. We have a few more brownies, and also lemon cake. And I have coffee and lemonade as well as tea. Any takers?"

Chapter 20

Emma

Paul was driving Emma home when he suddenly swerved over and parked. "Look up there," he said, pointing at the trees lining the road. "Some of your followers. Want to say hello?"

Emma moved her hand toward her seat belt latch and hesitated. "I don't have anything to feed them."

"When did you ever? You didn't mention feeding the crows at those softball practices."

True, she hadn't. But back then, she hadn't wanted anything from them. She'd just noticed them in passing, and enjoyed having a private joke with Robert.

As she failed to unfasten her seat belt, Paul unfastened his and twisted around to search the back seat. "Somewhere here . . . aha!" He held up a package of crackers, the kind vending machines stocked, and then dropped it back wherever it had come from. "I knew there was a good reason for my car to be a mess." He winked at her. "But wouldn't it be interesting to find out first whether they'll fly down and say hello without a food bribe?"

Emma took a deep breath and said, "All right." She unfastened the seat belt and got out, slowly enough that Paul was standing with a hand at the ready when she finished hoisting herself upright.

She walked over to the nearest tree, looked up at the crows, and felt foolish. But was that Robert's voice, very faint, in her head? Or was she just imagining him saying, "Go on, ask the birds to fly down to the pavement"?

She wasn't sure, actually, that she wanted a bunch of birds flapping around her. It made her think of that Hitchcock movie. Instead, she said, timidly and then at a more normal volume, "Hello, birds. It's nice to see you. Would you say hello to me?"

It seemed to her that a few of the crews looked at her. Nothing else happened, and she turned to go back to the car.

Then a single crow lifted off its branch, flapped down to the ground, let out a single "Caw!" and flew back up again.

She wanted to laugh, but it seemed rude. She swallowed the urge and moved toward the car. After a moment she heard Paul following her, before he moved ahead enough to open the door for her. As she nodded her thanks, he said, "Sure you don't want to try anything else?"

"Not today. Maybe I'll do the same again, in a different place, and see if at least one crow obliges me. And I'd like to read about what the actual researchers are up to, and whether the crows are inclined to go along."

"That all makes sense," Paul answered.

But he looked disappointed, so she stopped and said, "Please reach in and get a cracker for me." He smiled, the smile broadening into a grin, and leaned in to rummage in the clutter and come up with the package of crackers. She opened it, extracted one, and gave him back the rest before returning to the tree. She looked up at one side of it and swept her gaze through the thickly leaved branches to the other side, saying, "Hello again! I very much appreciated one of you saying hello to me before. Would any more of you care to do the same?"

This time, she hardly had to wait before at least a dozen crows fluttered down, landing in a close cluster and cawing in near-unison. Emma blinked back a ridiculous tear and unveiled the cracker. "Thank you so much! Here's a token of my gratitude. I'll come visit again soon."

As Paul drove her the rest of the way home, they chatted about nothing in particular until they reached her house. He sprang out and ran to open her door, actually bowing as he held it for her. This time she had no need to hold back a laugh, though it came out as an embarrassing giggle. As he escorted her to the door, he asked, "Did you mean it, about visiting the tree again?"

"Of course! I wouldn't have said so otherwise. I'd like to see just how much they understand. But I suppose that if I do have some special ability with crows, that won't be much good as far as the overall effort is concerned."

They said their goodbyes, and Emma went inside for a cup of tea and a session on her computer. Emma, on a computer! Wonders never ceased, for good or ill. Since the dangerous kind had come calling, it was time to make the most of the good.

Three days later, Emma received a report Rosie had forwarded from the crow research team. She drank about half her morning mug of tea before settling in to read it. By the time she had read all the way through, struggled with opening the attachments, called Paul for assistance, and finally succeeded, the rest of her tea had gone cold.

First of all, the team was working with ravens, not crows. Ravens were larger, and had longer beaks. But they were just as smart as crows, apparently.

Crows and ravens, left to their own devices, did dive-bomb animals and people occasionally when they felt threatened, say by the animal or person getting too close to their nests. They didn't usually do much harm — minor injuries at most, since their talons weren't all that sharp. Any damage came more from their beaks. It remained to be seen whether they could be trained to make such attacks . . . which would have its own down side, since the birds could pass knowledge down to their offspring. It would probably be necessary, the report said in its strange academic language, to "sacrifice" the birds involved in such studies and in any subsequent use.

Well! Aside from how unfair that was, just how did the researchers think they were going to have ravens all over the place attacking zombies, and then get them all to fly back somewhere to be slaughtered? Since ravens were smart, it seemed likely they'd outsmart the researchers as far as that plan went. Emma might just write to these people and suggest as much. Maybe they should stick with what the birds were already good at, dive-bombing and harassing. Like a shotgun blast, that kind of attack might distract the zombie long enough for the person it was attacking to get away. Was there any way to have enough ravens all over that every zombie attacking anyone would get them mobbed by big sharp-beaked birds? Could they descend on the zombies and herd them away from people?

Maybe the zombies would be weakened enough by not having people to eat (did they actually eat people, or just kill them and move on?), or just be discouraged enough, to give up and go back to their graves.

Emma kept reading.

Previous work with crows or ravens had shown that they could recognize individual faces and be trained to respond to particular ones. Some earlier researchers had put on caveman masks and then captured and caged a group (a "murder," wasn't it?) of crows, and from then on, for eight years or more, the crows in that neighborhood had dive-bombed and scolded anyone wearing that mask. The crows who'd actually been caged had even taught their chicks about the nasty, dangerous caveman! So now, the researchers were coming up with zombie masks, using artificial intelligence to digest all the photos and videos of zombies and come up with some sort of general zombie face to use. And they were watching the videos and practicing their "zombie walks."

She could just imagine a passel of boys showing off their zombie walks to each other, making vulgar comments and laughing it up. If she were there, she'd be hard put not to yell at them: *This isn't a GAME! People are dying! A young girl I know died!*

Hmmm. If she was going to have any chance to make a difference to this effort, she would need to be there, somehow. She just needed to figure out a way to make them invite her. Maybe Paul would have some ideas. Or maybe she would, once she thought about it some more.

Rosie

Paul had told the group about Emma's rapport with crows — at some length, and with repetitions of "I wouldn't have believed it if I hadn't seen it." The actual facts he related didn't impress Rosie quite as much as they'd apparently impressed him, but they were enough to intrigue her. If she could observe the actual experiments researchers were conducting, what could she learn and bring back to the team? Should she in fact request that one or more of them be allowed to visit? Or would their presence perturb the experiments?

And then, to her considerable surprise, she learned — from Emma herself — that Emma had gone ahead and asked to observe. Looking over the email Emma and Paul had composed to send the researchers, she chuckled, and marveled, at the picture they had presented: little old lady, harmless and basically past-it, is so impressed by what they're doing and would so much like to take a peek! Would the important researchers possibly condescend to allow her a wee bit of access? And then a separate message from Paul, expressing his overflowing gratitude that the researchers had been so good as to promise them updates, and confiding how depressed his aging friend was (though he somehow gave the impression of being a relative) about what was becoming of the world, and how much she needed some evidence that things would come right, even after she was gone. . . .

They had, Rosie ruefully acknowledged, given an impression much like Rosie's impression of Emma when first they met.

And Paul had been savvy enough to include a copy of the message the man at the Migratory Birds Program had sent to

Rosie. Maybe, just maybe, he would be persuaded to let Emma come.

The gambit worked. Emma and her dutiful escort were invited to observe; and so as not to exhaust the frail visitor, they would spend a night at the facility, in a room more often used by governmental overseers or curious academics. And Rosie and the others would postpone the next meeting until Emma and Paul had returned and Emma had rested up enough to tell them all about it.

Emma

Emma hadn't been away from home for more than a few hours since . . . was it since Robert had died, or even longer? She would hardly have dared to travel on her own, and it hadn't even occurred to her to sign up with some sort of tourist group. But now she had Paul to carry her suitcase, drive the car, and generally ease the way.

Though Paul wasn't, it seemed, all that good with directions. They had to stop twice for course corrections, so thank goodness Emma had insisted on leaving earlier than Paul had suggested. They would arrive in early afternoon, with plenty of time to see what was going on. And on one of those stops, Paul had talked her into buying packaged sandwiches they could eat in the car. She couldn't remember ever doing such a thing, which made it part of the adventure. She ate carefully so as not to leave crumbs.

Finally, they were driving along a tall wire fence with some sort of green fabric on it, hiding what was inside. As Paul looked for the gate, Emma leaned against her window for any trace of birds. And soon, there they were! — landing in twos and threes on top of the fence, croaking down at the car.

Paul glanced in that direction, chuckled, and muttered, "Queen of Crows." She didn't turn away to see his face, but she could hear his smile. Thought actually, the birds looked like the promised ravens, larger than crows and with long curved bills and wedge-shaped tails. It seemed her kingdom had expanded.

Emma hid her own smile against the glass.

Two long hours later, Emma was asking herself just why she had been so eager to come. Everything she had seen matched the descriptions in the reports the researchers had sent. Her back and her leg were aching. It was hot enough that she wished she'd been bold and gone without stockings. And while she'd both feared and sneakily hoped the ravens would show up to escort her around, they were kept in enclosures fenced at the top as well as the sides, and Emma and Paul were kept outside them. And none of the facilities or equipment they'd been shown was actually in use.

Well, maybe she could do something about that.

She leaned more heavily on her cane and said, in a quavering voice, "This is all so interesting! When will we be seeing the actual experiments? I *do* hope I won't have to go lie down before that happens." And then, after a strategic pause, "Oh, no! Have I overstepped? When we were invited, I *did* think the idea was that we would see your exciting work actually happening. I'll feel a little silly, coming all this way, if I was wrong. But if that wasn't what you meant . . . ."

Their guides looked at each other, clearly uncertain. Emma threw in a little sigh.

Finally, one of them cleared his throat and said, "We do have an exercise with the masks coming up. Did you read about the masks?"

"Of *course!*" Emma said eagerly. "I read all the reports as soon as I get them, and then read them again! The way you make the masks sounded so clever! I'd love to see them."

"Come this way, then. We'll be starting in a few minutes. I'll take you somewhere you can wait more comfortably."

Presumably a place she could finally sit down. Emma could have kissed him.

After about half an hour, they were led to one of the larger enclosures. Thankfully there was a bench outside, not exactly comfortable but much better than nothing. About twenty ravens were brought and released in the space and allowed to settle on the framework that served in place of trees. They croaked and squawked in almost musical tones, with an occasional rap-tap-tap call similar to a woodpecker at work. And then two disguised researchers came in.

The zombie masks struck her as somewhat crude, but combined with the stagger-shuffle the researchers used, they were enough to send chills down her spine. And the ravens reacted with new sounds, sequences of short shill calls. But Paul, looking closely, muttered, "Those aren't really right."

It took Emma a moment to remember why Paul actually knew what zombies looked like, and then it hit her. He had actually been there when a zombie attacked Janna and killed her. How could she have forgotten? She put a timid hand on his arm as she asked, "What's not right about them?"

Paul stood up and leaned against the fence, bracing himself with his arms. After about half a minute, he said, "Their walk is too ape-like. They're swinging their arms. They shouldn't do that. And they're not looking straight ahead, like the one I saw. As for the masks, they're dry, no slobber or — or blood near the mouths. And there's no hair showing. For that matter, the clothes are wrong too. They should be in tatters."

In fact, the researchers' bodies were completely covered in padded suits and the masks covered their entire heads. Presumably this was for protection from the ravens, who had descended in a mob and were squawking and pecking at the researchers, driving them toward the door through which they had come. It was clever of the birds to herd them like that. But then, ravens were clever.

Clever enough that if they were trained on these masks and outfits and gaits, they might not respond to the real thing? Or clever enough to draw the connection between imitation and reality? There was no way to know without a more accurate test.

Speaking of herding, one of their guides was coming back to fetch them. Emma thought quickly as he approached, and said as he reached them, "I was so interested when I read about how you would make the masks and learn how zombies walk, and it's a thrill to actually see it! How do the researchers who've actually seen zombies think these outfits and behavior compare to the real thing?"

The guide looked confused, then at a loss. "I don't know whether any of us has actually *seen* a zombie. I mean, how many people have? But we've seen some photos and videos, which should be good enough."

Emma looked at Paul. Should she have asked him whether he was willing to talk about it? But there hadn't been time, unless they waited and hoped for another opportunity. With genuine timidity, but realizing it would also make her persona more convincing, she asked, "Paul, dear, are you able to talk about it? I know it hasn't been very long . . . but think how much you could help this important work."

Paul swallowed, then did it again. She could see his Adam's apple bobbing. And his teeth were clenched. Finally he relaxed his jaw enough to say, "I should talk to someone, if possible. Because from what I'm seeing, there are some things you should know. But I only want to do this once. So please take me to someone who can actually make decisions."

In the end, he had to tell the story twice, the first time to an assistant to the man in charge. But the second time the assistant took detailed notes, and then a video as Paul did his best to reproduce how the zombie walked and ran. He had to stop once and ask where a men's room was, and when he returned, it looked as if he'd splashed his face and maybe rinsed out his mouth. It took long enough that Emma asked where she could sit down. Once she'd done so, a young man who'd been hovering around the edges of the tour sat down beside her and tried to make conversation. He seemed to want to talk about some other project, one working on drones that could smell zombies and fire weapons at them. Apparently the bird research team was eager to achieve useful results before these rivals could. Emma rather hoped they would, if only because she had her special connection to crows and knew nothing whatever about drones.

By the time they were finished, there was nothing else for them to see that day. The guide took them to the staff cafeteria, where the food was edible if not really appetizing, and then to their room. She'd been wondering what she would do if there was only one bed, but there were two. Paul disappeared into the bathroom without a word, and she soon heard the shower running.

While she waited for her turn, she sat in the one chair, but was too restless to read the book she'd brought. She went over to the window instead, watching what was left of an undramatic sunset. She was only briefly surprised to see a couple of crows fly down and perch on the ledge of the window. Or were they ravens? Were the ravens allowed to fly around at night, or had they escaped? It must be hard to keep such intelligent birds confined. And the birds' calls sounded more like what she'd heard earlier than like a crow's cawing.

She gave it no more thought as Paul came out of the bathroom and tipped a nonexistent hat. "Your turn, milady!" he announced cheerfully. Either he had shrugged off the distress he had suffered earlier, or he was good at pretending he had.

"Your majesty, you mean," she said grandly, and went to wash her hair.

Emma had hoped that someone would follow up on yesterday's meeting before they left, but no one did. They were shown one more part of the facility, where ravens with longer, stronger beaks were bred with each other, though it was unlikely, they were told, that even their offspring would be able to cause enough damage to stop a zombie for good. The current aim was to have them herd zombies away from their victims, or at least delay them long enough for the victims to get to some sufficiently sturdy shelter.

"Is there any program underway to build shelters like that?" Emma asked. But they got no clear answer, so she assumed the answer was no.

The young man who had chatted with Emma walked them back to their room. He and Paul seemed to get along nicely, and he looked grateful to have someone's attention. They were talking about ravens and crows and drones, but she knew Paul would tell her if any of it was important, so she let her mind drift instead of listening.

After their guide had excused himself, they packed the car and were headed home by late morning. They'd had a breakfast of clumpy oatmeal and muffins at the cafeteria. This time, they agreed, they would stop for a real lunch, something substantial. Emma had privately decided to treat herself to dessert, maybe even pie.

Two hours later, they pulled into the parking lot of a diner with a large and busy parking lot, hoping the many customers were a good sign. Paul got out, started to walk around to Emma's door, and stopped short. He called out something and pointed toward the edge of the parking lot. Emma got out on her own and came over to see what was worth fussing about.

The three spindly trees bordering the parking lot were full of large dark birds, to the point that the smaller branches were bending toward the ground. And from their size and their low-pitched calls, they sounded like ravens.

By the time she and Paul had lunch and came back to the car, there were four trees full of ravens.

Did she want to do any checking about whether the research facility was missing any birds? No, she decided, she did not.

Emma tried to see the sky through her window as they drove, but she couldn't see much of it. She did get an occasional glimpse of what might be a raven, but that was all.

They'd been listening to the radio, taking turns choosing the station. When Paul pulled into her driveway and turned the radio off, she thought she heard bird calls. Again he got out first, and opened her door. She saw his face, amused and a little wondering, before she got all the way out and could look around.

They had followed her home, all the birds she had seen at the restaurant. Even as she watched, another bird, then a second, flapped up and landed on the grass, since the street had few trees.

Emma stood there feeling like someone thrust onto a stage and told to recite a speech from Shakespeare, or at least the Gettysburg Address. "What should I do?" she whispered to Paul.

Paul just smiled at her. "I'm sure you'll think of something."

Emma looked at the birds again, gulped, and said in a shaky voice. "Thank you so much for coming." How absurd, as if she was the hostess at a cocktail party! But she went on. "The time may come soon when we can . . . work together. I hope you know on what — stopping zombies, or at least protecting people from them."

The ravens remained silent, except for one squawk that she chose to take as encouragement.

"And we can get crows to help too. There seem to be more crows in these parts — " But she was interrupted by a chorus of squawks, sounding for all the world like an indignant *No!* Maybe ravens and crows didn't get along. Maybe it was some sort of family quarrel. She would have to seek out some crows separately. Meanwhile, she would need to stay in touch with the ravens. "Anyway. Maybe . . . could you do whatever you need to, find good places to stay and find food and all that, but keep in touch? One or two of you could, um, check in every day or so. That way, when something's about to happen, I can ask you to help. Would that be all right?"

Nothing happened for almost a minute until, a few at a time and then in a tremendous flock, they all rose into the sky, circled, and flew away . . . except for two who perched in the lone tree in the yard. They must be staying in case of sudden trouble. Emma bit her lip, then managed to smile. "Thank you!" she called to the birds. She turned to Paul, beaming at her side. "And thank you so much for the ride, and for coming with me and talking to the people there."

"It was the least I could do." Paul looked suddenly sad, and then fierce. "I'll do whatever I can, whenever I can, until all this is over."

Would it ever be over? Paul was young enough to think so. She put out her hand for him to shake and then went into the house.

Chapter 21

Millie

"I'm still in awe of how brave you're being." Sofia gave Millie's hand a squeeze. Millie waited a few seconds, hoping Sofia would let go. She did so just before Millie would have reached her limit and pulled her hand free. She was too nervous and too keyed up to want comforting.

In fact, she would have preferred to be alone until it was time to "meet" with Rosie. But Sofia looked soulfully at her and said, "I could stay. I wouldn't mind, if you could use the emotional support."

Millie bit her tongue. Sofia deserved better than for Millie to snap, "I don't need a crutch." She waited until she could say politely, "That's very good of you. But you don't need to." And when Sofia seemed ready to repeat the offer, she allowed herself to add, "I don't need you to."

Sofia's eyes widened. Then she nodded, slowly, and said, "I'm glad to hear it."

Rosie

Sam had been making first contact for all the sessions, and usually hung around to take part. Rosie asked him to be present (so to speak) for her first brainstorming session with Millie as well, to make certain she missed nothing Millie was saying.

So here the three of them were, with Rosie at her usual table and Sam and Millie in whatever environment they'd deemed suitable for the occasion.

Actually, it might help to know where they were. So she asked, and Millie answered. "I'm in the coziest bed, sitting up with pillows behind me and a handmade quilt in pastel colors over my legs. Because you said what I needed to do was maybe like lucid dreaming. And Sam is sitting in a chair next to the bed."

Hmmm. That didn't exactly fit what Rosie had in mind. "That sounds lovely, and appropriate for certain kinds of practice later," she said diplomatically. "What I've thought of doing actually involves you making different settings and adding some elements to them. If you'd feel comfortable traveling around in that bed, that's fine. Otherwise, you may want to start out somewhere more . . . neutral."

After a pause for some exchange Rosie still couldn't hear, Sam said, *All right. Millie has just taken us to a big grassy field with trees around it. What should she do next?*

"Thank you, Millie." She could thank Sam as well, but that would get cumbersome. She'd do that later, when they were done for the day. "That's actually a good starting point for the exercise. Are there any animals visible?"

This time Millie spoke for herself. *No, none. I hadn't thought of it, but I don't usually put animals in. Should I add some?*

"Yes, please do. You can start small — maybe a squirrel."

As Rosie sat waiting to hear how Millie was succeeding, she started to feel strange — as if she were sitting at her table, seeing the usual fussily carved chairs and maroon velvet-patterned wall paper, but was somewhere else at the same time. Was she having a stroke? Falling asleep? What was going on?

Then she took in the intruding scene and realized it was a wide field of lush grass, surrounded by trees, with a squirrel hopping from one of the nearer trees to the next. Then came Sam's voice, amused, even smug. *How's that, love?*

"Sam, you marvel!" she exclaimed. "You're showing me what you and Millie are seeing! However did you manage it?"

Sam chuckled. *I simply realized I could. It's not so different, really, from talking to you. You aren't actually hearing me, after all, just sharing the words I'm thinking. Now you're also sharing what I see.*

Rosie pulled her thoughts back to the matter at hand. "Millie, that's an excellent squirrel. I was imagining something static, and you've already included movement. Well done! Let's move up in size to a larger animal."

She didn't know whether Sam lost his focus for a moment or whether the scene itself blurred, but soon enough it resolved itself again, with the same field now inhabited by a majestic stag. It bent down its crowned head and grazed, while the squirrel scampered down one tree and up the next.

"Thank you, Millie! Now an animal on its hind legs, like a bear."

Millie made a sound of dissatisfaction, a sort of grunt that went oddly with how Rosie imagined her. *I've never seen a bear standing up. Not even a picture of one, that I can remember.*

Sam interrupted. *I'll show you how they stand. Like this.* Rosie's view changed as he stood up. Was he trying to look frightening? No, Millie giggled. That was another thing Rosie hadn't imagined her doing. It was starting to sink in that Rosie's conception of Millie had been unduly limited.

Sorry! gasped Millie, and frowned in concentration as a bear wavered into view, a brown bear with its paws up and its mouth open in a snarl. Rosie heard Sam clapping and joined in.

"Great! Now, it's time to come up with a person. It can be someone you know, or someone famous, or someone you just dream up. Ready?"

Sam was looking closely enough at Millie that Rosie could see the twinkle in her eye. Moments later, the view jerked as Sam, apparently, jumped backward — looking at a replica of himself. Rosie studied it as Millie laughed in a high-pitched tone that suggested underlying hysteria. They had better end this session soon.

Rosie hadn't seen Sam in so many years . . . . She had assumed his afterlife self would look older, and he did, but only a little, more muscular, more mature. Still, she had to admit, eye candy. And now the view jiggled slightly as Sam laughed along with Millie.

Rosie let herself laugh too. Millie's effort deserved it. When they had all gotten the laughing out of their systems, she said, "Let's stop for today. When will the two of you be available to resume?"

Millie said, much more soberly, *For me, there's nothing more important than this, and I don't want to wait any longer than I have to.*

Sam added, *Rosie, you let us know when you have time, and I'll make myself available.*

The next lesson would have less laughter in it. But Rosie saw no need to say so. Instead, she signed off with, "It won't be long — a couple of days, on this end. I'll be in touch."

The next time they met, Sam showed Rosie a forest with a small clearing in it. *Millie feels this would be the best setting for what she senses is coming,* he said in a tone she'd have to call grim.

Millie had called it. But they could start slow. "Millie, please have someone — someone you like — come out from behind the trees."

At first, Rosie thought the figure slipping from behind a tree and walking forward was Janna, and her heart twisted at the thought of how Millie and Janna would have met. But looking closer, she saw that the girl was thinner and had different hair. It must be Jeri.

"Just to be sure I know what's happening," Rosie said, "That's an image you've made of Jeri, isn't it? Jeri hasn't come here to tease me?"

Millie smiled a little. *No, it's my made-up Jeri. She'd tell you so, but I don't know how to do that.*

Rosie thought quickly and said, "No, I don't think we'll need to do that. But practicing with some sound would be good. How about the bear again, and a roar? It doesn't have to be the same roar a bear would actually have."

Millie looked down and fidgeted. *I can try, I guess. Hold on.* The Jeri image vanished, and a bear emerged slowly from the trees. It stopped and opened its mouth. Nothing else happened for half a minute or so, and Rosie was preparing to regroup when the bear let out a roar worthy of a lion. In fact, it sounded just like a lion.

"Great! You did just what I asked. Now let's all take a moment to relax. Millie, you could do some breathing or stretching, or just add something to the setting that makes you smile."

A few flowers popped up among the roots of the trees, yellow and white and blue ones, half hidden as if shy.

Rosie got up, stretched out her back and neck, and made herself a cup of tea. Then she thought how incongruous it was, almost rude, to drink tea while someone was straining and making herself vulnerable, trying hard to do something difficult and disgusting, and left it on the counter. She returned to the table, sat down, and said, "Are you ready to continue?"

Rosie heard Millie take a deep breath and let it out in shaky puffs. *Yes. I think I know what's next. It's time to imagine a zombie.*

"I think so, yes."

Looking at Millie, her vulnerability so obvious, Rosie felt even more than before the outrageous unfairness that this harmless, inoffensive woman should have been victimized in so personal a way. She imagined, just as Millie must have so often imagined, those mild eyes inhabited by a mindless yet demonic force, those neatly trimmed nails ragged and more like claws, the tentative gait turned into an onrushing shamble.

And then she saw it. Because Millie had not, as Rosie had expected, conjured up some anonymous undead corpse, but had formed the one she could picture in the most detail, the one she most feared. Her own.

And it was terrifying.

Her view jolted as Sam recoiled. Millie whimpered. Rosie, hoping neither of the others could see her, stuffed her hand in her mouth, then removed it as she realized she just might vomit. "All right, you can stop!" she shouted.

For a breathless few seconds, it seemed Millie might not be able to. But then she gasped, set her hands on her thin hips, and stared at it until it crumbled into dirt.

No one said anything for a little while. Then Rosie said, her voice as steady as she could make it, "I believe I'll get myself a cup of tea. After that, we could keep going, or we could wait for another time."

Millie shook her head. *No. I don't want to wait. It won't get any easier. But I'll try having some tea.*

Rosie reheated her tea, considered getting something to go with it, realized what a profoundly bad idea that would be, and returned to the table in the living room. Settling back down, she took a sip and said, "Would either of you like a longer break, or should we continue?"

Sam answered in a voice obviously thickened by tears. *We should continue*, he said, as she wished she could hug him. *Millie's ready too.*

"Yes. Well. I'm afraid what I have in mind next will require Millie to bring back that same zombie. If it helps, you'll be putting it back where it belongs, if you can. I want you to call forth that zombie and *command* it to go lie down in its grave. If you know what your grave looks like, or may look like, then make that too. In fact, why don't you start with that — the grave, but not filled in, with a pile of dirt nearby."

There was a pause before Millie said, *I know where I wanted the grave to be. I don't know if it is. I . . . didn't have any way to make sure, anyone who would check. But I can make it the way I hope it is.*

"Yes," Rosie said as gently as she could. "That'll be fine."

The forest faded into mist, slowly replaced by a small cemetery like an American version of one in an English village: boulders piled up into a fence, modest graves with moss on them, bouquets of flowers partly obscuring the letters carved on tombstones. In the corner, at the end of a meandering row of graves, was the one that mattered now. She couldn't, from Sam's vantage point, read the inscription on the stone, but she could see that it was short. That might reflect reality, or simply Millie's expectation that no one would have much to say about her when she was gone. A mixture of anger and sorrow threatened to distract Rosie from the work at hand; she pushed it down.

And there came the obscene mockery of Millie, shambling through the open gate.

Millie's attempt to stand tall would have been funny in a less charged context. She stood very straight, with her shoulders up near her ears and her chin pointing up in the air, as she pointed to the grave and said in a shaky but loud voice, *Go there!*

The zombie dragged itself over to the foot of the grave, and stopped.

Millie suddenly slumped and put her face in her hands. The zombie disappeared. Before Rosie could decide what to ask and how to ask it, Millie lifted her face, her expression somewhere between embarrassed and bleak as she said, *I'm sorry. I'm sorry! I just couldn't do it. The thing is, I know that when I try this for real, the idea is for me to be inside the thing. And I'll be trying to lie down or to make it lie down — in my grave. It's ridiculous, when that's just where I want it to be, but . . . I used to dream about being buried alive. When I tried to order the body to lie down there, I couldn't stop thinking about how I'll feel, if I get that far, and I . . . lost focus. You've been helping me so much — I'm so sorry.*

"No, Millie, don't feel that way!" Rosie exclaimed. "You've been working very hard, and you've done *very* well! I never expected you to get so far in just two sessions." All true, but what would help? "We'll stop now, and before next time, I want you to imagine lying down in the grave as being like lying down in that lovely bed you were in. Imagine being tired — and you probably will be! — and lying down in the coziest possible place for a good long rest. Will you try that, later on, after you've done something very pleasant and completely different?"

Sam walked over to Millie, put his arms around her, and let go of the visual, leaving Rosie disoriented in her living room. *I'll make sure she has a change of scene and something appropriate to do. Check back in with us in a couple of days.*

"Will do," Rosie said, and sank back in her chair.

That night, Rosie decided it would be only fair if she dreamed her way through what she was asking Millie to do. She ran through the scene in her mind three times as she got ready for bed, placing her consciousness inside the zombie, completing the task at which Millie had faltered. As she climbed into bed, she recalled the advice she had so glibly given Millie.

Predictably, she found it somewhat harder than usual to fall asleep.

She started with a pleasant, inconsequential dream, a quick flight over the ocean, alternating with dives into the sea admiring an unlikely coral reef, then landing on the warm sand and stretching out on a luxurious towel. When a handsome fellow her imagination had apparently supplied turned up to join her, she allowed herself a frolic with him before she let the dream fade out. Then, after a transition that must have been NREM sleep, she found herself in the forest where Millie had conjured the zombie, and prepared herself for its approach.

She almost let herself wake when what appeared from beneath the trees was her own ghastly corpse, partially decomposed, stumbling and moaning toward her. Of course, she told herself. She could hardly have the experience Millie had undertaken if she entered any body but her own. She took a deep breath as if diving back into the ocean and surged inside.

She hadn't tried to imagine what the inner experience of a zombie might be like. If pressed, she would have said she didn't expect it to have any. And indeed, there was a blankness around her, an emptiness. How could she direct the creature, compel it to do something, without something to grab onto?

She could, at least, see out of its eyes, though the view was blurry, maybe from the nameless liquid that had been seeping from every orifice. She concentrated to create a path to the cemetery. (Had Millie thought about how to get her body there?) Then she lifted the creature's leg to step onto the path.

Instead, the creature veered off to walk back into the woods. And she had no idea how to wrest control of it and take it where it needed to go. She tried, and tried again, as the zombie went deeper and deeper into the forest. Finally, she gave up and pulled herself out.

Or tried to. But she was caught, like an insect caught in a sticky puddle, like a dinosaur wallowing helplessly in a pit full of tar.

Panicked, she jerked herself awake, panting and trembling. She clumsily threw back the covers, wrenching her arm, and tumbled out of the bed, running for the bathroom as soon as her feet hit the floor, turning on the cold water to splash it wildly on her face, making sure she was awake, wide awake, blessedly awake.

Chapter 22

Millie

Millie hated the way her session with Rosie had ended. It was too much like all the times she had tried things — or more often, wanted to try things — when she was alive. Sam being kind to her about it only made things worse, especially when he called in Johnny and Sofia to cheer her up. They had left the forest clearing behind, but none of her special places felt right, and she didn't want to take the feeling of failure back to her home. And she knew time was passing for the living, with every day putting more of them in danger.

They ended up on a cliff overlooking a vista of crashing surf on jagged rocks, as unsettled as her mood. Millie sat at the edge and stared at the view, filling her lungs with the salty air and her ears with the surge and ebb of the water.

After a while, Sam beckoned Sofia and Johnny for a quick consultation before he approached Millie and said, "Sofia and I will take ourselves off. Johnny will stay for a while, if that's all right with you."

She nodded, and they vanished. Johnny sat down next to her and said nothing for a few minutes. Then he asked in his calm, quiet voice, "I know, in general terms, what you're hoping to do. I'm a little hazy on the details. Do you want to talk about it?"

Did she? It might do her good to refocus her attention on her goal, rather than on the latest setback. "I'm going to try to go back inside my body, which is a zombie now. As for how to get there, the plan is that I'll do what I do when I make a new personal place, or go somewhere I want to be, except — except this will be somewhere I don't want to be at all." She shrugged, and found herself able to smile a little. "That's the stumbling block, so far."

Johnny leaned back on his hands. "This is a good spot for thinking. Or for not thinking. It's one of Sam's places."

She hadn't even wondered. "Please thank him for me, if you see him first."

They sat a while longer before Johnny said, "I imagine we don't know whether anyone's done it before — gone back."

"No." She chuckled a little. "So all this drama may come to nothing. But I have to try. And even if someone tried before and couldn't, this is different, isn't it? With my body already out of the grave and moving around? I'm hoping that'll make it easier. And if it doesn't work . . . well, I'll know I tried, and I won't have lost anything."

"True enough."

Now that she was calmer, she could think through the plan and look for any other difficulties. All too soon, she hit on one. "How will I know I'm really there?"

Johnny wrinkled his forehead in puzzlement. "How will you know?"

"I recreated the scene here, the forest and the zombie and the cemetery. I made it as real as I could — real enough to send me into a panic. How will I know if I've actually managed to go back, or if I've just made it up again?"

"Hmm. Good question."

They sat in companionable silence — silence except for the waves, and the call of a seagull.

"How about this?" Johnny eventually asked. "It might be a good idea if someone is with you. Here, that is. That way, if you're still here instead of where you should be, we can let you know."

She found herself relaxing despite the task ahead. "That's a very good idea." And then, daring: "Are you volunteering?"

She could have sworn Johnny looked at her with pride as he said, "Indeed I am. Who else would you like to have? I'm sure Sofia would want to assist, if you don't object. And possibly Daniel, who's bound to care a great deal about whether you succeed, and will want to increase the chances of it."

Millie took one more look at the dramatic, restless scene around her and stood up. "Let's find out now. Because I don't want to wait. I won't learn anything else by waiting, or get any braver. I need to do this now."

Johnny was right, as he so often was. Both Sofia and Daniel showed up. Though Sofia diffidently suggested, "Since we'll be waiting here after you disappear, if you do, maybe we could wait somewhere more comfortable than this cliff top. Like a garden?"

Millie imagined being in Sofia's place, watching Millie disappear and having no way to know what was happening to her. She would be nervous — no, more than that. Maybe even terrified. "Of course," she said. "Do you have one in mind?"

Soon they stood in a garden of some kind, though she had no attention to spare for its details. Daniel, who had joined them last, was as pale as she had ever seen him, and was shifting from foot to foot. "Would you mind," he asked abruptly, "if anyone else joined those of us who are waiting? After you go?"

He probably wanted his wife there. Millie didn't know her well, but . . . "That's fine. After I go."

And there was nothing else to wait for.

Except to figure out how to disappear. One method occurred to her. "Johnny, Sofia, Daniel," she whispered, "I want you to look at me, and think of me fading into mist. Try to see me vanishing. And at the same time, I'll think of my body, the way it must look now. I'll think of myself staring out through its eyes."

Sofia had taken her hand, and seemed reluctant to let go of it. Millie twitched her fingers as a gentle request. Sofia took a shaky breath and stepped back.

⸻◆⸻

Sofia

Sofia watched Millie squeeze her eyes shut and clench her fists tight. She was muttering something to herself, or at least her lips looked as if she were, but Sofia couldn't hear what she said. Millie was trying her hardest to do this seemingly impossible thing. And it was time for Sofia to try to help.

She stared at Millie, and imagined — no, imagining wasn't good enough. It wasn't imagining when she made a special spot. It was *making*. So now, she had to look at her friend, the woman she'd tried so hard to help all this time . . . and *make* her disappear.

It was like doing something with a muscle, but trying to do it on purpose instead of instinctively. Like trying to speak, or breathe, when she was scared and felt like she'd forgotten how. She had to try to relax — but she had to hurry. Because Millie was doing something that probably took all her strength, and she couldn't keep it up too long.

Sofia counted softly to herself, as she did when she practiced yoga. Breathe along with the count . . . steadily, steadily . . . easily . . . that was it. Now, as she breathed, reach out to Millie, the way she reached for a meadow or lake or sunrise she wanted to see . . . . Blur her edges into mist, soft, gentle mist, mist reaching out . . . reaching in . . . an outline made of mist, nothing else . . . and now, a breeze, a warm, caressing breeze, blowing through the mist, carrying it away, away, away . . . .

And Millie was gone.

Sofia gasped and crumpled into a heap. She wanted to call Millie's name, to call her back, and she mustn't. She bit her tongue instead, and fought to get her breathing under control again. Only when she felt past the crisis did she look around at Johnny and Daniel. And call to the twins, Janna and Jeri. To Robert, Emma's son, strong enough to reach Emma through the divide between the worlds. To Sam.

Millie might need them. And Sofia needed them, right now.

Millie

Millie felt very strange. Thick-headed, disconnected, disoriented. Was she sick? But no, she was dead, and how could she be both dead and sick? And why did the world keep lurching around her? And what was coming from her eyes, that smeared everything she could see?

Now she was hearing something, as if a radio had been slowly tuned to a station. A peculiar station, because a voice, a strangely familiar voice, was repeating strange words.

BRAINS BLOOD LICK BLOOD CRUNCH . . . BITE BONES SKULL . . . HUNT FIND HUNT FLESH BITE LICK GRIND CRUNCH

That voice — could it be her own?

And why wasn't she frightened?

She had always wanted peace, security, safety, and so often had been unable to find it. Even in . . . wherever she had been, somewhere different, when she had known she was safe, some part of her hadn't believed it. But now, even with the strange words like a background chant, there was something soothing about . . . wherever she was now. As if there was nothing to think about. Nothing to worry about, or be afraid of. She could just lie back and be carried, and think about nothing at all.

She lay back, carried along, at peace in spite of the uneven gait of whatever was carrying her, the words repeated over and over like a lullaby . . . .

But it wasn't really comfortable, with the lurching and stumbling. And something was niggling at her, trying to get her attention. A memory of some chore left undone. She had never liked leaving chores for later. They only got more tire-some when she did that. What hadn't she gotten done?

It felt like swimming through soup, thick soup, to try to remember. But it had something to do with where she was. She had come here, to this strange place, for a reason. Had she come to feel safe? To be at peace?

No, that wasn't it. . . .

Whatever the reason, it was about going somewhere else. Where else? And why did it matter?

An image, faint and blurry, floated into her mind. A place to rest, another place to rest. If she could go there, the lurching would stop, and maybe the voice. She could picture it, a sort of field, but with stones sticking up all through it, and a fence around it. But how to get there?

Then she knew. Her body knew the way. It had been there before, had made its way from there to wherever it was now. But did it want to go back there?

Could she tell it what to do? It was carrying her, but would it listen to her? All she could do was try. The words that came to her seemed strange, but whatever impulse suggested them, she would listen to it.

Go to bed, Millie said softly, almost humming, to — to what? Her carriage, her caretaker, her prison, herself? *It's time to go to bed. It's time to sleep.* And indeed, the light around her was dim. Dusk must be falling. Close enough to bedtime for a young child, and some instinct told her to treat the creature as one. *Playtime is over. Go to bed and get in so you can sleep.*

The jolting ride changed direction. In the right direction? She didn't know. She lapsed back into the comfort and peace of being carried. No more decisions, no more thinking. At least, not until they got to the little fenced field.

There was something in the way. Something cold, metal, bumping into the — her? the creature's? — knees. The creature kept pressing on the metal thing until the obstacle toppled forward. The chanted words slowed down and came to a stop.

This was a graveyard. The bed she had told the creature to find was her grave. They had to reach the grave, and lie down in it.

Why? Why was that better than being rocked and cradled as the body went its way?

The words. The words that started again, more slowly, in what passed for the creature's mind. If the body kept walking around in the world, those words were things it would want and things it would do. She remembered, now, that she had come here to stop it. It was her body, and so it was her job to stop it. Then she could go home, her new home, not the bed beneath the marker.

She spoke to her body again. *You've had a long, long day. Years long, many years. And now it's time to sleep.*

New words, now, from her body. *NO WANT TO WALK HUNT FLESH BITE LICK CRUNCH*

No, she said firmly. *You weren't supposed to be doing that. It wasn't your fault — something made you. But it's over now. Now it's time to sleep, where you belong.*

DON'T WANNAAAA.

Yes. It's time. You're going to lie down, like a good . . . body. You need to lie down. But first let's find your bed. Come with me. Let's find the right place to sleep.

The creature dragged its legs forward. She tried to read the gravestones through the slimy stuff covering the eyes. Surely she would recognize her name. But the creature shuffled past one stone and then another, and "Millie" was on none of them.

Wait! What was that? *Stop. Turn — no, the other way. Let me see.*

The grass was torn away, and dirt had slumped into the hole. Splintered planks of wood must have been the cheap pine coffin. At one end of the hole stood a stone saying, "Millicent Williams," and then the years. The years were right. The name wasn't. Her full name was Camille, but everyone — well, the people, not that many, who had known her had known her as Millie. Whoever made the stone should have had her identification, but maybe no one had brought it to them, and they'd guessed.

The creature was turning away. *No, go back. We're here. This is your bed. Don't you see, the mess you made getting out of it? But that will make it easier to lie down again. Let's lie down now.*

DON'T WANNAAAA!

And neither did she, that was the trouble. She'd always hated the thought. She'd never been so glad as when she opened her eyes in that other world, that other life, and found herself standing, looking around at the big lovely room with the coffered ceiling and the arches and the warm breeze blowing the scents of flowers toward her.

She wanted to go back there. She didn't want to lie down in that hole in the ground. But first one, then the other.

Let's get in. Let's start by crouching down. That's right. Would you like to play in the dirt first? You can take it in your hands and throw it in the air.

WANNA PLAY. DON'T WANNA LIE DOWN.

A mistake, perhaps, to say anything about playing. But she could let it play for a minute.

It threw the dirt in the air, and some of it landed in her hair. She wanted to shake her head, but she couldn't. After two more throws, she said, *All right, now, that's enough playing. Time for bed. First one leg, then the other.*

Slowly, lurching downward now, the creature climbed into the hole. It squatted at one end of it.

PLAY TOMORROW?

She couldn't cry. Neither could the creature, it seemed, but she wanted to cry, or the creature did. *We'll play together, in a place that's meant for playing. It'll be like dreaming, except you never have to stop. You sleep, and I'll play for both of us. All right?*

The other words started up again, but faintly, as if from a long way away. *BITE LICK CRUNCH . . . .*

No. You did that. Most bodies never get to do that, but you did. Now it's time to lie down like a good body. I'll do everything else. I'll take care of everything. You rest. Now lie down.

Slowly, slowly, the creature toppled over. It was on its side now, curled up like a baby.

That's good. Very good. Now you can relax. You don't need to go anywhere. Stay right here and go to sleep.

One by one, the little twitches and shuffles came to a stop. The creature sank into stillness, lying in the earth.

Now what? What should Millie do?

How could she get home?

Chapter 23

Emma

Emma was asleep, deep asleep, when a sound blasted her — not awake, but into a dream. It was Robert — and oh, to see him! To see him healthy and whole, big as life and smiling at her! She wanted to do nothing more than look at him and hug him tight, so tight he would never leave her again. But after only a few seconds, he held her away from him and said, "Mom, I'm sorry but you have to wake up! Paul is trying to reach you — it's time! Millie made it into her body, but now she needs your help, yours and the ravens'. Wake up and answer the phone!"

"Oh, no, Robert, I love you, stay with me . . . ."

He gave her one more squeeze and a kiss on the cheek, and then her arms were empty and she was awake. And the phone was ringing, just as Robert had told her. She stumbled out of bed and hurried for it — how long had it been ringing before she woke up? Would the caller still be there? "Hello?" she panted.

"Emma, I'm so glad I caught you!" It was Paul's voice. "Have you had breakfast?"

It was embarrassing, but she admitted, "No, I just got up. Do we need to do something? Go somewhere?"

"Yes and yes! Rosie just heard from Sam." Emma almost interrupted him to tell him she'd heard from Robert, but he was going on, his words climbing over each other in his haste. "Millie made her attempt and succeeded in getting inside her body. She's managed to get it to the cemetery, but Sam thinks she may need some help there. He isn't sure what kind, so he wants both sides of the team to be ready. I can come get you in ten minutes. Can you be ready that soon?"

Emma usually took her time picking out her clothes, but she could dispense with that ritual. "Maybe fifteen. And could you bring me something to eat? Something that won't make too much of a mess?"

Paul chuckled. "Come on, you've seen my car. You could treat crumbs like confetti and it wouldn't make much difference. I'll bring you a couple of toaster pastries. See you in fifteen."

She was standing on her front step in less than fifteen minutes. As Paul drove up, tires squealing on the pavement as he stopped, three ravens rose up out of the tree, squawking and flying in a circle. In all the hurry, she'd forgotten about the ravens. But now, as Paul got out and opened the passenger side door of his car, she said to them, "Please come along, with some of your friends, if you can. We may need you."

Rosie had somehow found out the location of the cemetery and shared it with Paul. The way Paul drove there, Emma kept a nervous eye out for police. But what she saw out the window was a growing escort of ravens. And when Emma insisted, Paul pulled over near a field where she saw crows gathered on someone's lawn, and Emma got out to make her plea to them, trying not to sound as hurried and panicky as she felt. As she talked, she brushed the crumbs of her hasty breakfast off her skirt, and some of the birds hopped over to peck at them. When they drove away, a small cloud of crows flew beside the car — on the other side from their larger cousins.

After what might have been forty minutes or so, but felt twice as long, Paul pulled into the driveway, gravel flying, and was out of the car before Emma even unfastened her seat belt. He helped her out with a bit more energy than was comfortable. As soon as her feet hit the gravel, he started looking around. "It's in a corner near the fence. Can you see any grave that looks right?"

Emma looked, more slowly than Paul had, and pointed. "That pile of dirt. Let's check there."

Now, after all the rushing, Paul wasn't moving as if he was in a hurry. She actually passed him, and then turned back quizzically. "What is it?"

Paul's answer came slowly. "If we're right, and if Millie has succeeded, what do you think we'll see in that grave?"

Oh.

"Millie's body."

"Not just that. A body that's become a zombie. That's what's lying there — we hope." He sighed and then trudged onward, still slowly enough that Emma could keep pace with him. The birds came with them, crows flying to trees, ravens circling above her, a few of each hopping along the slightly overgrown grass.

When they reached the pile of dirt, she glanced at Paul and then took charge. "We'll have to shovel it back in. Do you see a shovel anywhere?"

"Over there, near the shed." His steps quickened as he fetched it, slowed as he brought it back.

They had reached the grave. And Paul probably thought he had to be the first to look. Emma held her breath, took Paul's arm for balance, and leaned forward.

The body she saw below was filthy. That was what she noticed first. It was lying on its side, in something close to fetal position, so she couldn't — didn't have to — see its face, but she could tell that its eyes were closed.

She straightened up and said to Paul, "It doesn't look too bad. You should look, I think."

Paul stepped to the edge of the grave and looked down. His shoulders relaxed, and he said, "You're right. It doesn't." He wrinkled his nose. "It smells awful, though."

The smell was horrible, now that he'd called her attention to it — like nothing she'd ever smelled, a smell like rotten meat and an outhouse and damp earth all mixed together.

Paul was still looking. "Is Millie — the real Millie, her spirit — still in there?"

Emma shivered as she said, "I don't know. But it wasn't her spirit that made the body move and — and attack people. We'd better bury it, and tamp the earth down extra firmly."

Paul nodded and held up the shovel. "I'll get started. I shouldn't need help, as long as I rest if I need to."

Emma resolutely shook her head. "No, we need to get this all the way done as soon as we can. We'll take turns. But you can go first."

The birds, above and beside them, seemed to watch closely as the shovelfuls of earth fell softly into the grave. If there had been a coffin, as Emma supposed there had been, it had been reduced to the pieces of wood she had barely noticed when she first looked in. It was a gentler process without the clatter of dirt clods on a lid.

The body didn't stir as the dirt gradually covered the feet, the legs, the knees. Paul had started to breathe more heavily, and she tapped him on the shoulder. "My turn."

She had to take smaller amounts of dirt at a time, but she could still see the progress she was making. Knees, upper legs, the lower torso. She stopped when the dirt reached the chest. "Your turn again."

Millie

Someone was filling in the grave. It was getting harder for Millie to stay calm, with the dirt falling down. She felt as if she would suffocate, even though the body wasn't breathing. But she needed to make sure the body stayed put. *Feel that?* she said. *Someone is giving you a blanket, to make sure you're all cozy and comfy.*

The dirt had reached the chest. The shoulders. The neck. The face.

And then it started at the feet again, making the dirt deeper. And if Millie had been in control of the body, it would have started shaking.

More dirt, and more. It must be two or three feet deep by now. And then someone was hitting the dirt with something, probably a shovel, to make it firmer. To make it harder to climb out.

Millie knew her panic might be contagious, might make the creature want to move again. But she couldn't help it. And it was happening.

AFRAID AFRAID NEED TO GET OUT

Helplessly she felt the body uncurl. The legs start to kick. An arm reach upward, upward, through the dirt that was still loose. A leg kick again, over and over.

Emma

Paul, holding the shovel with the flat side down, suddenly jumped back and cried out. "It's trying to get out! What should we do?"

Emma peeked and saw the dirt-covered arm breaking through the dirt, and the flat surface Paul had just tamped down starting to crack and shift, a foot starting to show . . . and then came a rush of wind and sound, the ravens swooping downward, the crows a little behind, all of them cawing or letting out ravens' shrill series of calls; and then the ravens with their long sharp beaks striking at the arm, at the foot, again and again.

Millie

Something was happening, something that distracted her from her panic. She could just feel something touching her foot and her arm, something sharp. And there was noise, croaking and squawking along with short shrill calls. Was it birds? The crows or ravens Emma had been talking about, or vultures? Did even scavengers eat zombies?

The creature was recoiling, pulling its limbs back into the grave. *HURT SHARP HURT SCARED*

Oh, my. It's hurty and scary out there, isn't it? Come back inside where it's safe. You can rest here, and nothing will hurt you.

The creature curled up on its side again, making a snorting sound almost like crying.

There, there. It's all right now. You're safe. You can go back to sleep.

And there was the dirt again, more falling to replace whatever the creature had shoved away, and then the shovel tamping it down. Millie was still frightened, but not nearly as much as she had just been, when the zombie had tried to climb back out of the grave.

She waited, and waited some more. Surely it was time. She wasn't going to stay here. It was time to let someone else take over on this end, and to go home.

She tried to pull herself out without disturbing the creature. That was the last thing she wanted to do — except to stay here forever.

She pulled. She tugged. She felt something start to happen. And then it stopped happening. She didn't know how. She didn't have the strength.

She needed help! But she couldn't call for it, or the creature might wake up. And if she panicked again, it might wake up anyway.

From what felt like far away, she recalled the memory of special breathing. Yoga breathing, Sofia had called it. She wasn't breathing now, but she could remember what it felt like. She could calm herself down enough to reach out for help. To reach out to Sam and the others who must be waiting and listening.

She imagined breathing, slowly and deeply.

She reached.

<hr>

Janna

Soon after Millie had disappeared, Janna and the rest of the team had answered Sofia's summons. Millie had just disappeared, Sofia told them, and Sofia had made, or returned to, a garden, loosely planted and barely tended, full of spring and summer flowers mixed together, on a day of warm spring weather. They sat there in a circle, while Sofia concentrated and then asked all of them to do the same, to try to see what Millie saw and hear what she heard. She said she had made Millie dissolve into mist, so Johnny suggested they bring that mist back and then try to see through it. It took a long time, or that's what it felt like to Janna, as she wondered what was happening to Millie, all alone with a zombie to try to control. But finally, the mist turned into a sort of bubble with a picture in it, and they were watching a horrible version of Millie lurching along.

It must be scary as hell, to go back like that. A little like seeing your twin sister in a hospital bed, thin as a skeleton, and not knowing what would happen next. The memory must have made her go pale, because Jeri scooted closer and gave her a squeeze.

They watched the zombie make its way to the cemetery and break in, stagger to Millie's grave and start to leave again, crouch down and play with the dirt . . . and *finally* climb in. Millie wouldn't be seeing anything but dirt, now. What was happening up above? They all thought about that until the view pulled back, far enough that they could see Emma and Paul show up, and the birds they brought with them. "Cool!" Jeri exclaimed. Janna was inclined to agree.

And then they all gasped, or called out, "Oh, no!", when the creature started to fight its way back out of the grave. And gasped again, or clapped their hands, or cheered, when the birds attacked and drove it back in.

That looked like the end of the exciting part. Emma and Paul finished filling in the grave and packed the dirt. They waited a little while and then walked over to the fence, leaning against it close together, panting. Meanwhile, Millie wasn't doing anything. They were back to seeing what she saw, and all she could see was darkness, and there was nothing she could hear. But Janna felt something, a feeling coming from outside her. Millie's feelings. Worry. Fear. Panic.

Sam jumped up from the circle and shouted, "She's scared! She thinks she's stuck! She needs our help!" And then, eyes wide, "She's trying to stay calm. But if she doesn't get out of there, and she's scared enough, the zombie might get scared too. It might wake up and climb out again, and the birds might not be enough to stop it, if it's more scared from her fear than from whatever they did to it. We have to hurry!"

Johnny was always so calm. He looked concerned, but he asked in an almost soothing voice, "How do we help? What do you think we should do?"

Sam looked around jerkily as if searching for inspiration. Then he stopped, shut his eyes tight, and held his hands as if pulling on a rope. In a few seconds he stopped, huffing and puffing, and said more quietly, "I can't do this alone. All of you get in a line behind me, like you were going to pull someone out of quicksand, and think about Millie. Remember some conversation you had, something that impressed you or surprised you. And if you can't think of anything like that, just picture her face. If you've noticed her getting stronger and braver, the way I have, then think about that. And then grab onto the person in front of you and *pull*."

Daniel hurried behind Sam, and then Sofia, and then Robert. Janna got in line behind Robert, and Jeri followed and grabbed her tightly around the waist. Janna searched her memories for anything about Millie. She hadn't been there when Millie told the terrible story of finding out her body had killed someone — but other members had been impressed by the courage it took to tell it, and the fact that she hadn't asked for sympathy. She'd heard Rosie echoing Millie later, but she hadn't had much of an impression of her until — was it the worst moment of Janna's life, when the zombie killed her, or the second worst, because the worst had been Jeri's death? Or the third worst, because of how soul-destroying it had been to watch her mother grieving . . . . She pulled her mind back to the question at hand. She had met Millie, finally, when she arrived here. Millie had been patient and kind, and had shown Janna one of her own special places, and helped her reunite with Jeri there. And that place had been so lovely and peaceful. Millie must have a beautiful soul, to have made it. And she must know how much it mattered, to be surrounded in beauty and peace.

Millie deserved every good thing. And she did *not* deserve to be stuck in a stinky, slimy, decayed body, just because she cared enough about people to go back to it and make it stop killing them!

Janna thought about all those things, and gripped Robert's waist, and *pulled*.

Millie

Millie made herself remember steady breathing, in, out, in, out, until she had control of her fear. She fell into something like a trance, if a brittle one. If she concentrated enough, there would be no room for thoughts or fears or the passage of time to break through. Three counts in . . . five counts out . . . .

And then, something grabbed her — grabbed *her*, not the zombie body in which she was trapped. It startled her out of the trance, startled her as much as pain would have, but there was no pain, just a pull — jerky at first, in fits and starts, and then steadier and stronger. And familiar, somehow. She needed to go with it. She needed to let go of where she was, and go back where she belonged.

Carefully, as if she were relaxing the grip of her hands on a cage . . . come loose, let go . . .

But wait — had she done what she came for?

She was still wondering when one more mighty tug left her floating, and then sailing, away.

She found herself sitting in the garden.

Everywhere, colors bloomed and scents mingled and drifted on the gentle breeze. It was the greatest possible contrast to the stench of the zombie and the clammy closeness of earth. And her friends clustered around her, exclaiming at her reappearance, gazing at her as if unsure she were really there, reaching cautiously out to touch her. Daniel stood a little apart, looking both relieved and somber. Millie looked at her friends, at this flower and that, trying to understand that she was here, she had made it back — no, *they* had brought her back.

Sofia was the first to actually hug her. "Are you all right? You did so well! You were *amazing*!"

"Was I?" She looked at Sofia, once Sofia let go, and at the others. "Did I do enough? What if my body gets back up again, like it started to do before?" She looked around at the garden, breathed in the warm and fragrant air, felt the sun-warmed metal of the bench on which she sat. She forced out the words: "Should I go back? Should I . . . stay there, so my body will? I never expected a place like this, and I've already spent a lot of time here. Should that be enough?"

They all stared at her in shock. Johnny recovered first, saying, "Let's see what's happening there, before you make any decisions." He gave a sort of wave, and a portal opened, soft at its edges. There was the cemetery, and the grave, a packed mound of earth. Emma and Paul were standing near the fence, and Emma was looking up at a small cluster of trees. There was something odd about the trees — they had thickly clustered black splotches all over, and the thinner branches were bowing under them.

After sight came sound, a lot of croaking and cawing. It must be birds in the trees, dozens of them, maybe even a hundred per tree, crows or something similar; and they were calling to each other, or maybe to Emma. What was Emma saying? Millie listened hard, and could just hear it. "Thank you so much. You did just what we hoped. Would we be asking too much if we asked that you keep watch, or find a way to fetch others to do so?"

The birds — some bigger than crows, though just as black — rose from the tree and descended again, like a giant nod. Four of them flew to the grave and stationed themselves at its corners.

Paul spoke this time. "Thank you. If there's ever anything we can do for you, for any of you, I hope you'll find a way to let us know. We'll be going now, but you know where to find Emma. Maybe a couple of you can follow us and see where I live, so you can find me too."

Two birds left one of the trees and flew to the nearby car, perching on the hood and looking back as if expecting Emma and Paul to follow. Which they did.

Emma and Paul got in and drove away, the crows bobbing along beside. Back in the cemetery, the grave lay peaceful and still.

Johnny waved again, and the portal closed, leaving only the beauty and tranquility of the garden and the people sharing it.

They sat in a quiet in which the distant drone of bees and the soft movement of the breeze formed the gentlest of backdrops. Into this hush Sofia said, "You've done all anyone could ask, and more than you would ask of anyone else. We all hope that others whose bodies have been taken by this scourge will follow your brave example. If Daniel, here, were to do so, and then ask us the question you asked, would you think he should sentence himself to an eternity in something far worse than solitary confinement?"

Millie breathed in sharply. No wonder Daniel seemed burdened! But of course, he would be one of the next to volunteer. The thought of him, with his dapper clothing and trimmed beard, forcing himself into the decayed and hideous remnant of his former body made her want to retch. She looked up at him, her heart in her throat. "No! I'd want him to come back as soon as he could."

Daniel smiled sadly at her as Sofia said emphatically, "There, now! We'll have no more talk like that. So we can go back to celebrating your return and admiring your courage."

Millie had to smile at that, and to blush. But that couldn't be the end of it, not quite. "All right. But . . . if someone else arrives because my body got back out of the grave and killed them, I'll have to go back."

No one argued, but no one agreed. She would leave the matter there. For now, they were right. She had done enough.

Chapter 24

Rosie

R osie was waiting, if the anxiety-ridden restlessness consuming her could be given so placid a name, as Paul's car finally pulled into her driveway. He opened the passenger side door for Emma, giving her his arm in a positively courtly manner, as Rosie hustled to her front door and flung it open. Emma was beaming, what could only be pride making her stand almost straight, and lifting her chin to look squarely at Rosie. Rosie opened her mouth to demand a report, but Emma was already saying, "She made it! The thing, her body, went into the grave, and we filled it in —"

"And Emma's birds pecked at it when it started to get back out again, and it settled back down!" Paul had his arm around Emma's shoulders and gave her a little squeeze as he spoke.

If Sam had been sharing Rosie's vigil, she'd been too tense and distracted to realize it, but now she heard a long breathing-out of stress, and then an earnest *Well done, all of you! Please tell Paul and Emma how glad and grateful we are here! And that includes Millie! She's back!*

Rosie waved Paul and Emma inside and conveyed the good news. She invited them to sit down and talk about what should come next, but Paul and Emma looked at each other smugly, and Paul said, "Just a moment — there's something we left in the car." He ran out to the driveway and was soon back with a bakery box. Carrying it in and placing it carefully on the table around which they usually met, he pried it open with a flourish to reveal a cake, with the word *Congratulations!* in multicolored script atop its creamy chocolate frosting.

"We were ready to grab a plain one," Emma said with what Rosie would have to call a grin, "but this one simply called out to us!"

Diane had been working on the accounts in the small bedroom she had chosen as her office, but she heard the happy clamor and joined them. Over slices of what proved to be German chocolate cake, they brainstormed how to make the most of this achievement. Sam sat in, so to speak, after apparently somehow getting hold of his own slice of cake: *devil's food, if that shocks any of you.* Rosie felt him smirk.

Paul, with a waggle of his eyebrows, called it "groundbreaking." Swallowing his latest huge mouthful, he elaborated. "After all this time and flailing around, we've found something that can work. Now how do we scale it up?"

Diane had brought a legal pad — somehow, she managed to be efficient while using pen and paper for most tasks — and tapped her pen on it. "Our current reach is limited to cemeteries at least one of us, and preferably two or more, can get to. With our various other responsibilities, and even if those weren't a factor, we simply can't get to all the places zombies have emerged. So we need more people, spread over a much wider geographical area."

Emma seemed to be fading from her initial energy back into her old timidity. Maybe the efforts of the day had too heavily tapped whatever had been driving her during these past weeks. But she said, if shakily, "Can our spirit friends get in touch with more people, the way Robert got in touch with me?"

Sam was slow to respond, but finally said, *I'm afraid we've been slacking off, after the surprising success in your neck of the woods, and how much you've done once we made contact. And, I suppose, how little seemed to be coming of it. But now that we know what you all can accomplish, we'll step up our efforts.*

By the time all of them except Emma had finished a second slice of cake, they each had their assignments. Paul and Rosie would post on all their social media, which in Rosie's case included a Facebook group catering to mediums, another for small businesses, yet another for professional women, and finally one for lay folk interested in spiritualism. Diane would write up a flyer to be posted in libraries, senior citizen centers, and any particularly tolerant houses of worship. And Emma, emerging partway back out of her shell, undertook to post the flyer at the library she knew so well. "And if someone — maybe Diane? — will drive me to other libraries, I'll put it up there too. Oh — while I'm doing that, I can try to find crows or ravens to talk to." Diane nodded agreeably at the first request, but her eyes brightened at the second.

People were pushing back their chairs when Rosie had another thought. "Paul, could you contact Rabbi Horowitz? It's an insular community, and I suspect few of his people are on social media. You may be one of the few outsiders the rabbi might listen to. And he's already shown himself open to the supernatural."

At first, Paul looked put-open, a mulish expression forming on his face — before he stopped and stood very still. "Janna was willing to talk to him, as hard as she found it. I'll do it for Janna."

Thanks, Paul. That's really sweet of you, came Janna's voice. Rosie thought of passing it along, but decided not to complicate the moment.

Emma

As they left the third library on Diane's list, Emma knew she was walking too slowly. But Diane didn't seem impatient, merely saying, "It's a nice long drive to the next one. You'll be able to rest up."

Emma did more than rest. She fell asleep, lulled by the low note of the engine and the steady forward motion of the car. What woke her was a cawing sound outside her window. She found that her head was resting against the window, and turned enough to see three crows flying alongside, flying in straight lines — that must be why people said, 'as the crow flies'! — almost close enough that they could have pecked at the glass.

She blinked, shook her head a little to clear it, and asked Diane hesitantly, "Could we pull over for a minute, whenever you can?"

Diane looked first confused and then concerned. Did she think Emma felt sick? or needed to pee, and planned to squat alongside the road? Emma made haste to add, "There are crows following us. I want to try to talk to them."

Diane's expression shifted to excitement. "How marvelous! I'll find the first spot I can."

Emma had hoped for trees, but at least the wide shoulder had a low metal fence dividing the shoulder from the road. The crows settled on it; Emma leaned against the hood of the car. She looked over her shoulder at Diane, still behind the wheel and thus allowing Emma some privacy (not counting the crows). She cleared her throat and began. "I don't know if you know who I am, or anything about me. Or about the creatures, the zombies, who've been coming out of their graves and attacking people. But we're trying to stop them, and it turns out birds like you, and ravens, can be a great deal of help."

The birds looked at her with their dark beads of eyes as she stammered through her account of what birds had already done. She had no way to know whether they understood her as well as other crows had, but she would assume so, and say everything there was to say. "So I'm hoping you could tell the other crows — and ravens, if they'll let you talk to them — around here, and as far as you can comfortably travel. And that you'll ask them to help, if they see anyone refilling a grave. To peck at any creature that's trying to climb back out of it. Or even trying to fight its way out of a grave in the first place." What could she promise them in return? "And we'll try to make sure you always have enough to eat. And you'll be welcome to live near anyone who understands what you're doing."

She fell silent, and the silence was anticlimactic. Was that all? Should she just get back in the car?

One of the crows, the one closest to her, fluttered up from the fence and then back down. The one next to it did the same, and then the third. That was all the answer she was likely to get, and it was much better than none.

"Thank you so much! — for listening, and for anything else you plan to do."

The crows just sat there for half a minute or so. Then they rose as one and flew away. Emma made her way back to the car, not sure if she was shaking from reaction or fatigue, and climbed back in. "I guess we can go to the next library now."

Diane stared at her before saying, "That was amazing! I've never seen anything like it. I hope you're proud, very proud, of what you're doing, what you can do."

Emma thought she might be blushing as she said, "Thank you. How many more libraries do we have on the list?" She hoped there weren't too many. She was eager to get home and talk to the ravens who kept watch around her house, the ones she thought of as "hers." She hadn't explicitly asked them to spread the word. It was time she did.

⚊⚊◆⚊⚊

Paul

Paul hadn't gotten snailmail that wasn't either junk or a bill in some time, maybe not since the letter from the rabbi. When he saw the envelope with an unfamiliar return address, something long and governmental-looking, he thought at first it might be the bird research program under a new name, updating him about their progress. Maybe they wanted to thank him for his suggestions about the masks!

When he opened it, he found out differently.

Dear Mr. Johnson:

Consulting available records, we see that you are among the few individuals who have visited the project investigating tactical uses of certain corvids, under the auspices of the U.S. Fish and Wildlife Service Migratory Birds Program. We are contacting those visitors to inform them that this effort has been superseded by the substantial progress we have achieved in designing, producing, and equipping unmanned aerial vehicles (UAVs) to detect and attrit the cryptids that have allegedly been responsible for certain casualties in a range of locales. . . .

He had to read that sentence a second time to make out the meaning. UAVs were drones. This must be the program that chatty fellow at the bird research facility had told him about, the one they were trying to beat to the finish line.

Our test results, both simulations and field testing, are sufficiently definitive that the procedures for mass production of these UAVs are already underway, with a predicted success rate sufficient to render any reliance on unpredictable wild fauna entirely unnecessary.

Field tests? Did that mean the drones could actually find and stop zombies? That would be great news, even if it meant he and Emma and Emma's birds might not have much left to do.

Paul hadn't given much thought to that fellow since he and Emma had left. But he had gotten the man's phone number, and when he finished reading the letter, with its confident predictions and boasts, he found the number, texted to make sure the man was available, and called.

The man didn't quite say, "You remembered me!!" but his surprise and pleasure was almost as pitiful. As soon as Paul explained the letter he'd gotten, he broke in with, "Those bastards! Is *that* what they told you? What was the date on the letter?"

Paul checked and told him.

"Well, maybe they didn't know yet. Or maybe nobody in that outfit tells anybody anything. But they really didn't say what actually happened when they tried the things out?"

It was a sorry enough tale. The drones had in fact found a couple of zombies, or maybe it was three or four. But it turned out zombies were less impressed with drones than the Bureau of Whatever was. They'd ignored the ones that shot bullets or dropped some sort of gas grenades. One drone, the most expensive kind, had an onboard laser, and that did set the zombie on fire. (Paul couldn't help but feel vindicated.) But the people nearby didn't exactly appreciate flying machines starting fires in random places, even for that good a reason. So there were angry phone calls and petitions, and that part of the effort was on hold.

Paul thanked his informant and asked, "So how's your project coming along?"

It took a couple of heartbeats before the man said, "It's doing fine. We're starting to write up the procedures for field testing." And then, as what sounded like an afterthought, "They redid the masks after your visit. You had something to do with that, didn't you? Thanks."

As Paul put his phone away, he rolled his eyes and thought, *Looks like our gang will still have work to do for a while yet.*

Emma

Rosie had given her own and Diane's names on the flyers as the people to contact, but someone at the library, probably in a misguided attempt to be helpful, had directed an inquiry to Emma instead. Emma thus received a letter in an expensive envelope, with a return address showing what looked like the name of a law firm. She opened it carefully, unfolded the equally expensive paper, and read the convoluted prose.

Dear Ms. Wells:

My firm represents the North Side Peaceful Haven ("Haven") and the Association of Suburban Funerary Establishments ("Suburban"). My clients have received a disturbing report as to the activities of you and certain of your acquaintance . . . .

She waded through it all and then reread the final paragraph.

Therefore, to avoid the filing of a complaint, Haven requires you to restore its grounds, including without limitation the grave of Millicent Williams, to its original and pristine condition; repair any and all damage done by the birds you have attracted to the property; and to undertake in writing not to trespass on the Haven grounds at any time in the future. Midwestern similarly requires the same undertaking as to all its members' facilities.

Please contact us, or have your counsel contact us, to make the necessary arrangements.

Instead, Emma took a deep breath and started on an email to Rosie.

Dear Rosie,

Something upsetting, but also ridiculous has happened. We should probably discuss it at the next meeting, but if convenient, I'd like to get your thoughts on it first . . . .

She had expected to get an email, if anything. When the phone rang, she assumed it was another company trying to sell her something or pushing a scam. But she answered anyway, and almost failed to recognize Rosie's voice, so surprised was she to hear it.

"Emma, I'd like to see that letter and go over it with you before our next meeting. Would it be all right if I came over?"

She hadn't had anyone visit, or come to her home for anything except essential repair work, in years. How many years? She'd lost count. When had she last cleaned the house? It might have been weeks ago. "I don't know . . . ." On the other hand, she had more important things to think about. "Yes, that'll be all right. That'll be fine."

Rosie seemed sincere in admiring Emma's little house. And she'd brought chocolate éclairs. While Emma took as tiny nibbles as she could manage (éclairs didn't lend themselves to neat nibbling) so she could make the treat last, Rosie read the letter, commenting under her breath. "'Peaceful Haven' — not so peaceful when zombies are sprouting out of it! . . . So they weren't 'disturbed' until we and Millie came along to fix things? . . . 'Pristine'! Are they *kidding*? . . ." Then she slammed the letter down on the table. "And would you believe this isn't all the nonsense that's been coming our way? More legal threats based on local government ordinances about desecrating cemeteries, animal lovers furious that we're 'exploiting' birds . . . . And of course, we're all supposed to be con artists."

Emma put down what remained of her éclair. "What do we do? Do we have to hire a lawyer?"

Rosie took a big bite of her own éclair. "I have a paralegal friend who can help write a response to this pile of crap, once I explain what's going on. We might need an actual lawyer later on, depending how things go, but if we do, I'd bet we'll be able to crowdfund the expense. Which brings me to the other thing we'll do, ASAP."

After talking to the paralegal, Rosie got in touch with Paul, and with Janna and Jeri, as the youngest and presumably the most social media savvy, of their combined team. Their posts on every forum she and Paul could reach varied somewhat, based on the customs of the users, but were all fundamentally similar.

Can you BELIEVE this?!

We've finally, after unprecedented effort and one woman's amazing courage, found a way to stop a zombie — to put it back in its grave, apparently to stay. And what does the cemetery that was supposed to be in charge of that body, and an association for such cemeteries, have to say about it? "Thank you, thank you, thank you"? "Good job"? Please do it again"? No, not at all! Unless that's what "stop it or we'll sue" means.

As we've already posted, we need as many people as we can to join this effort. So please — get in touch and promise your help. And make sure your local cemeteries and government officials KNOW that we have your support!

Of course, many people angrily accused them of making it all up, of exploiting the pain and fear that was spreading faster than the zombie phenomenon itself. But the controversy led to more attention, with articles and posts quoting Rosie's initial wording. Among the nasty and sometimes threatening responses, there were a few, and then more, that offered appreciation and even help. Diane set up a separate contact email for cemeteries, or their visitors, to use in letting the team know about disrupted graves. People started signing up to go to cemeteries in various cities and towns during an intervention, to do whatever might be necessary or helpful. Some cemeteries started leaving shovels handy, and even replacing them when they were stolen.

Their reach was expanding.

Chapter 25

Daniel

It was Daniel's turn. There had been a delay, none of his doing, while the living team members had found and persuaded two people to go to the cemetery, and Emma's network of crows had crept eastward until it reached as far. But now he had no more excuse for delay, and his fear was no excuse at all.

He hadn't been so terrified since he was nine years old. A kindly aunt had paid for him to have new clothes — a suit, just his size — and he knew the bullies would target him. They'd pound him into jelly, and the new suit would get covered in blood and dirt, which would never come out. He hadn't had another new suit until he was sixteen and spent his first wages for it.

He was in no real danger, this time. No matter what happened, he would return to this place of beauty and peace, whole and unhurt. And surely, putting his errant body where it belonged would exorcise whatever was causing him to create phantoms based on it.

Assuming he could return at all. It had seemed like a near thing, bringing Millie back. Would there be enough people helping him, rescuing him?

"Yet another reason I should be there," said Ruth.

"I don't want you to see that. To see me like that."

She patted his hand, as if he were fretting about some trifle. "I won't be seeing you. Surely you don't believe that transformed castoff is *you*."

He shook his head violently, frustrated at her refusal to understand, or to admit understanding. "It'll look like me, except horrible. A profane, warped image of me." Why did the idea of Ruth seeing that frighten him? "I'm afraid you won't be able to forget it."

Ruth sighed, and for a moment, she looked old and weary. "My dear, do you imagine you were a vision worth remembering when you were dying? Or even when you had the flu so badly and couldn't keep anything down for days — were you at your put-together best?"

She didn't realize how different, how much worse it would be. For that matter, he hadn't seen the thing himself. But he'd seen the hideous travesty that was Millie's walking corpse, and it was all too easy to picture what his own must look like. The phantoms he'd created were proof.

He was so deep in his inner visions that it took a moment to see Ruth's expression, the gentleness and the hesitation. It was the way she always looked when she had bad news for him, news she knew she could handle and feared he couldn't. "I've seen them, dearest. Here, since I came. I've seen them lurking behind trees, appearing and disappearing behind you as you walk."

"You saw . . . what . . . ."

She took his hand in both of hers and held it tight. "I saw what you fear, just as you imagine it. Whatever is waiting for you, whatever I'll see when I observe and stand by, I doubt it will be much worse."

Daniel felt his shoulders slump as he surrendered. "All right. If you really want to stay, then stay." And with the end of the argument, he had no further defense against what he had agreed to do.

Daniel was not accustomed to failing. When it occurred, it confused him. He had tried to conjure what his body would be seeing, and to place himself behind those eyes, but nothing happened. Why not?

His fear, of course. He was trying to ignore it, but it was too strong, and too close to the core of him, to be ignored. He would have to accept it and let its energy carry him along.

And yet he failed again.

What had gone wrong this time? He looked around and met Ruth's eyes, filled with embarrassment and, most unusually, remorse. "I think I interfered," she murmured. "We were supposed to imagine you vanishing, and I didn't *want* you to vanish. Not so soon after I'd found you again!"

He took her in his arms. "Then pull hard, when it's time to bring me home. And I'll come home to you."

She did. And he did.

the chronicler

For every spirit inspired by Millie's courage, or ashamed not to follow her example, there was one who found the idea outrageous, or too appalling to contemplate, or simply not their problem. Among the latter, one, a Mr. Sandhill, neatly summed up the common attitude: "I had nothing to do with my body refusing to stay where I left it! I was buried properly, six feet down, with a headstone and all due ceremony. If someone, or something — an asteroid, or a virus, or whatever the hell it is — has gone and stirred my body into wreaking havoc, it's not my responsibility to risk going back into it, and maybe being implicated in one or more murders or even getting stuck in it."

Daniel concealed his shock and said earnestly, "No one's saying it's your fault, or that you had anything to do with your body being hijacked, any more than I did when it happened to mine. But you're in a unique position to put a stop to it."

Mr. Sandhill tossed his head. "Let me guess. It's the only thing anyone has tried — going back into their own body. But how do you know that has any greater chance of success than a stranger going in? Shouldn't you try that too? Maybe it works better!"

Millie

When Daniel came to Millie, approaching slowly as if carrying a great weight, or as if afraid of her, she knew it had something to do with the creatures. She burst out, "Has my body gotten loose again?"

"No, nothing like that." He hesitated. "You know not everyone whose body has been . . . taken wants to do what you did. It was heroic, and not everyone can contemplate being a hero."

As if he hadn't done it himself! She'd heard that not everyone was willing, and hadn't been surprised. At times she was more surprised that she'd done it herself. It had been an emotional decision, driven by guilt and grief and outrage and protectiveness, and she could hardly expect everyone else to be so irrational. "Have you figured out any other way to stop them?"

She'd expected him to say they would have to give up, and was prepared to bolster his spirits until he changed his mind. Though it was hard to believe that anyone who had his determination would surrender before trying absolutely everything. She was relieved, at first, when he said, "Someone did make a suggestion."

But why did he stop there, instead of explaining? "And it's one you don't like. But you think it might work."

He shook his head, energetically enough that his well-groomed hair stirred. "I have no idea whether it'd work! And it may be dangerous. Even more so than what we did."

What on earth (now there was an appropriate phrase) could it be? . . . And then, suddenly, her stomach sank as if it had started down to earth without her. Because she knew. She opened her mouth, and couldn't force the words out. On the second try, she was able to say, or rather to croak, "They want other people to go into their bodies, and try to take them back to their graves.”

Daniel closed his eyes and nodded.

What popped into her head first was a practical objection. “How would we even know where to go? Where the grave was?”

“They’d tell us where it is and what it looks like. And if I have anything to say about it, they’ll be right there with the extraction team, giving details and saying if the body is heading in the wrong direction.”

Millie started shaking. They stared at each other until Daniel burst out with, “We don’t have to do it! It doesn’t have to be us!”

Millie thought about that. It didn’t have to be them, to be her. But . . . the relief she’d been feeling, as if all the nastiness and ugliness and fear were behind her, there was something about it that didn’t fit. It was like a child’s primer about paradise, promising that everything would be wonderful forever and ever, no more pain, no more trouble, no worries, no cares. She couldn’t picture it. She hadn’t lived it. Even when the world didn't force worries on her, she’d made her own, put her own clouds in the emotional sky. Maybe there was a way to sweep away those clouds and still be herself, still be human. She could think about it later, after she’d done this one more thing, this thing that was like real life.

She didn’t know how to explain all that to Daniel and have it make sense. So she just said, “Of course we don’t have to. I’m even less responsible for someone else’s body being . . . corrupted than when it happened to mine. But I still feel some of the other feelings. It still feels like an outrageous thing to happen. And I know now that the creature does have emotions that aren't hunger or rage. I felt for my own body a little the way I'd feel for a child someone had hurt, and I was . . . *right* to feel that way. I feel the same way, or almost, for any other body trapped in that nightmare."

The look on Daniel's face was what a condemned man might have if he'd thought his sentence had been commuted and then found out differently. She took a deep, slow breath, and when she'd let it out, she said, "So I'll go first."

Daniel stared at her, then grabbed her shoulders and looked in her eyes. She was too surprised to react in any way as he said, in a hoarse voice, "I should argue, and I can't. I can't. But — we'll be watching every minute. And I swear to you, we'll get you home."

She met with Mr. Sandhill, whose body she would be trying to rescue — because that was how she thought of it, how she had to think of it to keep the terror at bay. He found it hard to meet her eyes, and was sullen about it, but he told her all about where the cemetery was, and he described the grave site and the ornately carved stone in detail. She had the impression he had actually seen it and had a great deal to do with its decoration. It had probably given him comfort in the face of the fact that he would someday die. Maybe that was why he found himself unable to confront the reality that had clawed and crawled its way out of that grave.

Then they had to wait while the slowly expanding network of living helpers found someone to fill in the grave. Two people would be better, but one would do. And one person was all they could find, unless they wanted to wait longer. It was up to Millie.

She would have liked to wait, and to spend some time in her seaside retreat, or visit the ice cream parlor, before the attempt. But there was no way to be sure what the delay would mean, back on earth. The creature might attack someone while she was smelling the sea air or licking a chocolate-covered spoon.

The hardest part, so far, was finding the body. No one was sure, yet, how far a zombie could roam, though the evidence suggested their maximum range might be between 200 and 250 square miles. Rosie and the other living team members had used the man's name to find a photo of him, and a zombie report, complete with security video, that might be the creature his body had become. But even if Millie wanted to ask the team members to scour the area — and she had no intention of putting them in danger that way — and if it were found, she had no way in. They would need Mr. Sandhill's help to begin the process, to open the door so Millie could slip through.

Sam and Daniel went back to tell him. She didn't know what they said, or whether they ound some way to pressure him, even to threaten him. But he returned with them, grudging but also cringing a little, as if embarrassed or even ashamed. All too soon, they were assembled in the same garden she had come back to the last time, and they were ready.

Millie stood by, with Sofia and Johnny beside her tense and silent, until Mr. Sandhill flinched and said, "There. It's right there." And then, his voice higher-pitched, "It's hideous! Oh, I can't bear it!"

"Now," Daniel ordered as Millie left her friends and put a hand on Mr. Sandhill's arm. "*Right now!*"

And then she was in some confused state between afterlife and undead, and then she was inside.

BITE HUNT BITE LICK CRUNCH FLESH

She had heard words like that sometime, somewhere. Wherever she was, had she been here before? But something was different. Whatever was moving was moving differently. And the voice saying the words was deeper.

And she was sad.

As soon as she said that to herself, she realized the words had changed.

LOST SCARED LOST

and then,

LOST SCARED WANNA GO HOME LOST

She had been somewhere like this before. And she had helped the . . . whatever it was to go home. She could help this poor, frightened, lost creature, the way she had helped the first one.

There, there, dear. Poor lost boy. I'll find out where home is and take you there, and then you can sleep.

LOST SCARED LOST TAKE ME HOME

Yes, I'll take you home. I just need to find out where it is.

Somehow she had already known, the last time, where home was. She thought she'd recognize it, if she saw it. But how to get there?

Now a different voice, very different, and coming from somewhere else, somewhere farther away. *You need to find Arbor Street. There'll be a sign.*

A sign. Signs were something you saw and understood. But she couldn't see well. She was looking through something lumpy and streaky.

The new voice sounded frustrated. *All right, just turn around slowly and stop when I tell you. . . . Stop! Go that way. Keep going. I'll tell you when to turn.*

She turned her attention back to the lost child. *Do what I say, and we'll get you home.*

WANNA GO HOME TAKE ME

You and I have to work together. Start walking, straight in front of us. That's right. And as the other voice interrupted with new instructions: *Now turn toward that big tree. No, the other way. Good. Walk some more. Now stop and turn the other way. That's right. Good boy. We'll get you home.*

SAD SCARED LOST HELP ME

That's why I'm here, to help you and get you where you need to go. It'll be all right. I'll help you.

Walking, coaxing the creature to go the right direction, reassuring it, comforting it . . . Millie was very, very tired.

There! said the guiding voice. *You're there. Now open the gate and go straight down the middle.*

Open the gate? How could she open the gate? How could she tell the creature how to do it? She would just have to try to explain.

You've done very well. We're almost there. Now, do you see that metal thing that's in our way? That's a gate. What you need to do —

Before she could go on, the creature lunged at the gate, slamming into it.

OWWW HARD HURTS OWWW MAKE IT GO AWAY

I can do that, but you'll have to help me. Do you know what your arm is? You have two of them, one on each side. Hold one of them out in front of you. Yes! Very good! That thing on the end of your arm is your hand. The little pieces are fingers. Can you move the fingers?

The fingers, crusted with dirt and some sort of dried fluid, wiggled wildly.

Good. Now reach your hand out to where there's something sticking out of the gate, a little smaller than your hand. Grab hold of it. You've . . . . She faltered as she realized just what the creature would have grabbed before. But she had to go on. *You've grabbed things before, to make them hold still or pull them closer. This won't come closer yet, but grab it — yes, that's right! Now, twist your hand — no, keep grabbing the thing and twist your hand, either direction. When you've twisted it as far as you can, try pushing on it.*

Nothing happened.

SAD TIRED WANNA GO HOME

It's all right. Grab it again, and twist it the other way, and push. Yes! See how it moves out of the way? You did that! Very good! Now walk through and keep walking until I tell you to stop.

About thirty staggering steps took them to a tall stone with lots of carving. It looked familiar. There was a messy hole in front of it, where something about the size of the creature had dug its way out of the ground.

That's the right one, the guide voice said. *Remember, if you can get in there and stay there for a while, someone will come and re-bury the thing. Then the folks up here can get you out. My part's over.*

She thought she heard some other voices, some sort of arguing, but nothing clear. She put it aside and said to the creature, *We're here! We made it all the way. Now climb down, first your legs — those are the things that touch the ground when you walk — and then the rest of you. Climb down, and then you can lie down and sleep.*

The creature lurched and tumbled its way to the bottom of the grave and collapsed into lying down.

HOME. FEELS LIKE HOME.

That's right. You're home. Now you can relax and go to sleep.

HELP ME SLEEP

How was she supposed to do that? There was one way, something mothers did. She'd done it once or twice, long ago, babysitting for a niece.

I'll tell you a story. That should make you sleepy.

But what sort of story could the creature possibly understand?

Once there was a . . . someone just like you. It had walked a long, long way, and it was tired and wanted to go home. But it didn't know where home was.

The creature's voice was already a little slower. *TIRED TIRED WANTED TO GO HOME*

That's right, it wanted to go home. Then a nice lady

(She deserved that, to call herself nice)

came and said, I'll help you get home. And the . . . the little boy was a good boy, and tried very hard to understand the lady and do everything she said. And because of that, the little boy and the lady found the boy's home. And he wasn't sad or scared anymore.

NOT SAD NOT SCARED

That's right. He was still tired, but he was happy, because he was home. He knew he could stay there, and be cozy and safe, and sleep in peace So he lay down and went to sleep. The end.

STAY SLEEP

Yes, that's right. You'll stay here, and you'll go to sleep, and everything will be all right.

LADY STAY

No, the lady had her own home to go to. So she told the boy a story, and he went to sleep. And when he was fast asleep, the lady went home.

NO YOU STAY YOU MY FRIEND YOU STAY HERE

Now she was starting to get frightened. Could this lonely child-creature keep her here? *No, no. I have to go home. I helped you get home, and now it's my turn. You know about taking turns.*

There was a silence, broken by approaching footsteps, and then by dirt falling into the grave.

See, there's your blanket, just the right kind of blanket to help you sleep. I'll stay until you're all nicely covered up, and then you go to sleep and I'll go home.

NO SLEEP LATER FOLLOW YOU GO WITH YOU

The dirt kept falling, and now she heard cawing. That would be crows. If only she could get the creature to stay where it belonged, it wouldn't have to get pecked. She didn't want it scared anymore, or hurt.

What to say to it? . . . She could tell it the truth.

You know what? Part of you is already where I'm going, waiting for me to come home. That's how things are supposed to be — you stay here and sleep, and that lets the other part of you be safe and happy too, in the other place, the place I came from. So you stay here and sleep, and I'll go find the other part of you and tell him what a good boy you've been.

The dirt had gotten thick enough that the new dirt falling made only a soft sound, a little like snow. She could feel the creature slowing down some more, and hear its voice getting softer. It was getting sleepy, just like a little boy at bedtime.

I STAY HERE AND YOU TALK TO ME THERE . . . I CAN SLEEP . . . AND YOU CAN STILL TALK TO ME . . . AND TELL ME STORIES

If she could have, she thought she would have cried. *Yes. If the other part of you wants me to, I can tell him stories. And the first story I'll tell him is how you found your way home and went to sleep, just the way you should.*

The creature's jaw made a cracking sound. Had it actually yawned?

Sleep well, little boy. Sleep well.

She waited for it to protest, or ask for another story, or ask her not to go, or say anything. It didn't. It just lay there under the dirt, as if the dirt were truly a blanket, a soft thick quilt.

Or as if it were a body, a dead body that would never need to move again.

She waited for anything else to happen. She could almost have fallen asleep herself, except the very idea made a jolt of fear start at the middle of her and want to work its way outward. She forced it back in. She mustn't wake the creature.

Finally, faintly, she heard Sam's voice. *"A couple of our new recruits are here. They say everything's quiet, and there are enough birds on guard. Now we can get you out of there.*

She came to herself in the garden once again, the warm breeze patting her cheek in welcome. She was lying in Sofia's arms, and Johnny was holding her hand. She looked up wordlessly at them as they fussed over her. She couldn't remember the last time anyone had fussed over her like this, but it had happened sometime. She must have been a child, and a young child at that.

Someone else bent over her, and to her surprise it was Mr. Sandhill, the man whose body she had just left. She sat up, Johnny giving her a boost, and said to him, "I thought you were leaving once you guided me to the cemetery."

Mr. Sandhill shrugged. "It didn't feel right to leave. I wanted to be sure you made it back all right. I suppose I'm the last person you want to see."

"No, I'm glad to see you. I have a promise to keep." He looked confused, and the others looked curious. "You may not know that I — and others, I'd guess, who do the same thing — can communicate with the creatures, a little."

Now they all stared at her wide-eyed, except Daniel, who nodded. She really should have confided more in those who had helped her. "It's how I've been able to control them," she explained. "It isn't a matter of, of brute force. And this one was easier than my own body, I think. Though it didn't want to let me go." She shivered. "So I explained about how you were here, and said I'd tell you that it behaved itself and went to sleep as I asked."

Mr. Sandhill looked down and shuffled his feet. "Did it . . . did it wonder why I wasn't there? Why I wasn't the one who came for it?"

For the first time since she'd met him, Mr. Sandhill looked as if he could use a pat on the shoulder or even a hug, but somehow Millie doubted he'd welcome it from her. She tried to put some comfort in her voice as she said, "I don't think it knew enough to wonder that. Instead, it helped it to know that its other half, so to speak, was somewhere nice and that I'd be talking to you."

"It didn't want to join me here?"

The truest answer would be, *Not exactly.* But she'd probably have to explain it, and she was too tired. So she simply said, "No, it didn't say it wanted that."

Johnny smoothly interrupted this exchange with "Let's talk about where we go from here. You've established that with courage and empathy, a spirit, perhaps any willing spirit, can retrieve a body that has become a zombie and restore it to its grave. We also have a spreading pool of people to fill in the grave, and of ravens and crows to discourage that body from rising again. Until we find the source of the problem, this could eventually amount to a stopgap solution."

Daniel turned away from him and then back. "The most important word in that sentence may be 'willing.' This solution is unacceptable if it is to be left to only a few people to take the risk over and over."

Mr. Sandhill's eyes were darting here and there, and was he actually trembling? Millie wasn't the only one to notice. Sofia moved toward him, put a hand on his arm, and said, "Are you all right? Is something wrong?"

"Yes." His voice was barely audible. "But I can try to put it right. Are there . . . are there other people who refuse to help, the way I did? Whose bodies are killing people, and they aren't willing to try to stop it?"

Daniel pulled out a list he'd apparently made. "So far, there are three who've refused outright, five who've evaded answering the question, and dozens whom no one has asked yet." He stood very straight, took a deep breath, and went on, "After I go back for the first of their bodies, there will only be two left in that first category."

Millie walked right up to Daniel and put her arms around him. He started in surprise, and then relaxed into the embrace, holding her tight. She could see a little over his shoulder, enough to know that Mr. Sandhill was gazing at her as if she held something special in her hand that he didn't deserve to share. He started to walk away, then turned on his heel and almost marched back. When he reached them, he announced, "I'll take the next one after that."

Daniel looked at him for a long moment and then put out his hand. They shook hands solemnly, and Daniel said, "I'll get you the information you need."

It was Mr. Sandhill — or Fred, as he'd eventually asked Millie and the others to call him — who suggested that if people heard about Millie's experiences, and about his own change of heart, they could probably get more volunteers. Millie, with assistance and some emotional support from her friends, started telling people about how she persuaded the creatures to return to and get back in their graves, while the group that had helped her get home instructed people on how to do that. Fred's account of how he'd shrunk from the ordeal, and how ashamed he had subsequently been, proved persuasive — especially after his turn had come, and he'd made it back safely.

It was wonderful, Millie thought, that Fred Sandhill was telling his story, trying to get others to follow his belated example. They needed all the spirits they could enlist . . . .

Chapter 26

Millie

And then came Alan.

Alan was a tall, fit-looking man in his mid-thirties, though there was no telling how old he'd been when he died. It had taken a while to track him down. Since the crisis became better known, many spirits checked in regularly, or at least occasionally, with the welcomers, who now maintained a list of zombie descriptions. Alan had not. Only when a friend of his did consult the list and found one description disturbingly familiar did the friend meet with that zombie's victim, and then cajole both the victim and Alan into meeting each other. He was incredulous and then appalled to hear that his body was running rampant. Millie had accompanied the victim to the encounter, and it took all her patience and tact to overcome Alan's initial disbelief, and the victim's understandable anger at that disbelief.

"Yes, I'd heard about the zombies," he explained to Millie and Daniel later. "But I never thought it could happen to me — that is, to my body. It's, it's . . . so utterly *unlike* me."

That was not so unusual a reaction, and they were used to helping spirits move past it. Before they could ask him whether he'd be willing to intervene, he interrupted them with, "Of course I'll go take care of this. It's outrageous, and the sooner I clean up this situation, the better."

Millie and Daniel talked the meeting over at a deli with giant sandwiches. It tickled her that Daniel enjoyed them in spite of how hard it was to eat them without making a mess.

At first, Millie struggled to define precisely what troubled her about Alan. Finally, dabbing her lips with the paper towel provided as a napkin, she said, "He seems . . . impatient with what's happened, and with the need to deal with it."

Daniel swallowed a large mouthful of corned beef sandwich and nodded. When he could speak again, he answered, "And he's quite sure he can 'clean up the situation' in short order."

Millie scooped up a small quantity of macaroni salad and put it down again. "I'll hope he's right."

The next morning, Alan appeared promptly at the rendezvous with the friends he had been instructed to bring. One, who looked like the youngest, had a deferential air, not so much towards her as towards Alan. The second had a sober, not to say stodgy, manner, quite a contrast with the jovial behavior of the third, who regarded Alan as an older brother might, a mix of friendly, amused, and protective. Millie and Daniel would remain with them, and Johnny had promised to come if summoned.

Alan, she saw, had dressed in obviously old, stained clothes, as if he would be soiling them further. He looked at the men who'd come with him and exchanged shrugs, then nodded to Daniel. "Instruct me, if you will."

Daniel spoke very deliberately, the way he did when ignoring discomfort. "You should imagine yourself inside your body, which will probably be standing or walking. Meanwhile, we and your friends will imagine you enveloped in mist and vanishing into it. When it comes time to bring you back, we'll form a chain as if you had a rope tied around your waist and we were tugging on it." He paused. "It may help to regard the zombie as a sort of child, temperamental and confused, in need of an adult to guide it back where it belongs."

Alan gave a short, firm nod. "A child, misbehaving. I can provide the firm hand misbehavior requires. This shouldn't take long."

Millie told herself that her own, gentler approach might not be the only workable method. If nothing else (what was she assuming?), this would be a worthwhile experiment.

It took longer than usual for Alan to disappear. For an awkward few minutes, he stood there tapping his foot, looking both self-conscious and irritated, while the rest of them stared at him and tried to conjure the necessary images. Millie had to imagine him as a child, and his outfit as play clothes, before she could put aside the cold stiffness of his current manner. But finally, his edges wavered and he faded slowly into the mist. She and Daniel formed the viewing portal, and they all gathered round to look into it.

What they first saw was Alan's body, shuffling through what looked like an abandoned lot. It came to a sudden stop, swinging its head back and forth as if trying to find what had disturbed it. Its round-shouldered posture abruptly went straight, almost as if electrocuted.

"You know," commented the friend with the brotherly attitude, softly but clearly, "It's not altogether Alan's fault that he has the proverbial stick up his butt." The deferential friend turned and frowned, probably offended on Alan's behalf, but the speaker ignored him. "Alan's parents were even worse, and they didn't know squat about raising a child, especially a boy. Any semblance of approval, he had to earn by doing and being just what they demanded. When you aim affection at him, he doesn't know what to do with it. But he's learning."

Meanwhile, the zombie stood still except for odd jerking motions of its arms, and then took a single stiff step. It swayed back and forth, and then stamped its foot, twice, three times. It had been silent since Alan entered it, but now it threw its head back and let out a roar, shaking its fists in the air.

Daniel turned to Millie and whispered, "How long should we give him before we haul him back?"

"A little longer. Let's see whether he seems to make any headway."

But there was no indication that he was, except that when the body went back to shuffling forward, it moved in a circle of sorts instead of a straight line. Whether Alan had induced it to follow that somewhat less dangerous route was unclear. They waited a while in case the zombie changed direction toward its grave, but it showed no signs of doing so.

Daniel shook his head and sighed. "All right, let's get him out of there."

Unlike the disappearance, the process of extracting Alan was quicker and easier than usual, as if he'd been less firmly anchored. In well under a minute he stood before them, flushed, looking both embarrassed and angry. He glanced down at his untidy clothes and waved his hand, rather like an irritable magician, to replace them with a clean and tailored jacket and slacks.

The brotherly friend gathered him in like a lost chick, even daring to put an arm around him, as the deferential friend asked anxiously, "Are you all right?"

Alan seemed to be searching for words. The third friend said calmly, "Give him a moment to collect his thoughts."

"There's little to tell," Alan said curtly. "I told the — the thing that I had come to take it back to its grave and ordered it to follow my directions. It refused and threw a tantrum. I tried to impose my will on it, to take over, and it felt for a moment as if I were succeeding, but in the end I did not."

Was there any point in suggesting the ways in which he could alter his approach? As Millie thought this, Daniel asked quietly, "Do you wish to make another attempt?"

Alan's flush had been fading, but the question revived it. "I suppose you have helpful advice to offer. But I don't think I'm well equipped for the task." For the first time, he looked lost and uncertain; and for the first time, Millie felt sympathy for him as he added, "You said I should think of the zombie as a sort of child. You were quite right. But I've never been good with children. I . . . never had much opportunity to act like one, and I've rather avoided them since."

She stepped up to him and reached for his hand. He let her take it. She squeezed it and said, "Thank you for trying. I know that takes courage, and that it was a very distasteful task."

He gave her the faintest of smiles. "Loathsome, I would say."

She smiled back.

He and his friends left without further discussion. She and Daniel looked at each other, Daniel looking as gloomy as she felt. "Well, then," he said, "we've learned something, something I for one am chagrined that I needed to learn. Not everyone is suited for this work. Possibly not everyone can become so. We'll just have to look harder for those who can handle it."

the chronicler

It would have mattered less if the birds could handle the zombies on their own. There were, after all, so many ravens and crows. Some of them were bound to see zombies emerge from their graves. . . .

In a well-manicured cemetery with rows and rows of nearly identical white markers, the recently mown grass covering one grave started twitching, then rippling.

In a tree near the wire fence, leaves stirred, and a black wing caught the sunlight.

The ripples in the grass became faster, almost frantic. Anyone standing near the grave could have heard a faint, muffled sound, something like a moan. And then a crevice appeared, as if the cemetery had been struck by a very small earthquake. And the moan became something between a gurgle and a howl.

One crow, then two, flapped up out of the tree. They flew to the grave and circled it, cawing, as a mottled, wriggling mass broke through the crevice and widened it. A policeman, or a coroner, might have recognized it as a hand.

One of the crows darted down and pecked at the hand. It jerked, and the fingers flailed. It drew partway back beneath the turf. But then the edges of the crevice heaved and crumbled away again, until the crevice was a trench, and a slimy arm with tattered cloth clinging to it shot out into the innocent sunlight. Both crows flew down this time, cawing and pecking, but the arm thrashed and knocked one of them out of the way before a shoulder and then a torso jerked and thrust its way up into the light.

The crows flew back to the tree, cawing, and then across the fence and away.

By the time they flew back with half a dozen others, the zombie had made its way out of the grave and was shuffling in a circle, waving its arms, making noises from moaning to wailing to whimpering to howling. The crows added their sharp cawing. The cacophony finally attracted the ground keeper's attention, and he walked closer. And stopped, and shouted, and turned around to run through the obstacle course of the graves.

The zombie shuffled into a walk, and then a run, chasing the man. The crows wheeled around it, circling its head, pecking it, flapping their wings in its face, cawing their loudest. The man reached his jeep, tumbled into it, and sped out of the cemetery, honking his horn and flashing his lights, fumbling for his phone. The zombie went back to its circular shuffle, then picked another direction, a straight paved path that led to a gate. The crows' harassment could not stop it from bashing itself against the gate, over and over, until the gate gave way.

Millie

Millie had been pessimistic and anxious after Alan's failure. She had feared that after all, it would be left to a handful of volunteers to spend all their time and strength inhabiting one zombie after another. But as Daniel had suggested, they continued to recruit other spirits, now taking more care to assess their personalities and readiness for the task.

And they had more success than she had predicted. Gradually, taking part in laying zombies to rest became a much-honored volunteer activity. Spirits whose sense of duty had been central to their lives, especially those who had served as first responders or in the military, were especially eager to take on this task. Members of religious communities were also well represented. There were even people who believed, or at least hoped, that if they brought a zombie back to its grave, their own bodies would never be taken.

Meanwhile, Paul, Rosie, and Diane took turns driving Emma to new places where she could talk to crows and ravens, asking them to spread the word to other locations in turn. There were still times that no birds were available, and the spirit persuading a body to lie still had to work harder and longer. There were failures, where the spirit had to be pulled out of a body that had fought its way out of the grave again.

But those failures were few, as the birds spread the word over a larger and larger area and raised hatchlings to know their tasks from the beginning. And feeding birds, crows and ravens at least, was starting to became less of an occasional eccentricity. They could hope it would end up as more of a civic obligation.

The afterlife team learned from the debacle with Alan. The brief exchange with him before his attempt had clearly been inadequate. Now they instituted systematic training, with the spirits who had succeeded in their interventions telling their stories and saying what they believed had been most effective. The training culminated with role-playing, supervised by the experienced spirits and featuring anyone with a flair for the theatrical.

It was Millie's turn to monitor a trainee. This time, it was a young woman named Barbara, slim and of medium height, with striking black hair and eyes. And Jeri, brimming with energy and mischief, would be playing her body.

Barbara clenched her fists, took a deep breath, closed her eyes, opened them, and stepped up close to Jeri, saying woodenly, "It's time to go to sleep now. I'll help you."

"No way!" Jeri replied. "You're no fun. Let's go eat someone instead."

Millie chuckled, but intervened to say, "Jeri, try to speak in even simpler phrases. But let's go on. Barbara, what would you say to that? Remember that the tone of your voice matters as much as what you say."

Barbara nodded and said in a lower, coaxing tone, "No, Barbie dear. It's not snack time. It's sleep time. Here, I'll take you there and tuck you in."

Jeri put her hands on her hips and whined, "Don' wanna! Wanna eat, wanna play!"

"I know, Barbie. But you've done your eating and playing. It's bedtime now. You're going to have a nice long sleep, the nicest you've ever had." And then, more sternly, "Now let's go."

Millie clapped. "Much better! Go on." She watched, with only a few more words of comment, until Barbara had coaxed Jeri into lying down, then sang lullabies until Jeri gave a big yawn and curled up as if to sleep.

"Excellent!" Millie told them. "Barbara, someone will be in touch shortly with details of your assignment. Next pair, please!"

Chapter 27

Millie

No one was surprised when Johnny volunteered to occupy a zombie and march it back to its grave. "Finally!" he exclaimed. "It's been way too long since I got to do a rescue."

The errant body was almost as big as Johnny, but Morris Melmoth, the spirit that had inhabited it in life, was gentle and timid, far from having the confidence to wrest control of it. He offered Johnny any help he could give, providing not only the location of the grave, but directions to it from all over the city containing it. "And of course I'll be there to help open your way in," he said earnestly. Millie, Sofia, Sam, Daniel, Robert, and the twins all promised to help bring Johnny home once the job was done.

Johnny's preparations were quite unlike Millie's or Daniel's or any others they had seen. Instead of visiting a favorite place or fortifying himself with a favorite food, he started doing vigorous jumping jacks, then imagined into existence a trail of tires lying on the ground and hopped through them at speed, then ran in place for at least five minutes, then dropped flat and did a series of push-ups, including twenty one-handed (ten with each hand). When he finally got up and faced his wide-eyed audience, he shrugged and said, "I used to play football."

Morris stepped up and cleared his throat. "Are you ready? I guess I am."

Johnny waited patiently, doing some sort of isometric exercise with his arms, while Morris located his body. "There!" Morris announced, and then somehow combined a frown and a flinch. "And it's close to some people, so please get down there *now*."

"Right-o," Johnny said as he squeezed his eyes shut. Nothing happened that Millie could see, and he said, "I'm having trouble getting in. Morris, can you hold the door wider, so to speak?" Morris nodded and closed his own eyes, standing very straight, muscles tense.

And then, suddenly, both Johnny and Morris disappeared.

At first, the group nervously watching could see no change. The big zombie lurched toward a group of teenagers around high school age, three girls and a boy. Two of the girls clutched each other, shrieking; one of them, and the boy, stood in front of their friends, the boy clenching his fists and the girl holding pepper spray in her shaking hand, both of them pale as ice. The zombie made a long, howling, moaning noise and took a step toward them.

And then it flung its arms up in a parody of surprise and fell flat on its face. Millie had at times been unwillingly exposed to football, so she knew what Robert meant when he said in an awestruck murmur, "Just like a linebacker taking down a receiver."

That must have been Johnny's doing. But if Morris had indeed been swept along with Johnny, what was happening to him? Millie thought back on her brief acquaintance with the man, hoping for some clue. Morris had been anxious to help, as if to make up for his failure to take on the task of actually reentering his rogue body. He would probably be overwhelmed, at first, to find himself where he had not intended to go, but she thought it likely he would soon enough try to make the best of things and contribute what he could. Was there any sign that this was happening?

There might be. Soft-spoken as Johnny was, he had a determined, energetic way of moving, but the zombie was taking its time getting up. Had Johnny's control faltered, or were he and Morris discussing the situation?

The zombie finally stood, and Millie stared at the image in the portal. She might be imagining it, but wasn't there some hint of Morris's body language in the zombie's posture? Certainly its arms were no longer hanging low or swinging as loosely as if its shoulders were dislocated. Instead they were close to its body, as if protecting it. And the zombie wasn't standing straight, as Johnny did, but it was hunched over in a different way than it had been before.

Beside her, Sam whistled in surprise. "Well, *that's* interesting. If everything works out, we can try doing it again on purpose."

They all watched, Janna and Jeri holding their breaths except when they squealed in shock or excitement, as the two spirits jerkily steered the body to its grave. It certainly appeared that they were taking turns, the body striding out boldly for a few minutes and then slowing to a faltering halt, only to start up again with small careful steps as if on uncertain ground.

Even the sounds the zombie made would change with the spirit controlling it, Johnny silencing it completely, Morris allowing quiet moans and gurgles to escape.

A burial detail had been alerted to the grave's location, and Millie expected to see them waiting at the other end of the cemetery where the zombie was least likely to notice them, accompanied by the usual ravens or crows. But instead, when the zombie lurched and zigzagged its way through the cemetery gate under Johnny's and Morris 's alternating control, it was to come upon a man and a woman digging frantically away at the grave itself. Two other people stood fretting nearby, and one of them, a young woman, said in a sort of stage whisper, "Someone's gone and filled the grave in!"

Robert let out a curse Millie could only hope Emma didn't somehow hear. Whoever it was had no doubt meant to be helpful, or at least thought that other visitors to the cemetery shouldn't be confronted with the unsettling sight of a grave disrupted from underneath. But it meant that the duo busy shoveling were right in the zombie's path.

The zombie roared, leaned forward, and lifted its arms, spreading its claws wide. The two people digging spun around to face it, eyes wide, frozen in place — not that running would have helped. The other two looked wildly around for a moment and then started screaming and shouting as they backed away in opposite directions. From the jerkiness in their movements and their pale faces, they knew very well the risk they were taking.

Would Johnny and Morris be able to restrain Morris's body? At first that seemed doubtful, the zombie turning from one fleeing person to the next as if choosing the juiciest victim. But then a black cloud of birds arose from the trees and swept toward the zombie, making sharp shrill calls as they came and striking at its face and hands with their beaks. The zombie squalled and recoiled, coming to a halt a couple of yards from the hole where the grave had been.

The birds pulled back and flew upward to form a circle rotating above the zombie, like a tame tornado. The two who had been digging, who had dropped their shovels, now looked down at them, but neither moved to pick one up. Millie could understand their reluctance to start digging again with their backs to the zombie waiting so close by. Instead they moved to join the rest of the team, who had now stopped running and come together a few graves away.

The zombie started to move again — but not toward any of the living. To Millie's astonishment, it came slowly toward the hole, picked up a shovel, and started digging. Awkwardly, jerkily, but whether from the strength in its body or the strength Johnny brought to it, it made good headway. Every once in a while, one of the birds swooped down toward the hole as if inspecting it, then returned to the circle overhead.

The zombie's digging got slower. Could an undead body feel fatigue, or was Johnny's control wavering? Maybe he had handed off to Morris. Yes, that would explain it. But Millie could feel her own tension echoed in the others watching with her, ratcheting up with every moment of delay.

The digging stopped. The shovel fell to the ground next to what had once again become a grave. Was it deep enough? The body bent forward as if inspecting its work — and tumbled inside.

Squeals of panic erupted from the pit, sounding like a trapped hog. Millie couldn't see inside, but she could imagine thrashing limbs as the zombie trying to climb back out. The circling birds came lower, diving down in twos and threes and then back up. The living team huddled together in urgent conference. And then, contrary to every expectation Millie might have, they walked slowly together toward the grave . . . singing. Singing a lullaby.

They came almost to the lip of the hole and kept singing, louder now. Johnny and Morris must have heard it, and while they were in no position to sing along, they could be silently echoing the song as they tried to soothe the creature. And it seemed to be working — at least, the hog-squeals faded into quieter wails and whimpers. By the time the song was over, there was no sound from the grave, and the birds had returned to their quiet circle overhead.

Minutes passed. The living team members looked down into the grave, maybe seeing the body settling down in whatever might remain of the coffin. Finally, one of the men heaved a sigh and picked up the shovel the zombie had been using, though his hesitation showed his reluctance to touch the handle. Beside him, the younger woman retrieved the other shovel, and they began filling in the grave. Close behind them, the other two started singing again, more softly — a hymn, it sounded like, with the words "Be Thou My Vision."

It was strange to watch the work and know that Johnny's and Morris's spirits were inside the grave, waiting patiently, or at least with determination, for the job to be completed. She remembered how hard it had been to wait. But at least Morris and Johnny had each other's company, not just the minimal mind of the creature they were laying to rest. Sam was right — it might be a good idea to have people do these interventions in pairs whenever possible, the spirit whose body was running riot and someone else willing to assist. They could try to pair people by their skills and strengths . . . .

Millie was lost in her thoughts to the point that she took no part in the retrieval effort. She jumped, startled, when the portal winked out and the two spirits reappeared, Johnny holding Morris's upper arm as if keeping him upright.

The group of spirits burst into applause. The volume of it surprised Millie anew; she looked around and saw that more watchers had gathered while she had been so fully absorbed in Johnny's and Morris's struggles. Surrounded by this warmth and admiration, Johnny, usually so self-possessed, looked flustered, while Morris beamed in shy delight. Johnny glanced over at him, then grinned, grabbed Morris's hand, and bowed over it. When he straightened up, he pointed at Morris and then joined in the applause, saying, "The rest of you couldn't hear it, but boy, can this fellow sing!"

Morris blushed, but soon recovered enough to reply, "Johnny too! We sang a lullaby duet!"

"I wish I could have heard it," Millie said softly . . . only for Sofia to tilt her head, look around at the crowd, and say, "How about it, people? Should we ask them for an encore?"

Johnny grinned at Morris. "What should we sing for this eager audience? Something livelier than a lullaby, I'm thinking."

Morris bounced on his toes and grinned back. Then he settled down and fingered his chin for a few seconds before saying, "How about "You Did It" from *My Fair Lady*?"

Johnny bowed. "As you command, my good sir!" And without further ado, they launched into the duet. Morris's voice was as good as Johnny had promised.

the chronicler

A new group, or perhaps it should be called a club, formed, spirits who had made the fraught journey. Of those, Millie was, for now, the only one who had done so twice, which gave her a status she could not help but find gratifying. As membership grew and came to include a greater variety of people, including those whose pursuits in life had been athletic and daring, their get-togethers became less likely to be all-inclusive: some of them might instead be off learning flower arranging from a woman who had been the upper housemaid for a duchess, while others would sky-dive from heights impossible in life, or scale the highest conceivable glaciers or volcanoes. But whatever their distractions and amusements, all of them knew that they had shown undeniable courage. And many of them knew, in their heart of hearts, that if called upon, they could show such courage again.

Of course, things didn't always go as planned.

Rosie

Rosie took an appreciative sniff of her morning pot of coffee, poured a mugful, sat down, and took a sip. Ah, morning coffee! And the air conditioning that let her enjoy it! She took another sip, opened her newspaper app, glanced at the headlines — and almost spat the coffee all over the screen. She scanned the story quickly, read it again more slowly, and called Emma. Did women Emma's age sleep late? She hoped not.

"Hello?" Emma's voice was shaky and uncertain, probably because she rarely received phone calls. But she didn't sound actually sleepy, at least.

"Emma, I'm glad I found you at home. Have you by any chance heard or seen any news this morning?"

There was a short silence, and then: "Oh. That."

Whatever Rosie had expected, that — or "That." — wasn't it. "You know about the ravens and crows attacking people? Regular live people?"

"Not just any people." Emma sounded defensive. "The birds were *defending* people. Other people, that some 'regular' person was attacking."

Rosie looked at the article again. Yes, down toward the end of the story, there was a reference to "claims" along those lines. And now Rosie was hearing the theme from the old *Superman* cartoons. It was a good thing Emma couldn't see Rosie fighting a smile.

"Emma, we really can't have ravens and crows doing that!"

"I've told them that isn't their job," Emma replied, still sounding uncharacteristically prickly. "But I can't really tell them what to do on their own time, so to speak. And it's not as if bad people should be allowed to go around hurting other people, is it?"

Rosie sighed, and hoped it sounded like sympathy instead of exasperation. "If ravens get a reputation as a public nuisance, it could be dangerous for them, and for what we're trying to do. Can you *please* get that message across to them?"

"I'll try. I'll talk to them very seriously." Now, finally, she sounded as meek as usual. Which was a good deal less meek than when Rosie first met her, and that was just as well . . . most of the time.

Chapter 28

Sofia

The rumors had started up again, probably arising from what some new arrival had revealed, and now they came thick and fast. An old woman, people said, had been shocked into a heart attack by seeing a child zombie staggering down the street and stalking someone's dog. Accounts varied as to whether the dog fought the zombie and tore it to pieces, or succeeded in running away, or died in the street. One person claimed the dog had approached the zombie wagging its tail before whining and backing away.

Sofia knew so many people, and was trusted by so many, that it was easy for her to gather these contradictory details. As frustrating as she found the confusion, she couldn't stop herself from trying to make sense of it. And of course Iris, her daughter, so knowledgeable for her apparent age, so caring and sensitive, noticed that something was the matter.

"Tell me! Why won't you tell me!" And then: "Is it because I'm too young?" And when the question called forth some flicker of an admission, the followup, hesitant, reluctance slowing the words: "If I let myself get older, would you tell me then?"

Sofia pulled Iris into a hug, holding her long and tight, trying to decide what to do. She settled the child next to her on the river bank and said softly, "I'm afraid what's on my mind might frighten you or make you sad. But I don't want to upset you or make you think I don't trust you by *not* telling you. What do you think? What do you want me to do?"

Iris pursed her lips in an exaggerated I'm-thinking face, nodding her head as she thought. Sofia held her breath, a leftover habit she had no wish to break. Finally, Iris said, "That depends. Is it about the child zombie people are talking about? Are you going to do something about it? Like you did before?"

Sofia tried to ignore the chill that ran down her spine. "Do you mean, will someone go inside the zombie? Or will I go?"

Iris thought some more, finishing with a decisive nod. "You'd be the best at it. Because you're such a good mom, and the zombie was still a child when it died."

Sofia was marveling at Iris' maturity when the girl's lip started trembling, and she buried her face in Sofia's lap. "But I don't want anything bad to happen to you!"

"Oh, sweetheart." She stroked Iris's dark curly head. "Nothing bad will happen. I've done this before, and so have plenty of other people. We look after each other and make sure everything's all right."

Iris's voice was muffled by Sofia's skirt. "But this time is different."

So it was. Different, and in some way worse. It wasn't, she reminded herself, worse for the living who might become victims of a larger and stronger creature. But worse all the same.

The attempt was different in more ways than Sofia had initially realized. It had become common, almost routine, for the spirit whose body was being so misused to go inhabit it, but neither Sofia nor anyone else would drag a child into that horror. It was bad enough that they had to tell her what had happened. Nor had either parent of this child arrived yet, and while they were trying to find some relative the child might have known in life, they'd been so far unsuccessful. Rather than wait to complete a search that might be fruitless, an unrelated adult would accompany Sofia instead.

The zombies of adults often knew the way to their burial sites, but they could hardly count on a child doing so. It had been quite a task to find out which cemetery it would be. The child, of course, didn't know, and she couldn't recall any graveyard her parents had mentioned or where she'd visited any older graves. But she did know the name of her town and her own last name. The living team had done research and found the child with that name who had died there eight years ago. And of the town's two cemeteries, one was within a few miles of the first sighting. Rosie had conveyed the location and directions to Robert, who had drawn a map for Sofia to study in case the body couldn't find its own way.

At least it would be Daniel, familiar with the task and dedicated to expiating his own blameless involvement, who would assist her. The two of them, and the various spirits who would help them return safely, gathered in the usual garden. The family with whom the girl had been living brought her in, cuddling her as she trembled, reassuring her, the teenage boy in the family glaring at Sofia and the rest of the circle.

Sofia had wondered whether a child spirit would have more trouble locating her wandering body, but it proved easier than for anyone before. Maybe children, with less sense of the future and the world outside their daily lives, were more body-centered, more tightly linked to the reality closest to them. Soon — too soon, Sofia couldn't help but feel — it was time.

◆

Millie

Millie clasped her hands as she watched Sofia and Daniel. Any moment they would disappear.

Sofia did. But Daniel didn't. It took a moment before he realized something had gone awry. Then he looked wildly around and said in a hoarse voice, "I couldn't — there wasn't enough room!" And then, "she's there all alone...."

"She can do it," Millie said as firmly as she could. "I was solo my first time, and I'm nowhere near as strong as Sofia. And physically, it's an easier task, moving a young child's body around. She'll be fine."

Something was happening in the garden, on the other side of the small pool with the koi fish and the daffodils Iris had appeared, panting as if she'd been running before she remembered she could get here faster than she could run. "Where - is she? I have to - wish her luck! I - need to - give her another - hug!" She looked right, looked left, peered across the pool. "I don't see her! Where is she?"

Daniel walked over to her and silently held out his hand. She narrowed her eyes at him, but took it, and he led her to where the others were standing and looking at the misty bubble showing the zombie and its surroundings. Iris leaned forward, looked in, and whirled toward Daniel, shaking her small fist at him. "She's in *that*? In *there*?"

Iris must have known what Sofia would be doing — didn't she? Millie opened her mouth without knowing what she would say. But Iris' anger had given way to tears. "I wanted to say goodbye! What if something *happens*?"

Millie knelt and opened her arms, and Iris crept into them, laying her head on Millie's shoulder, soaking Millie's shawl with her tears. After a few bittersweet minutes, Millie felt a tentative tap on her other shoulder and looked up to see a girl a little younger than Iris. It was Eleni, the child whose body Sofia had gone to save. Millie relaxed her embrace of Iris and sat back a little; Iris looked up and saw the other child. The two girls looked gravely at each other. Iris spoke first. "Why are you here? Do you know my mother?"

The other girl shook her head. "It's my body down there trying to hurt people. It tried to hurt a dog." Her voice shook. "Is it your mother who's gone to try to stop it?"

Iris nodded.

"Are you mad at me? Because I'm not the one who went?"

Iris looked at her gravely and said, "You aren't big enough. Zombies are strong. Stronger than they were before. It takes a grownup to make them behave." And then, with a brave attempt at confidence: "My mother can do it." She twitched herself loose from Millie's arms, and the two girls went to sit together next to the pool of mist, holding hands tightly.

◄◦►

Sofia

Sofia felt the moment when Daniel was torn away, and fought a moment of panic. Daniel was probably fine, back among the other spirits watching and wishing her well. She would find out later why he hadn't been able to come with her. She had more urgent business.

One immediate bit of good fortune: the child's body was not in the midst of stalking anyone, or any animal. Instead it was stumbling in a circle, whining.

And crying inside. Crying, and frightened, and lost.

It shouldn't surprise her. The two other zombies Sofia had entered, and the ones Millie had told her about, had been childlike. How much more so, a zombie that was also a child?

And yet there was something different, and disturbing. Something . . . almost animal. Did fewer years as a human being let a zombie revert more readily to an animal's state of mind? Had it tried to attack a dog the way one dog might drive another out of its territory?

Well, Sofia had calmed animals as well as children, dogs and horses and even feral cats. And she had best get started.

Eleni. I'm hear to help you. Let's start by your holding still for a minute. You'll feel better when you're not walking in circles.

The zombie snarled and whirled around faster, probably looking for whoever was talking.

I'm here with you. You can't see me, but I'm here, and I'm going to help you.

The zombie spread its fingers, with their claw-like nails, and thrashed at the air.

Talking wasn't helping, at least not yet. What else could she try? If she were working to calm and control an animal, she'd do something physical, something like stroking. Or she'd offer a treat, but even if there was something nearby, she couldn't pick it up until she got control of the body.

What could she reach? What could she touch?

She imagined stretching out a hand and gently stroking the warm fur of a dog. No, a puppy. She pictured her hand, and the soft fur, and a puppy's black wet nose. Would it lick her? Or bite her? She put aside that thought and concentrated on stroking, and on crooning a comforting murmur: *There, there. It's all right. I'll help you get where you need to be. You've been lost and scared, but everything will be better very soon.*

The zombie stopped circling, and the whining changed to a quieter whimper.

Only one person would be waiting at the cemetery, but for a child's grave, that should be enough. *Let's get going. Back where you came from when you first woke up. I'll help you find it. We'll go back there, and I'll tuck you in and sing you a lullaby, and then you'll go to sleep. All right?*

She didn't really expect it to be that easy, and it wasn't. But instead of trying to run away as an animal might, or growling, the zombie stamped its foot and then fell to the ground in what she could only call a tantrum, yelling, a howl that had thoughts along with it — *NO! WON'T! GO AWAY!*

Now that's enough of that. The stern tone had no immediate effect. What would she do if facing such a tantrum in the flesh? She might grab the child's hands and hold them down. Iris had responded well to that, as if being out of control frightened her and having her mother restrain her was ultimately reassuring. Sofia gathered her strength and took control of the flailing fists. When the child responded by bucking and kicking harder, she extended her control to the entire body. *You'll just make yourself tired. You're tired already, aren't you? That's why you're in such a bad mood.* She paused for a moment, struck by her truly epic understatement. *You're overtired, and thrashing around will only make it worse. Relax. Try relaxing one part at a time — left leg . . . left arm . . . .* She gave fervent thanks when the thrashing limbs slowed. *That's very good. Right leg . . . right arm . . . .*

The body slumped on the ground, an improvement of sorts, but now she had to get it on its feet again.

Good girl! Now, as a reward, we're going to play a game. How fast can you get on your feet and walk toward where you woke up?

Even knowing the resilience of children and the unnatural strength of zombies, she was startled at how quickly the body sprang upright. It swiveled its head this way and that, and then broke into a run. Bystanders scattered and screamed. Sofia sympathized, but told the body, *Oh, very good! You're doing so well! How soon can you get there?*

The creature tried to run faster, but its clumsiness defeated it. It tripped and fell flat, then started howling louder than before, twisting and flailing and pounding on the ground again. Sofia suppressed a sigh. *Oh, I'm sorry you hurt yourself.* She imagined rubbing the child's back. *There, there. You're not really hurt, but I'm sure that startled you. It's all right. Let's get up again. Do you know how to count? I'll count, and if you can, you count with me. When we get to three — no, five. When we get to five, you'll get up again, and we'll head where you need to go. Here we go! One . . . two . . . .*

It took two counts of five before the creature grudgingly climbed to its feet and shambled forward.

By this time, Sofia had given up any expectation that the task would be simple. That helped her cope with the busy construction zone that had sprung up along the path she'd prepared for. She studied the site through the zombie's bleary eyes. She could probably steer the creature safely through. That left the workers to deal with.

She hated to frighten them, but she had little choice.

You've been such a good girl. Would you like to roar some more, just a little more, before you go back to sleep?

She could feel the creature's pleasure and even something like gratitude as it waved its arms and roared and shrieked. The construction workers yelled in fear and scattered, even knocking over some wooden barricades and kicking cones as they fled. The creature bounced on its toes.

DID I DO IT RIGHT MOMMY

If Sofia had been breathing, the words would have stopped her breath. The wave of pity and sorrow almost shook loose her grasp, almost sent her reeling back to the garden full of spirits. But she managed to calm herself, and then to say, *Yes, you did it just right. But now it's time to stop all that and go back to finding your way to where you can sleep.*

It felt like hours before they entered the cemetery. The helper was hiding behind a rundown tool shed to avoid attracting the zombie's attention. The grave was a mess, so sadly different from a child's bed that she wondered whether she should tidy it up before urging the creature to climb inside. But the inside looked less disrupted than the surface, so she crooned to the zombie, *Here we are. Now we get back in bed, you and I. There's room for both of us. And once you lie down like a good girl, I'll sing to you. I don't know whether I know your favorite lullaby, but can you tell me what it is?*

The answer came, mulish and distressed at the same time: *DUNNO CAN'T REMEMBER NAME*

Well, then. *Can you sing just a little of it for me? Maybe I'll recognize it.*

The creature seemed eager to oblige, immediately humming a tune with a few garbled syllables thrown in. To her relief, it was a tune Sofia knew. The child's mother or father might have sung it in some unfamiliar language, but whatever allowed Sofia to communicate with what was left of the child seemed to overcome such barriers. *I know that one. I'll sing it to you, while you settle down and get ready to sleep. And if you're still awake, I'll sing it again.*

She was on the third time through, and the body had relaxed in the bonelessness of a child's sleep, when Sofia felt the tug that meant she was on her way home.

And then she was standing in the familiar garden, and an instant later, in Iris's arms. And from somewhere nearby, a child's voice, quiet and choked with tears, said, "Thank you. Thank you for stopping it." And then, even quieter: "Will it be all right now?"

Did Eleni mean everything, or her body? Sofia could hope for both, and share that hope without bothering with caveats. "Yes, sweetheart. Your body will sleep, as it should. Everything will be all right."

Chapter 29

Rosie

For some months, Rosie had kept a nervous eye out for dark four-door sedans and equally colorless men in suits. Lately she'd neglected that precaution, so it gave her an unpleasant jolt to collect the mail from her mailbox and see an official-looking envelope from "The Combined Interagency Task Force for Illegal Wildlife Trafficking." Had that been the agency name on the business card she'd torn up and thrown away?

She made herself walk at her usual pace back inside and put the rest of her mail down carefully in the usual spot before sitting down and ripping open the envelope.

Dear Ms. Dodd:

Rosie muttered, "What, no *Dear old fraud*?" Months later, those worlds still stung. She scanned the letter quickly, looking for dates when more federal agents would descend on her, or when she was ordered to appear somewhere and be interrogated or worse. She found none, and put the letter down while she leafed through the rest of the mail. Bills, fundraising appeals, one realtor asking if she was ready to sell her home, and a newsletter from an association of which she no longer cared to consider herself a member. She went back to the letter from Combined Interagency, et cetera, picking it up and carrying to the nearest armchair.

In regards to the investigation previously commenced concerning your possible activities in regard to the unlawful storage and transfer of restricted fauna and of weaponry regulated under . . .

What was that?

In light of the services you appear to have rendered to your community in the recent past, no further action is contemplated in this matter at the present time.

They were backing off?

They were acknowledging that she'd "served her community"?

She heard a rustling sound and realized she was holding the letter tight, and that her hand was shaking. She dropped the letter next to the chair, curled up with her arms around her knees, and let herself cry.

Rosie relished the slower pace that had come with the fall. While she still had her duties in the ongoing effort to control the creatures, she had time for such relaxing pleasures as a walk to admire the leaves, comparing their colors this week to last, picking up a few of the more vivid ones that had fallen and taking them home.

When she walked through her front door, Diane had a note for her, trading it for the handful of leaves. "Mrs. Fuyuko called, and she's very eager to attend another séance. Her oldest daughter is going to have a baby, and it's making her melancholy. She wants to tell her husband about the baby. Here's her number."

Rosie raised an eyebrow. "Don't we have the number in the database?"

Diane smirked. "If you have the number handy, you're less likely to put it off."

To be fair to herself, she had tried to reach this client as part of her initial restitution effort. But the woman hadn't called back — maybe busy with that daughter's wedding or relocation. Or she might have heard the message and forgotten about it, having some tendency to forget things.

At least Rosie was starting to get used to explaining how her sessions had changed. Someday, she might even stop feeling embarrassed and ashamed when she talked to old clients, but she was as good as ever at covering her feelings with a professional demeanor, if a less artificial one. No more unctuous profundities.

She thought of making a cup of tea first, then decided against it. She'd reward herself with tea and a cookie after she made the call.

Mrs. Fuyuko answered her phone in something close to a monotone. Was it Rosie's imagination or actual perception that made her see the woman as slumped in a chair, her hair uncombed? Rosie infused her words with the energy her client lacked as she said, "I hear you've been wanting to make an appointment?"

She listened as Mrs. Fuyuko's voice went from flat and colorless to tear-choked and rapid and ran down again. She replied, "Of course I can accommodate you. And I'm now offering solo and small-group appointments, which allows more time for a real conversation. Wouldn't that be nice?"

A hint of suspicion, long overdue if no longer merited. "That sounds expensive."

"No, I'm offering them at the same rate as the group séances you attended." Now for the tightrope-walking. "But they're different in another way. Since I last saw you, I've discovered I had greater abilities than I'd known before. The music, the incense, the lighting — I no longer need it in order to contact the spirits." Though she still used a candle, or her old standby the crystal ball. It helped her concentrate.

An anxious note, now, in the woman's voice: "What about Aya? Is she still helping you?"

Rosie grimaced. She'd done a little too well with Aya. Mrs. Fuyuko wasn't the only one who felt deprived at the thought of losing her. Maybe her new policy of almost-honesty could use a tweak, if it made the clients more comfortable. But Sam would tease and nag and berate her without mercy if she tried it. "Aya," she replied diplomatically, "is only one of many spirits whose benevolence, or their life debts, lead them to assist bereaved mortals like yourself. Lately, it is a gentleman named Samuel who has come at my call. His ability to find my clients' loved ones is unparalleled. Now, as to schedule . . . ."

As she ended the call, she heard a familiar voice, somehow both sardonic and fond. *You more or less told the truth there. My ability to find loved ones is "unparalleled" because you've never had anyone else doing it.*

She would have stuck out her tongue at him if Diane hadn't been nearby. *Would you rather I give Aya credit for what you do? Or maybe I should revive Thaddeus. He was an agreeable fellow, much less likely to sass me.*

Sam chuckled. *Good old Thaddeus. Gone, but not forgotten.*

Which sent Rosie's mind wandering to all those who were gone from her world, violently wrenched from it. And how she must not forget them.

Sam's voice again, more subdued. *Didn't mean to bring you down. You're doing much more than most people.*

Rosie chuckled. *And much more than you expected me to do. Don't bother denying it.*

Footsteps heralded the approach of Diane. "I'd expected you to be sitting with tea and cookies by now. What are you up to? Oh, I can guess. Chatting with Sam. Say hello for me."

Rosie relayed the message. Sam chuckled and said, *Blow her a kiss for me and tell her she's my sweetheart.*

How fickle of you. All teasing aside, do you have someone special up there, or over there, or however I should say it?

Sam took his time replying. *Not at the moment. Ask me again when you show up. No rush about that. You've got a lot more living to do. And a lot more to do, period.*

Rosie swallowed a lump in her throat as she told him, *So I do. Now go off and enjoy some eternal bliss while I get to it.*

Yes, ma'am! Later. She felt a quick kiss on the cheek, and then another on her lips, before he left. Rosie took a deep breath for composure and then turned to Diane. "All right, what's next?"

(that winter)

Emma

It had been around five months since that unforgettable day when Millie had regained control of her body and marched it back to her grave. Emma was still in awe of the courage that had taken. And she devoutly hoped and prayed that by the time she herself was laid to rest, whatever was causing bodies to rise as zombies would be discovered and stopped for good. In the meantime she could be proud of the part she had played, and was still playing, in keeping the menace under some degree of control.

Getting to spend time with Paul again was an added reward. He was always so kind and helpful, and he never — or very rarely — bristled when she asked him how he was doing, whether he was taking care of himself, or whether he'd met a nice girl. He must realize how much she ached to be able to ask Robert such questions. And since his own parents lived so far away, and he was estranged from them for reasons she would have to get out of him sooner or later, he might actually welcome her mothering him.

As today, when she gave him the scarf she'd knitted for him. She was getting better at knitting. He beamed, thanked her, and wrapped it around his neck, tucking it in securely. She even saw him stroke it now and then as he drove them to the cemetery.

It was one of the three she and Paul — and lately, even Janna's mother, once in a while — visited together regularly. The ones farther away took too long to get to, unless they went on a weekend when Paul was less likely to be working, and she hated to take up his weekends that way. Sometimes one of the others, Rosie or Diane or Meg, drove her instead. And they were, or rather Rosie and Diane were, still busily recruiting to find others willing to go to cemeteries in other towns and states and even countries. But those people could only check to make sure there were at least a few ravens or crows on guard, and thank them for being there, whether the birds could understand them or not. So far, they'd found no one else like Emma, who could definitely communicate with crows and ravens. Paul always insisted it was perfectly all right for her to be proud she could do that.

"Here we are." While she'd been woolgathering, Paul had turned off the highway and made his way to the small cemetery with the stone fence.

The lawn and even the graves looked almost cozy under their clean white blanket of snow. And of course the marker was different. They had all chipped in to pay for a better one. The new one was larger, and had engraved flowers at the bottom and top. And it had new words, so it now read:

Camille (Millie) Williams

And after the years of birth and death:

A brave lady, lovingly remembered

By now the birds — crows, it sounded like — were cawing up a storm, and half a dozen of them were flying in a circle above Emma's head. One crow mischievously perched on Paul's head and tugged at a lock of his hair with its beak. "Now stop that!" Emma scolded, and when the crow let go and lifted off, held out a handful of unsalted peanuts and sunflower seeds as a reward. That, of course, brought the whole flock down out of the trees, so she quickly scattered that handful plus another on the ground.

While the flock was feasting, she examined the grave. The heaped and packed earth had settled, naturally. There might well be new grass under the snow. She could see no sign that it had been disturbed in any way, let alone from underneath.

Satisfied, she returned her attention to the birds. "Thank you so much for being here. After all this time, it could be that the danger has passed, but I'd greatly appreciate it if at least some of you would stay a while longer." How much longer did Millie's grave need these winged guardians? She would ask Rosie to ask Millie what she thought.

As they returned to the car, Paul got a thoughtful look and said, as he opened the door for her, "I wonder whether, when the graves we know about have been undisturbed long enough, we should ask the birds to make the rounds of other cemeteries. In case of new zombies popping up, so to speak."

It was a good idea, despite his frivolous way of putting it. Such a good idea, in fact, that she was already doing it. Should she tell him so? Maybe another time. She wanted to let him enjoy the moment. And his next good idea might be one no one else had thought of.

There was a difficulty, of course. There always was. It was mainly about the ravens. Many people understood how important their presence was, but others found it hard to get used to masses of big, sharp-beaked birds hovering. Crows were easier to take. Everyone in the team kept spreading the word that having so many of the birds around was actually a good thing, posting as much of the relevant research as they could get away with (not that the governmental bodies were making that easy). It was at times like this that they missed

Janna's contacts with the younger crowd — though Emma, at least, missed her more for her fresh youthful energy. She could only hope that being reunited with her twin made Janna more reconciled with her abrupt removal from everything else she had known and loved. . . .

Emma put the grief aside for another time. Paul had actually given her an idea, though it would mean they, rather than the birds, would have to do the work. "Maybe we should be doing the same thing. Lots of people visit graveyards as a sort of hobby — to make rubbings of the stones, or to read them and see how old they are and whether they suggested any interesting stories. We could start doing it too."

Paul looked dubious for a moment, but then his eyes lit up. "Or maybe we can try to sort of enlist all those people, and ask them to keep an eye out for disturbed graves and let us know if they see any."

When he was older, maybe his mind would go first to the drawbacks of a plan. Maybe it was something people her age had to learn to do. Tentatively she said, "That would be wonderful, if they'd do it. But if we tell them why, they may start to worry about seeing signs of zombies. They may even stop going to cemeteries out of fear that they'll catch one coming up — and be caught by it."

Paul stuck out his lip a little — she couldn't ever tell him it made him look like a darling little boy — and said, "So we don't have to tell them why. We can come up with some explanation." At her starting to frown, he added, "We can ask Rosie. She knows how to tell people what they want to hear and make them do what she wants."

"But she doesn't do that anymore, does she?"

Paul smiled. "I'll bet she can still come up with something that's not quite a lie. Something just . . . directing people's attention away from the problematic part. I'll ask her, anyway."

Emma let it go. He might be right. And it would be such a help! It could even save people. That was what mattered most, saving everyone they could.

A Note in Closing

the chronicler

Toward the end of Shakespeare's *A Midsummer Night's Dream*, the sprite and jester Puck reassures the audience:

> *If we shadows have offended,*
> *Think but this, and all is mended,*
> *That you have but slumber'd here*
> *While these visions did appear.*
> *And this weak and idle theme,*
> *No more yielding but a dream.*

Believe this if you will. And if you are made of sterner stuff and still seek some comfort, know that there is hope.

We have not yet learned why it is happening. But we are learning how to stop it. How to bring our bodies home. How to put them to rest.

Acknowledgments

As always, I have many people to thank. I'll start with my beta readers, who perform a task essential to me as to (I would posit) most authors. For this book, they were, in alphabetical order, Hazzan Adewole, Margaret DeVere, Jill Franclemont, Maksim Kovalev, Brianna Prislipsky, Carolyn M. Smith, Fred Smith, Samantha Strong, and Elisabeth Zguta.

I am also grateful to:

— Danusha Goska and Otto Gross, plus various people participating in Authors Guild discussion groups, for their comments on the bird appearing on the book cover.

— Assorted members of the Monroe County Constitutional Conservatives and Confinement Facebook groups for answering questions about drones. (By the way, "Confinement" is the name of a science fiction convention, not a group with particular BDSM interests.)

— My daughter Alissa Wyle for her aesthetic and other reactions to cover as a whole.

— Last but far from least, my husband Paul Hager for letting me extract opinions on one after another excerpt and miscellaneous topic.

I did some research on topics including the social habits of corvids, the nature of golems in Jewish lore and legend, the meanings of tarot cards, and (of course) the supposed methods of creating zombies and of freeing oneself from zombiehood. However, I did not, as I do when writing historical fiction, compile a comprehensive source list. Feel free to ask me where I looked for information on any point, and I'll try to find out.

Finally, I tip my metaphorical hat to thesaurus.com, a site I visited frequently when I discovered I was using the same word twice in the same paragraph or even in successive sentences.

Author's Note

The subject matter of this novel was a surprise to me and to many people who know me. I don't watch movies or TV shows about zombies, or featuring horror in general. I didn't expect to write a book whose central features included zombies — until it occurred to me to wonder how spirits in the afterlife would react to learning that their bodies were running around wreaking havoc. Then the idea of writing about zombies went from unthinkable to irresistible. It is my assessment that despite this departure from my usual set of genres, the book that resulted is very much like my other novels in themes, tone, treatment of character, and other such factors. I'd be very interested in hearing whether my readers agree.

One of my beta readers suggested I explain how I came up with the idea of golems as a zombie-fighting option. The simplest answer (given that I can't directly question my subconscious, from which my ideas generally spring) is that I'm Jewish and have gradually, over the course of my life, become acquainted with a certain amount of Jewish folklore. It only occurred to me during the revision process that some video game or other might have included the same notion. A little research showed that the idea wasn't that unusual in the gaming universe.

Some readers may question my decision to leave the zombie problem less than entirely solved. This decision was not entirely unprecedented. I drew courage from a science fiction novel by a prolific and (at least at one point) well-known author, which featured a different deadly peril and ended with the threat still very much present. (I'm not naming the book or author in order not to "spoil" it.)

One decision I made early on and then questioned several times was to use the term "zombie" rather than some synonym. Part of that decision was the dearth of synonyms. I considered "revenant," but it's uncommon enough that I thought some readers would find it distracting, at least for the first few uses and possibly for longer.

About the Author

Karen A. Wyle was born a Connecticut Yankee, but eventually settled in Bloomington, Indiana, home of Indiana University. She now considers herself a Hoosier. She and her husband have two wildly creative adult offspring.

In addition to writing novels (science fiction, afterlife fantasy, general fantasy, and historical fiction including historical romance) and picture books, Wyle is also an appellate attorney (though quasi-retired). Her voice is the product of almost five decades of reading both literary and genre fiction. It is no doubt also influenced, although she hopes not fatally tainted, by her years of law practice. Her personal history has led her to focus on often-intertwined themes of family, communication, personal identity and development, the impossibility of controlling events, and the persistence of unfinished business.

Connect With the Author

Learn more about Karen A. Wyle by looking her up on
her author website, http://www,KarenAWyle.com;
X (aka Twitter), at https://www.x.com/KarenAWyle;
Facebook, at https://www.facebook.com/KarenAWyle;
Goodreads, at http://www.goodreads.com/kawyle;
or her blog, Looking Around, at https://looking-around
.blogspot.com/.

You can also follow the author on BookBub, at https://w
ww.bookbub.com/authors/karen-a-wyle, which will send you
alerts about new releases.

Like the book? Please tell readers! Online book reviews
are enormously helpful – and old-fashioned word of mouth
is terrific as well!

You can sign up for Wyle's monthly newsletter, including news of upcoming releases as well as looks at her writing
process and extras like excerpts and cover reveals, at Wyle's
newsletter signup link. This is accessible from her website
(bottom right corner of the home page).